writing on the wall

She knew what she was looking at as soon as she saw it. She closed her eyes and wished it away, but when she opened them again, she still held a dispatch flyer with West's face on it.

Was it a joke? Some kind of elaborate, awful prank? The picture of West was current; it looked like it had been taken from above as he was leaving the Bazaar.

> West James Donovan, age 19
> Height: 6 feet
> Weight: 165 pounds
> Dark brown hair, green eyes. Virus scars on the face
>   and thighs.
> Subject is wanted for the murder of Bridget Hannah
>   Kingston.

Murder? The absurdity of it made her wonder again if this was some kind of prank. The idea that West would kill the headmaster's daughter was so impossible, she couldn't imagine it.

Until it struck her that of course he wouldn't kill her or anyone else. The report of Bridget's death would show up in the databases before it happened. A dispatch flyer would be distributed—this dispatch flyer—and stop the crime before it was committed.

They'd stop it by putting her brother in front of a firing squad. Not their father's squad, of course; that would be too cruel. But West would be executed.

viral nation

shaunta grimes

BERKLEY BOOKS, NEW YORK

THE BERKLEY PUBLISHING GROUP
Published by the Penguin Group
Penguin Group (USA) Inc.
375 Hudson Street, New York, New York 10014, USA

USA I Canada I UK I Ireland I Australia I New Zealand I India I South Africa I China

Penguin Books Ltd., Registered Offices: 80 Strand, London WC2R 0RL, England
For more information about the Penguin Group, visit penguin.com.

This book is an original publication of The Berkley Publishing Group.

Library of Congress Cataloging-in-Publication Data

Grimes, Shaunta.
Viral nation / Shaunta Grimes.—Berkley trade paperback edition
pages cm.
ISBN 978-0-425-26513-0 (pbk.)
1. Time travel—Fiction.   2. Corporate power—United States—Fiction.   I. Title.
PS3607.R55685V57 2013
813'.6—dc23   2013007612

PUBLISHING HISTORY
Berkley trade paperback edition / July 2013

PRINTED IN THE UNITED STATES OF AMERICA

10 9 8 7 6 5 4 3 2 1

Cover art by Blake Morrow.
Cover design by Diana Kolsky.
Interior text design by Kristin del Rosario.

ALWAYS LEARNING   PEARSON

prologue

"Keep her away from me."

James walked toward his wife with their newborn daughter sleeping against his chest, her body a warm spot through a shirt he hadn't changed in three days. "You don't mean that, Janie."

"I don't want her near me." Jane's features were swollen almost beyond recognition. Sores, seeping and open, covered skin that had been a source of vanity—more his than hers—only a week ago. Talking caused the corners of her mouth to crack.

His own skin ached to the muscle in sympathy with hers. Like they shared the same body. And he was so angry. So goddamned *bent*.

They were supposed to be safe here, in the mountains where the fleas that carried the virus couldn't live. The president had told them so.

Told the whole country, so that desperate and already sick people stampeded to higher elevations. Nothing could hold them back. They came like a revival of the Gold Rush, blinded by the need to move westward and upward into the Sierras.

"Hold her, Jane. It's too . . ." *Late anyway*. He couldn't bring himself to say it. He wished to God it weren't true.

His wife had brought the virus home from the hospital along with their new baby. Clover, they'd named her. Jane said it was a good name for a baby born in spring.

It was nothing more than bad luck that the virus came to the hospital at the same time their Clover did, but Jane blamed herself all the same.

She'd rear-ended a pickup truck on the way to the supermarket. Her water broke and Clover was born two weeks early. If the baby had come on time, in the first part of May instead of middle April, they would have known better than to go to the hospital.

Ten days ago the virus was something that happened somewhere else. Obscene but distant, like reading in the *Reno Gazette-Journal* about a hurricane in Florida or a tornado in Kansas. Closer than an earthquake in Haiti, but still not their worry.

Not something that could touch them beyond a general grief for the suffering of fellow human beings and an uptick in gasoline or food costs.

Now it was everywhere. It was in their living room, on the narrow bed he'd moved down from their son's room for Jane when she couldn't climb the stairs anymore.

Their son West, only three years old, was already feverish, his lymph nodes swollen and hot. It would come for Clover next. And James, too. Maybe even tonight.

Except Jane's body had filled Clover's with immunities that could keep her healthy longer than him.

The thought that he might die before Clover did made it difficult for James to breathe. It made him want to do something reckless and unthinkable. He had to be healthy enough to care for his baby or she'd be left to die alone.

He wouldn't let that happen.

Jane moaned, low in her throat. Her skin decomposed, even as he watched.

His wife didn't deserve this shredding of her body while her mind refused to blunt. She'd find no relief, not even in dementia, until she was dead.

For the first time since they were seventeen, there was nothing he could do to protect her.

The world had collapsed around them while they told each other everything would be okay. The virus was only the icing on a cake with layers of energy crisis, climate change, recession, xeno-phobia, and a short but vicious civil war between the midwest-ern and southwestern states over the need for illegal migrant workers on the farms and the desire to keep them out of the border states.

The media called that cake the Bad Times.

Until Jane got sick—was it just three days ago? Yes, just three days ago, when the air wasn't thick with the scent of her dying flesh. Until the first sores came, James, like everyone he knew, assumed that a return to good times was coming.

"Please, take her out, James. It's not too late. It's not."

But it was. Jane would die tonight, if there was any mercy left in the universe. His boy had maybe two days. By morning, West would be wracked with pain, just like his mother. Within a week, it would be over for all four of them, one way or another.

James kissed the top of Clover's head, felt her feathery dark wisps of hair against his lips. She smelled new, when the rest of the house stank of a B-grade slasher movie.

"It's time, isn't it?" he whispered to Jane.

Her eyes, wildly green in her ravaged face, filled with tears. "I'm so sorry."

"Not your fault, baby. It's not your fault." He laid Clover against Jane's body. His wife was too weak to fight, so she wrapped a fragile arm around the tiny bundle and curled protectively against the baby, like an oyster around a pearl.

How could Jane have lost so much weight so quickly? Under a worn nightgown, her rib bones felt like splintery artifacts against the back of his hand.

The doctor who'd told them that Jane had the virus wore a full-body hazmat suit and something that looked like a cross between an astronaut's helmet and the gas mask James had been issued in Iraq before West was born. She sent them home from the clinic with what she called a "pain kit."

Prescription painkillers and a bottle of liquid narcotics for the children. And a box of prefilled syringes.

"For when the pills stop working," she'd said.

She had a case full of the kits and a box of red plastic quarantine ribbons on the floor of her examination room.

They went home, stunned, with one of each and no follow-up appointment. Everyone knew that no one survived the virus.

All that remained was managing the pain and praying for a miracle. They were left to take care of each other because no one would risk infection to care for them.

Jane had not stopped praying, the words falling off her lips and, as far as James could tell, on deaf ears. Still, he couldn't stop himself from doing it now. *God, give me the strength to do this.*

He shook a dozen small white pills from the bottle. She wouldn't be able to swallow them; her throat hardly let sips of water through. So he crushed the pills into a fine powder with a gray stone mortar and pestle that they'd bought on their honeymoon in Cuernavaca.

They'd ridden horses there. Jane learned to balance on her knees across a pony's bare back, arms thrown wide to the wind. She had no fear then. She wanted to do everything, try everything.

James found applesauce to stir the powder into.

Jane held the sleeping baby and murmured to her between bitter spoonfuls. After she took the last bite, her throat still worked, maybe trying to speak to him or say good-bye to Clover. Maybe just reacting to the agony of so much swallowing.

Somehow, he'd expected an instant end to her pain. It didn't happen that way. Her breaths started to come in hitching hiccups, so far apart that between each he was sure she was gone. Her body rattled as her blood pressure plummeted. Her system was nearly empty but released anyway, adding to the sick-house stench.

But she didn't die. He'd made her pain worse.

He fumbled for the box that held the syringes, his heart pounding and hands shaking. The needle went through the skin of her upper arm before he could think about what he was doing.

He didn't even know what he'd given her. Morphine, maybe. Some stronger relief than the pills. Did she need more? He picked up another syringe, noticing for the first time that the doctor had given him four.

Enough for a quick, semi-sanctioned death for his wife and children. For him. *Law & Order* reruns called a man who did what James could see no way around doing a family annihilator.

Jane gasped another breath, then one more.

And then her eyes closed, the green dulling before they did, and James panicked. "Jane!"

The quiet in the house was shattered by a pounding on their front door that made his heart thud hard enough to send a wave of nausea over him. Clover screamed as she was startled out of sleep.

He put the used needle down and grabbed the baby, because he didn't want her disturbing Jane.

She's dead. I killed my wife.

She might wake at any moment, maybe from the pain caused by the sores, or because her swollen throat wouldn't let her take a breath.

She's dead. Oh, God. Forgive me.

He'd lost his mind, sometime in the past minute. Was that all it took? One minute?

"Who is it?" he called, unwilling to look through the peephole and see someone he knew covered in open sores.

"Dr. Hamilton."

He opened the door just as the doctor jerked away the plastic quarantine ribbon from the jamb and let it bounce down the front steps. When she turned back to him, he saw an oozing bandage in the hollow of her right cheek. She wore blue jeans and a pink T-shirt, instead of a hazmat suit. Without her mask, she looked ill and exhausted.

Beyond the doorway, the street teemed with people, and noise he'd somehow missed until now. Car horns honked. Children banged wooden spoons into pots and pans, like they were scaring off evil spirits on New Year's Eve.

"What's happening?" He felt dim. Like he'd already half followed his wife to wherever she'd gone when her eyes closed. Somehow he'd completely forgotten there was a world outside this house.

Jane believed in heaven. Said God believed in him, even if he wasn't sure he believed in God. He wanted to go to her.

No.

Not before the children. Them, and then him, and they'd all be together again.

The doctor came into the house when James took a step back.

"You can't be here," he said.

The doctor reached into her bag and pulled out a hypodermic needle. "It's over. It's finally all over."

She removed the plastic cover from the point and walked to the bed where Jane lay. The applesauce dish and used needle sat on the table next to her.

It didn't take long for the doctor to realize it was too late. James couldn't make his throat work to get out a confession before the doctor felt for a pulse and let out a sad sigh.

"Oh, James," she said.

He was going to prison. He knew it immediately. But whatever was in that syringe might help West. It looked like the kind of implement a cartoon doctor might wield: oversized and filled with an icy blue substance. "West is sick."

James, still holding his daughter, started up the stairs to where West lay listless in his bed, the boy's sweet, small face already marked with sores on his fever-flushed cheeks.

The doctor swabbed West's arm with antiseptic and pushed the sharp point of the wicked-looking needle into his skin. The boy didn't even whimper, a sign of how deeply the virus had invaded his body already.

"It'll take a while," the doctor said. "And he'll need a shot every day. You all will. I'll leave enough for you to inject until he's well enough to come to the clinic. Let's call it a week, okay?"

"And then he'll be better?"

The doctor had lost her glimmer of joy. She'd meant to save the life of a young mother. James felt numb.

"The drug is a suppressant. It'll keep the symptoms away and stop healthy people from contracting the virus. But everyone needs a shot every day. Forever."

The doctor stuck James in the hip. The suppressant burned like hot tar as it worked its way through his veins. "Oh, my God."

"You'll get used to it." The doctor rubbed the spot she'd injected, encouraging the medicine to move more quickly, and then used a third needle on Clover's fat little thigh. The thick substance formed a bubble under the baby's skin, too viscous to move easily.

Clover startled, her arms and legs opening wide, and her mouth twisted in a silent screech before sound finally escaped in a high-pitched wail.

"I'll send someone for Jane," the doctor said quietly. "I'm so sorry."

"No, Daddy," West moaned when James sat on his bed two days later to administer the boy's third shot. The sores were in the creases of West's groin now, and one had started in the crook of his right elbow in the night.

James tortured his dying son with jelly-thick medicine that seared as it pushed through a needle as thick as a juice box straw. Before Dr. Hamilton showed up, James was ready to move West and Clover on to whatever came next in order to save them from pain.

Now he shoved needles and medicine that burned like acid into them, all because someone had given him a glimmer of hope.

"It's making you better, buddy. I know it hurts, but you need it."

West's thin arms were bruised where the first two shots had gone in. Like a miniature junkie. Would the treatments be less painful in the boy's thigh? Maybe James should try his hip?

In the end, he was afraid to deviate from what the doctor had shown him.

How could West's little body endure this day after day? James gave his son a stuffed koala bear to squeeze, then pushed the needle into his skin and depressed the plunger.

West cried, and James reminded himself that on the first night his son had been too ill to notice how unpleasant the suppressant was.

By the end of the week, West's skin was healing, his lymph nodes were smaller, and he began to have a spark of energy again.

For the next month, James and his children spent hours every day in line at the clinic for their suppressant doses. And James prepared himself for his inevitable arrest. He'd murdered Jane with his inability to withstand her pain. He deserved to be punished.

There was no one else to take care of West and Clover. He and Jane were both only children. Their parents were all gone, either dead or, in the case of Jane's father who had walked away when his daughter was twelve, deserted. Probably all dead, now.

Most of every day was spent trying to figure out how to take his next breath without his wife. He didn't go to work. He didn't even bother to find out if he still had a job.

Day after day, no one came to arrest him. Maybe there were too many dead to focus on the actual cause of death for virus victims. Too many changes happening all at once to spend any time noticing one mercy killing.

Maybe there had been so many mercy killings that arresting all the guilty survivors was impractical.

Whatever the reason, no one came, and he couldn't find the courage to turn himself in.

His children needed him, he told himself. There was no one else.

News trickled in over the radio. Two scientists, Ned Waverly and Jon Stead, had developed the suppressant. In order to administer it to those who had survived the virus, each state gathered its residents into a central city.

In Nevada, that city was Reno, where James, West, and Clover already lived, so they weren't uprooted the way the survivors who traveled in caravans from the southern and eastern parts of the state were.

They didn't have to move into the home of a dead family. Sleep in their beds, eat their food at their tables. The process of bringing in the displaced was quick and efficient. There were so few left, fewer than twenty thousand in Nevada, and nearly half of those younger than twelve. The virus had scared both the fight and the flight out of all of those old enough to think about either one.

"We had it better than most states," his only surviving neighbor said as she cooed over Clover. His daughter didn't like to be held—she stiffened like a hard-limbed baby doll—but Mrs. Finch didn't seem to care. "The mountain states all had it better."

She was right. The drought-devastated plains states, which had already badly lost their war, had been nearly depopulated. The states where staple crops were easily grown were hit the hardest, the radio announcers said. Not just by the virus, but by the fallout of the war fought on the country's best soil.

James heard, six weeks after Jane died, that crews were picking through Reno, removing dead bodies, sanitizing houses, making a place for the surviving Nevadans who'd stayed in the state. Five thousand left the state, according to the radio. They went back to where they came from. Mostly, that meant California, since a decade's worth of floods, courtesy of melting glaciers in Greenland and Antarctica, had sent people streaming east over the mountains to Nevada. Some were shuttled to the states that didn't have enough people left even to populate one city.

"A recruiter came yesterday," James said to his neighbor. "They want me to join the crews."

Alba Finch had lost her husband, her children, and all but one grandchild to the virus. Isaiah was West's age. The two boys played in the place on the living room floor where Jane had died.

"I'll mind the children," Mrs. Finch said, without looking at him. Not for the first time, James wondered if she had her own secrets.

The government was building a wall around part of the city. The better to monitor daily suppressant dosing, the mayor said. The better to ensure that no one went out and brought back the virus. Martial law, the president said. Just until things settled down.

"I can't stand to think of them in the foster houses," James said.

The government commandeered a gated community built just as the housing bubble was bursting. Rows of houses no one had ever moved into. A ghost neighborhood. Each three-thousand-square-foot micro-mansion with granite countertops and renewable bamboo floors would be filled with orphans and the children of people who were needed to work rebuilding society.

"No," Mrs. Finch said. She kissed Clover's forehead and the baby arched back, her face red with an impending squeal. "I wouldn't have that."

Two months ago, the world had made sense. Now there weren't enough people to manage the farms and ranches that fed the country. There were whispers that even if there were, the land wasn't producing. Those who had survived were prostrate with grief and largely unskilled in the tasks of making a first-world nation run.

The United States of America was no longer a first-world nation, anyway. The virus had leveled the playing field.

There was talk about some kind of portal under Lake Tahoe. Submarines and time travel, a science-fiction fantasy reported by breathless radio voices that captured the imagination the way that Seabiscuit and James J. Braddock had during the Great Depression.

Two months ago, most everyone believed the Bad Times were temporary. Hard, scary, but not lasting. Not forever.

James didn't think anyone believed that anymore.

chapter 1

So far as the colleges go, the sideshows are
swallowing up the circus.

—WOODROW WILSON,
PRESIDENTIAL ADDRESS AT ST. PAUL'S SCHOOL, JUNE 3, 1909

SIXTEEN YEARS LATER
WALLED CITY OF RENO, NEVADA

Clover centered the envelope, which was the first
personal mail she had ever received, against the bottom edge of a
worn, woven placemat that was centered against the edge of the
kitchen table.

Rectangle on rectangle on rectangle.

Delivery stamp on the right, the Waverly-Stead Reno Academy's
return address on the left. Her own name and address front and
center, written with thick blue ink in a sharply slanted script. *Miss
Clover Jane Donovan.* She liked that. It made her feel important.

It was a skinny letter, feather light in her hand. Whatever the
Reno Academy had to say to her could be said on a single sheet of
paper. She was pretty sure whatever it said, what it meant was that
she had tested well enough to qualify for higher education. Waverly-
Stead, the Company that was the center of every aspect of life in
Reno and all of the fifty walled American cities, wanted to train

her for some useful profession beyond farming or learning to work a sewing machine in the clothing factory.

Maybe learn to be a researcher in the massive downtown library that was the center of everything good that happened in her life. She touched the edge of the envelope. It felt substantial. Expensive. Like the shoe box filled with her mother's old letters, worn smooth and soft with a thousand readings, stashed in the trunk at the foot of her bed.

Not at all like the flimsy recycled paper West sometimes brought home from the Bazaar. They rationed that paper like it was dipped in gold.

She liked the way the envelope felt almost like cloth as she ran her finger from the top left corner to the right, again and again.

She closed her eyes and rocked as her fingerprint rasped against the grain of the paper.

"Aren't you going to open that?"

Clover's heart lurched once, then settled as she took a breath out of order and it caught in her throat. She ignored the question.

West tossed his pack to the floor and sat in a chair across from her, already dressed for the day in blue jeans and a light blue shirt that buttoned down the front, the collar of a white T-shirt peeking out at the neck.

Every other day of the week, he wore brown. For the dirt slingers, he'd said before his first day of work at the cantaloupe farm nearly three years ago.

She started to rock again, to bring herself back into balance, humming this time.

"Clover," West said. And then, when she opened her eyes, "Don't glare at me."

She reached back and yanked her collar inside out, abruptly ending an angry exchange between the back of her neck and a stiff, itchy tag. "I need the scissors."

Who came up with the bright idea to put tags in clothing anyway? Sock seams, too. How hard could seamless socks be to make? She wiggled her toes and rocked a little faster.

"Scissors," she said again, holding out her other hand to her brother.

West pushed his chair back, the metal legs scraping across the tile floor, and across her eardrums, too. She twitched against the sensation and held the tag farther from her skin as West cut it off.

Something soft and heavy pressed itself against her shins under the table. Clover reached down to pat Mango on his cream-colored head. The bulldog rubbed his broad forehead against her jeans, then propped his jowly chin on her knee.

Her rocking slowed and then stopped.

West reached for the letter. "Do you want me to read it first?"

Clover put her palm down on it. "Not likely."

She lifted the envelope and tapped one end against the table, then tore away the edge and shook the letter out.

We are pleased to inform you that you have been accepted to the Waverly-Stead Reno Academy's fall term, beginning Monday, September Seventh. We have reserved a bed for you in the Girls' Dormitory. An orientation and registration interview are scheduled for Monday, August third, at eleven in the morning. Please attend.

The letter was signed *Adam Kingston, Headmaster.*

Scrawled across the bottom was a handwritten note. *Your entrance exam scores were extraordinary, Miss Donovan. I look forward to having such a bright student enrolled in the upcoming semester.* Signed with the initials *A.K.*

Clover read the letter through twice. It didn't surprise her. She graduated primary school at the top of her class. Adam Kingston would have been an idiot not to accept her.

It was good to know he wasn't an idiot.

"I'm sorry, Clover," West said.

"Sorry about what?" She petted Mango's head. The dog lapped his broad, slobbery tongue over the top of her hand and pressed his weight more firmly against her legs. That was part of his job. The pressure helped her focus.

West sat in the chair next to hers. "I know how much you wanted this."

She handed him the letter. "I got in."

"Are you kidding me?" He grabbed the paper and read it. "You even got accepted into the boarding program. Come on, Clover. Smile at least!"

"I'm happy." She showed her teeth to prove it.

Most everyone graduated from primary school and went to work for the government. They worked on the farms, like West, or at the Bazaar handing out rations. They preserved food for the winter, or so it could be sent to the other cities that couldn't produce enough to feed themselves. Or they worked for the Company doing menial labor like guarding the gate or rocking babies in the Company nurseries.

Now that the children who'd survived the virus were older, there were far more babies than there used to be.

The Academy was for people whose tests showed an aptitude for research or medicine or leadership. Engineers who worked with water treatment and electricity were Academy trained. Travelers—Time Mariners and Messengers—were as well. That was the most coveted, and most elusive, track. Doctors and other scientists were Academy trained, too. Even artists came through the Academy, although Clover was pretty sure she'd flunked that part of the exams.

"Do you know how hard it is to get into the Academy?"

"They didn't take you," she said. West's face fell, and Clover wished she could take the words back. Not because they weren't true, though. "No one is good at everything."

"No, they aren't." He looked for a minute like he wanted to strangle her, and then like he wanted to hug her. She was happy when he just leaned back and crossed his arms over his chest. "I'm proud of you."

"I know." She pushed her chair back. "I need to go to the library today."

Maybe she really would be a librarian when she left the Academy. She loved the library more than any other place in the city.

West studied her for another long moment. "Come on, then."

When Clover stood next to West, she came up to his shoulder, same as she did their father. West had the same habit James Donovan did of yanking his hand through his dark brown hair until it stood up like a porcupine asleep on his head.

Would their father ever find out she'd been accepted into the Academy?

Clover grabbed her pack, already full of books, and followed West to the back door.

"You need to comb your hair."

West shot her a quick salute and opened the door for her.

She clipped Mango's lead to his harness with her free hand and went out into the heat.

"There you are!"

West stopped and made a low clucking noise with his teeth and tongue so that Mango would notice and stop Clover, too. She'd say she could go alone to the library, but West needed to see her turn down the road toward the big building on Center Street.

In a month his little sister would be in boarding school, and he wasn't sure what he'd do with all that freedom. Swim in it, maybe.

Their next-door neighbor, Mrs. Finch, was in her seventies. She had looked after West and Clover since their father was recruited to the crews, soon after the virus took their mother. Her grandson was West's best friend. Isaiah was denied entrance to the Academy and joined Waverly-Stead's guard training program at sixteen. His grandmother had a stroke a week after he moved into the training barracks. Now West looked after Mrs. Finch.

She reached a palsied, soil-covered hand into the pocket of the kind of front-snapped cotton dress that old women had worn forever. Her small stack of ration coupons were bent and tattered paper rectangles the city used and reused until their print was worn completely off. Each was worth a pound of produce or meat or grain. She also had one for the tiny bit of oil, sugar, and salt she'd be allotted for the week.

"I was beginning to think you weren't coming this morning, West." Her face screwed up to the right when she spoke. At least she could speak now. And the nearly constant drooling from the first year had passed. West was relieved when she started to look like their Mrs. Finch again. He knew Clover was, too. Mrs. Finch was the only mother his sister had ever known.

Every Wednesday since he turned eighteen and was old enough to get into the Bazaar, West picked up Mrs. Finch's rations with his own. He wasn't late this morning. He'd never been late, but Mrs. Finch still acted like he was going to let her starve every week.

"I'm sorry, Mrs. Finch," he said as he took her coupons and slipped them into his own pocket. "I'll be around with your rations this afternoon."

She knelt back on a small cushion, lurching to the right and then finding her balance, in front of a bed of lettuce. "I'll have some cabbage soup for you and Clover. Maybe some bread, too, if I get myself inside to get it rising."

Even though she'd had a stroke, Mrs. Finch's front yard was a jungle of produce. Pumpkin vines twined around stalks of corn and beanpoles; sunflowers lined one side of her house. She fed the seed-filled heads to the chickens that pecked in a fenced area under an apple tree. It was too early for ripe apples, but West and Clover would eat themselves sick on them in the fall.

Her garden made the neglected patch in West and Clover's backyard look pathetic. Her contributions to their food stocks kept them from being more than skin and bones.

"Let's go," Clover said from beside him.

"Good morning, Miss Clover," Mrs. Finch said to her. Loud and slow. "And how are we today?"

Clover was easily three times as smart and ten times as well read as anyone West knew. Mrs. Finch included. Maybe Mrs. Finch especially, since she still greeted Clover the same way, every time she saw her.

Clover said, just as loud and slow, "We're fine."

Mrs. Finch blinked at her, then looked at West, who shrugged one shoulder. The old woman had practically raised Clover. If she didn't know the girl by now, she never would.

"I was just telling West I'll have cabbage soup for the two of you this afternoon."

"My brother doesn't like cabbage soup." Clover shifted her weight from one foot to the other and flapped her free hand two or three times. "I'm late for the library."

"Clover." West looked at Mrs. Finch, whose nearly black eyes bulged out of her coffee-colored face enough to look painful. "Thank you, Mrs. Finch."

He took Mango by the collar and walked away, knowing Clover would follow. Hopefully before she made some comment about how Mrs. Finch's eyeballs looked like boiled eggs.

"Slow down," Clover called, practically running to keep up. "Let go of my dog!"

West let Mango go and shortened his steps. They walked together for a while in silence.

Their street was lined with brick houses, each sitting on about an acre of land. This neighborhood had once been more densely populated. The crews, in the old days, tore down houses to give more land to those that remained. Before the reconstruction there were two neighbors between them and the Finches. With something like fifteen thousand people living in a city built for ten or twelve times as many, there was room to spread out.

And need for the room, because the government rations alone weren't enough to feed a person. Everyone grew some produce. Some people kept backyard chickens and even dairy goats, if they were lucky enough to win a pair in the Bazaar. West and Clover had two laying hens in a pen in their backyard.

"Are you going to the Bazaar while I'm at the library?" She asked every week. The answer was always the same, but she still asked.

"Just to pick up our rations and Mrs. Finch's."

"We need candles," she said.

He had thirty-five chances each week to win extras. Twenty-one he earned working at the cantaloupe farm, plus Clover's minor ration of fourteen. Each ticket was traded for a token that he gambled for candles, toilet paper, soap, a butchered chicken. Maybe if he was lucky, some extra energy for the week. Anything above and beyond their bare-bones food rations. On Wednesdays, he pulled for Mrs. Finch's fourteen elder ration extras, too.

"Reading by candlelight isn't good for your eyes, you know," he said.

"Just get some, okay?"

He didn't answer. He had exactly zero control over what the machines gave him. Some weeks he came home with so much he could barely carry it, others with nothing more than their basic rations.

Clover waved over her shoulder as she turned with Mango toward the library. From behind, she looked more like twelve than sixteen. Her black hair was cut short, in chunky layers. She had a habit of hacking at it with scissors when it started to bother her. She wore their mother's red Converse high-tops and blue jeans cuffed at the ankle with a standard-issue white T-shirt.

She was so thin. He hoped for some meat, instead of the candles she wanted. The virus, which many expected to affect the chicken population, had jumped from humans to cows instead. They were endangered now and pampered like pets on dairy farms. It was hard for West to imagine that once upon a time people ate them. A pound of lamb or pork would go a long way, though.

West watched until his sister was out of sight, then walked the other way, toward the Bazaar.

There were two things he could count on every Wednesday morning. An unpleasant twinge of resentment when he traded a backbreaking week of hard labor for barely enough food and energy to take care of his sister. And passing by the Kingston Estate on his way to the Bazaar, where he knew Bridget Kingston would be somewhere near the gate.

The Kingston Estate was as big and grand as its name implied. A large white house and a smaller guest house sat on maybe two acres of land with stables between them. The estate had housed the current headmaster since the Academy opened fifteen years ago. First a man named Norton, and for the last four years Adam Kingston and his daughter.

A trio of horses looked up from where they ate alfalfa in a front pasture when West walked by. Beyond the buildings, the land dropped off into a ravine, leaving a backdrop of city below and mountains beyond.

The house was well kept, with walls repainted bright white by government workers every third spring and set off by the deep blue shutters and a red front door. Very patriotic. A wide porch wrapped around the front and both sides of the house.

As West came close, Bridget stood up from the bench swing that hung from the porch rafters near the front door. She wore her honey-colored hair swept away from her face and pulled into a high ponytail. The curled ends of it brushed the back of her neck.

Passing on his way to the Bazaar was the only time West saw Bridget since he'd graduated primary school and become a dirt slinger three springs ago. They rarely said more than "good morning" or "hello" to each other. There was more caught in the space between them, but it stayed there. West convinced himself he was fine with the slow progression. He'd be about forty before he was in a position to offer Bridget anything more than a simple greeting.

It hadn't always been that way. Before Adam Kingston was headmaster, he was just a teacher and West's father was a guard. A guard's son could be with a teacher's daughter. This guard's son had time to fall in love with that teacher's daughter, in fact, before things changed. Bridget moved with her father into the estate and that was that.

"Morning," she said. She wore a pair of Academy gray pants that she'd cut off and neatly hemmed into shorts, and a white T-shirt that set off her long, golden limbs.

"Morning," he answered. God, he was an idiot. She was the headmaster's daughter. He smelled, constantly, of manure and rotting melon. He buried his hands in his pockets and quickened his pace.

"Are you headed for the Bazaar?" she asked as he passed by.

"Yes." He stopped walking but didn't know what else to say. He looked for something anyway. Anything to draw out this moment. "You, too?"

"I don't get my own rations until November."

Of course. He knew that she was seventeen. Her father would pick up her rations along with his, and those of anyone else he supported. He would never let his daughter near the Bazaar. West didn't blame him.

"Have a good day, Bridget." He liked saying her name. It felt sweet on his tongue. It always had.

She smiled, her cheeks flushed just a little, and he walked away.

"You're in a good mood."

West turned and smiled when he saw Isaiah walking toward him. "What are you doing here?"

"Got the day off and thought I'd get my grandma's rations for her."

"I'm just on my way to the Bazaar." West balanced himself back on a garden wall, his thick-soled boots making it difficult, and reached into his pocket for Mrs. Finch's ration coupons.

Isaiah took them, then pushed West's shoulder until he lost balance again. "Saw you talking to Bridget Kingston. She why you're so smiley today?"

He hopped back on the wall and walked backward a few steps. "Just saying hello."

"Watch yourself, West. That girl is way out of your league."

"Don't worry. That's not why I'm happy today." Not mostly, anyway.

"No?"

"Clover got accepted into the Academy. Boarding and all."

Isaiah stopped walking, and West did, too, after a few more steps. "So you going to join the Company?"

There were only two things to do in Reno. Work for the Waverly-Stead Company, or work for the government. Company work for people as young as West required living in the barracks, at least for training. He couldn't leave Clover, so West worked for the government raising cantaloupe to be sent by train to feed people in other states.

Are you going to join the Company? wasn't a real question. All

West had ever wanted was to work for Waverly-Stead, just like his father.

"As soon as she's settled in, I can apply," he said.

Isaiah ran a hand over the stubble growing on top of his head. "School starts in what, a month?"

"About."

"You could start training the next day."

West's stomach tightened. He could start the process now. Today. That letter was for Clover, but it sure changed his life, too. He'd been taking care of her since he was sixteen and she was thirteen. Since their father was promoted from guard to executioner, part of one of the five-person firing squads that were the center of the most efficient law enforcement system in the history of the country. People convicted of future capital crimes were brought from every state's walled city to Reno so that their sentences could be carried out. Executioners were required to live in the Company barracks, and promotions within the Company weren't something anyone could turn down easily. Their father signed guardianship to Mrs. Finch, but it was West who had taken care of not only himself and his sister, but their guardian as well, until Clover's care passed to him officially when he turned eighteen.

"You've waited long enough," Isaiah said.

Hell, yes, he had.

West received a similar letter to Clover's from the Academy a few months after he convinced his father he could take care of his sister. By then it was clear that, official documents aside, Mrs. Finch couldn't even care for herself. He declined the invitation. What else could he do? Foster City was supposed to be a perfect system, allowing children to be cared for so their parents could do the work of recivilization. Somehow he'd known that system wouldn't work for them. Foster City would have chewed his sister up and spit her out. But now that she was accepted into the Academy herself, he had his life back.

chapter 2

She got to go to heaven four days early.

—BILL CLINTON,
ON HIS MOTHER'S TRIP TO LAS VEGAS FOUR DAYS BEFORE
HER DEATH.

A man at least as old as Mrs. Finch stood, ramrod straight, just inside the big library building. Clover stopped in front of him, as she had a thousand times.

"Morning, Clover," he said. "Help you find anything today?"

A large whiteboard stood next to him, and someone had written that day's class offerings on it. "Any good classes today?"

"One on preserving meat. Another on making soap."

She'd taken those already. More than once. "Looks like the first-aid class has a new teacher."

"Yes, indeed."

Clover wandered off, holding Mango's lead in her right hand. At the last minute, she remembered and turned back. "Thank you, Tom."

The old man's wrinkled face softened into a smile. "Pleasure."

Clover inhaled as she walked among the shelves of books. The library's scent of dust and old paper filtered through her as she lifted her free hand and let her fingers trail along the spines of a row of art books. The world changed just as she was born. It had shrunk to the size of the city. But these books let her see what it used to be.

She picked one full of prints of Georgia O'Keeffe's work. Cow skulls and desert landscapes. Clover traced the petals of a huge flower that held secrets she didn't quite understand. Then she slid the book back into its spot, where she knew she could find it anytime she wanted it, and went to look for books on beekeeping. If West couldn't get her candles, maybe she could make her own.

The Waverly-Stead building and the Bazaar sat across four lanes of Virginia Street from each other. A huge arched sign, declaring Reno *The Biggest Little City in the World*, bridged the road. Back in the day, the buildings must have used as much energy between them every day as the whole rest of the city combined did now.

West passed with Isaiah under the sign and through the heavy double doors into the Company's headquarters. The artificial cool inside gave him goose bumps as they walked along the marble entrance to a large wooden desk.

The woman behind the desk stopped typing when they approached, her fingers curved like claws over the keyboard. "How can I help you?"

"I'm here to apply for guard training," West said. "Please."

The receptionist was maybe forty. Her light brown hair was teased and fluffed to an arrangement that didn't move when she turned her head. Pitted scars on her cheeks meant the Company had saved her life.

West had the scars, too. He rarely thought about them, but they marked him as a survivor. The woman glanced from his eyes to his right cheek and back.

"Take the elevator to the third floor, honey, make a left and then a right, and you'll see the recruitment offices at the end of the hall," she said.

West and Isaiah walked toward the elevator together. The Bazaar had a bank of them, too. No other building in Reno except for the hospital had enough energy reserve to save people from walking up stairs.

"You'll get a packet to fill out, and they'll want a start date," Isaiah said as the doors slipped closed.

Just like that, the long wait to start his life was over. He pressed the button for the third floor and rocked on his toes as the elevator lurched upward.

He looked at Isaiah in the mirrored elevator door. His friend wore guard uniform pants, mottled with shades of green and brown, and a white T-shirt the same as West's.

All work was important. Without farmers, no one ate. But West was so ready to do something really interesting, he could barely hold it in.

They found the recruitment office easily enough. Isaiah had been there before, of course, three years ago. West hesitated before opening the door, feeling like he was crossing some sort of threshold, but when he did, he found just a room. A table inside the door held a stack of dark blue and white folders.

"Take one," a man behind a desk said without looking up from his work. He flicked his wrist toward some chairs a few feet away. "Sit there and fill it out."

The packet inside the top folder was thick, with a couple dozen pages stapled inside. "Can I bring this back?" West asked. "My sister is waiting for me in the library, and I still have to get to the Bazaar—"

The man held up a hand, and West swallowed the rest of his rambling.

"Fill out the first page. We'll set an appointment for your interview. You can bring the balance of the application two days before that date."

"Thank you, sir."

The old man's sharp blue eyes darted back to the work West had interrupted with his question.

The short form asked for West's vital statistics and had a statement for him to sign that notified him that his name would be run through the Company database. If it came up attached to any violent crime that would happen in the next two years, he'd be punished swiftly and justly. He filled the page out quickly, signed it, and brought it back to the officer.

The old man made him wait several minutes before taking the page and asking, "And what date are you available to begin training?"

West took a deep breath. *This is it.* "September seventh." The day after his sister started classes at the Academy.

"Okay. You'll come for your interview on the—" The man tapped the eraser end of a pencil against his desk as he flipped through the pages of a calendar. "Third at one thirty in the afternoon, and bring your full and complete application anytime on or before the first. We will run your name through the database during your interview, do you understand?"

"Yes, sir. Thank you." West turned to leave and nearly plowed into Isaiah standing behind him.

"A late start," Isaiah said as they exited the elevator a few minutes later. "But you're finally becoming a man, my friend."

After they'd made their way out of the building, they stopped at the median, in the center of four lanes of blacktop, to let a group of little kids on bicycles and their teacher pass. "What's the training like?"

"The hardest thing you've ever done," Isaiah said. "You'll want to die before it's over."

Isaiah entered training at sixteen, directly out of primary school. West was nearly twenty and had been working a farm for three years. "I think I'll survive."

"Remember that when you're running ten miles on an empty stomach at four in the morning after two hours' sleep."

"In my bare feet, through the snow?"

Isaiah laughed.

They made their way to the Bazaar's entrance and West pushed the dark glass door open. Carnival music, full of organs and horns, blared loud enough to compete with the noise of thousands of gamblers. The machines whirred and clanked, and when someone won a leg of lamb or a pair of wool socks, bells and sirens went off.

This was why he'd given up the Academy. Clover would never be able to walk through the door to the Bazaar to pick up her own rations.

Primary school classrooms had overstimulated his sister to the point of catatonia some days. On a good day, he'd come home to find her curled in a corner of the couch, humming frantically to herself with her face buried in a book. Other days, he'd find her rocking and banging the heel of her hand into her forehead.

The noise, the crush of people, the smells of the Bazaar would incapacitate her. He didn't have to worry about that now. For the next four years, all of Clover's needs would be taken care of.

West and Isaiah passed by glassy-eyed people frantically yanking on the slot machine arms and went to stand in line at the cage to turn their extra tickets in for gambling tokens.

"Let's play craps," Isaiah said.

"It takes too long."

"Clover got you on a curfew?" Isaiah bumped him with his shoulder, and West pushed him away.

He did feel lucky today. "Fine. One game. But then I'm already late."

Isaiah walked to the cage window when the man in front of them left with his handful of tokens. "We both know your sister could spend the rest of her life in the library and be perfectly happy."

"In the library, yes. Sitting outside waiting for me? Not so much." West cashed in the six tickets he'd received the day before. Three earned, three for his day off. As a general rule, he played his tokens as he got them. He was trying to feed himself, Clover, and a large dog on what amounted to about enough to feed one person. If he won a loaf of bread or a pound of carrots, they needed it as soon as possible.

Isaiah had a week's worth of extra tickets for himself, plus the fourteen his grandmother received as an old-age pension from the city each week. Living in the barracks, he didn't draw food rations.

"I can't wait around for you to play all those," West said.

"No worries."

West shoved his tokens into his pocket and followed Isaiah to the oblong table, lined on three sides with people, their faces red and slick with sweat as they cheered on the shooter and then followed the dice down the table with their eyes. Isaiah elbowed his way to the front, and West followed in his wake.

The dealer across the table from them was dressed in fishnet stockings and a pink satin leotard cut over her round hips to her narrow waist on the sides and nearly down to her belly button in front, barely containing her cleavage.

The dice bounced off the rail and rolled partway back before stopping. The dealer's bleached-blond curls bobbed as she called, "Shooter rolls eight the hard way!"

Some groans, one whoop from somewhere near the head of the table. The dealer at the center of the table, a man wearing a jester's hat with bells on the tips and a skintight, slightly obscene metallic purple jumpsuit, raked in the dice while the fishnet girl and another wearing shiny black shorts and a red tasseled bra mucked up the bets.

The jester used his stick to push the dice toward the next shooter, but flipped his hook and took them back when the music changed and the lights in the room dimmed before one bright beam shot down from the ceiling.

The deafening noise that defined the Bazaar's gambling floor dulled, and everyone at the table craned their heads back to look up. West included.

"Ladies and gentlemen!" A deep, rumbling voice boomed over the speaker system. "Overhead, for your viewing pleasure, the Flying Phoenix!"

The room stayed silent for a moment as a girl in crimson velvet encrusted with crystal stones unfurled from a wide, white silk ribbon. She dropped from the ceiling with dizzying speed, then caught herself with a wrist trapped in the silk and spun in a wide circle over them.

"Christ," Isaiah said. "Look at those legs."

They were long and flexible, each one tipped with a satin slipper. Clear stones on the velvet caught the lights and her dark hair cascaded around her as she spun.

The show was over in five minutes, and West knew another one would happen every half hour. Maybe another aerial show. Maybe jugglers on stilts making their way between the machines, or trained poodles jumping through hoops in the circus ring that rose from the center of the main floor.

Anyone who had an entertaining talent could earn a few extra tickets by performing at the Bazaar.

When the lights and music came back up, the shooter who'd rolled the eight handed the dealer back the coupon he'd been given for his win and took another token.

"Just a pound of mutton," he said to the woman next to him. "We can do better."

"I'm going to the machines," West said to Isaiah.

"Come on, I'm the next shooter. Then you. Then we'll go tug the bandits, okay?"

Isaiah smiled and laid a token down without waiting for West to answer. The shooter threw something that made everyone at the table groan and the female dealers lean precariously over the table to collect the house wins.

"Okay, okay, okay." Isaiah moved into position and placed a bet as the jester slid the dice to him. "Daddy needs a new pair of shoes."

He picked up the red cubes, tossed them around in his palms, blew on them, and sent them flying. The dealer in front of West, the girl with the huge breasts, winked a heavily made-up eye at him, then looked back at the bets in front of her.

"Hot damn!" Isaiah smacked the heel of his hand on the wooden rim of the table, sending an empty glass balanced there tumbling to the floor.

The winking dealer handed him a coupon, her fingers lingering a little longer than necessary. Isaiah slid his long brown fingers down the length of the girl's hand, palming the slip of paper. He waved it at West after he read it. "Sweet!"

Ten units of energy, West read before Isaiah slipped it into his pocket and placed another bet. Ten hours of power to one sixty-watt bulb.

His run lasted two more rolls, and then it was West's turn. He placed his first bet of the night on the Don't Pass line because he needed to get out of there. He tossed the dice without Isaiah's fanfare. They landed on snake eyes. Everyone else at the table had bet the Pass line and grumbled as the dealer handed him a ticket for a pound of potatoes.

He left his bet and waited while more Pass line bets were placed, then rolled again. The dice tumbled, bounced off the far side of the table, and landed on snake eyes again. The dealer in the center reached for them with his stick, lifting his eyebrows as he slid them back and West took another ticket, for a loaf of bread this time.

"Sure you don't want to go for the Pass line?" Isaiah whispered in his ear. "You aren't going to pull that out again."

West ignored him and threw the dice. He nearly came out of his skin when a lighted siren blared and twirled over their heads. Some of the other players had switched their bets to the Don't Pass line. The man who'd turned in his pound of mutton wasn't one of them, and he lost his last token.

"Winner, winner, chicken dinner!" the jester called out, and handed West a card from his breast pocket.

One live chicken, it read.

Isaiah elbowed West in the ribs. "Good eats at your house tonight, right?"

Not without his rations. West threw the dice again and finally lost his token.

"Okay," he said to Isaiah. "It's been fun, but I really need to get out of here."

Isaiah looked back over his shoulder at the dealer who'd been flirting with him. He turned back to West with a grin on his face. "Do me a favor, man?"

West sighed and held out his hand. Isaiah reached into his pocket and put his grandmother's stack of ration cards into it.

"I owe you one."

He owed him at least a hundred, but who was counting? "What about her extras?"

"Oh." Isaiah tore his eyes from the dealer who looked like she belonged between the pages of one of the magazines they sold in a dimly lit store at the back corner of the sixth floor. "Right."

He reached into his other pocket and handed West the energy coupon, one for a length of the homespun cotton cloth made in a factory in Ohio and shipped to the Bazaar by train, and one for a cantaloupe. Great. "Just give her these."

And then he was gone, pushing his way back to the craps table.

He would probably have a chance with the dealer, too, West thought. Girls had always liked Isaiah. He watched his friend bend his dark head toward the woman and saw her smile, ignoring the table until the jester goosed her.

He walked to the nearest bank of machines and put a token in one. The reels spun, and when they landed on nothing special four times, West went to the elevator. An operator, dressed in a tuxedo complete with top hat, grinned at him when he entered through a set of wide golden doors.

"What floor?"

"Produce." West would go to the second floor, walk from room to room, and gather the fruits and vegetables that were the bulk of their diet, and then the third for the couple of pounds of meat that were supposed to feed them for the next week.

There should have been plenty. The farm West worked on grew enough cantaloupe to keep the whole city fat and happy. But the Bad Times had ruined the country's farm belt, and whatever food could be produced in each state was distributed by steam train to help feed the cities that couldn't support themselves.

Isaiah thought the live chicken was funny. But a laying hen would add to the two they already had and give him and Clover some extra protein each week. Mrs. Finch had a rooster. If he could pick a broody hen this time, they'd be able to raise some meat as well.

Or maybe they'd just roast this one up. They'd never had an extra chicken to butcher, but he thought he could figure out how it was done.

Mango lifted his head and woofed when West turned the corner and came walking toward the library, his pack full and heavy on his back. Clover closed her book and stuffed it into her own pack.

West lifted a small metal cage toward her and the chicken inside it squawked. It was small and brown, with a black head. "Is it an egg chicken or a meat one?" she asked.

"Egg."

She'd like to eat the animal's meat, but if it would lay, then they'd have food for lots of meals. "Did you get candles?"

West shook his head. "Not this time."

Clover shouldered her own pack, refilled with books, took one of West's bags, and picked up Mango's lead. "I got a book about beekeeping."

"Clover."

She hated when he said her name like that. "What? We could have our own honey, and wax for candles, too."

"You'll be in school in a month."

"It doesn't hurt to know things. I won't be at school forever."

Clover tried to match her strides to West's, but his legs were six inches longer than hers and she couldn't do it. She took shorter, faster steps. Her red sneakers slapped against the concrete, like a song almost.

Wednesday was her favorite day of the week, and the library was her favorite place in Reno. Once her pack was filled with books, she went to hear the new first-aid instructor teach about setting bones. And then she connected their laptop computer into the library's nets and took a look at the classified ads.

"Someone in Little Rock is looking for a husband," she said to

West. "Healthy, age twenty-six, red hair and blue eyes. Good cook and seamstress. One five-year-old son."

"Trying to marry me off to an older woman?"

Clover ignored him. "And I saw a message from Albany, New York, that said, 'The only thing we have to fear is fear itself.'"

"Roosevelt," West said, finally slowing a little for her.

"Why don't you ever read the ads, West?" They were the only way that the cities had to communicate with each other. The only thing that widened the world a little bit.

"I don't have time. Besides, I have you to filter out the best for me."

Good point. Also, she didn't particularly want him hanging out with her in the library, trying to tell her what books she should read or classes she should take. "Why would someone quote an old president in the ads?"

"Haven't got a clue."

Clover adjusted her pack. "I think I'll go for a run when we get home."

"Mrs. Finch has soup for us. And bread, if we're lucky. That way we can keep the loaf I won today and use it tomorrow."

Clover made a face. West stopped walking altogether.

"What?" she asked.

"You shouldn't have said that I don't like her soup. Sometimes it's the only thing that keeps us going."

"But you don't like it." Clover doubted anyone in the world actually *liked* cabbage soup.

"That's not the point."

She didn't argue. He was right. The point was, free food is free food. And Mrs. Finch was their neighbor. "Fine. I'll eat it. And then I'm running."

Running was Clover's favorite thing to do, after reading. She loved the way the cement felt hard and unforgiving under her feet until she reached the park and the dirt path that wound its way alongside the Truckee River.

She liked the wind in her face and how it smelled like water. And the way Mango ran beside her, keeping her company. But most of all she liked the way the steady pace untangled her thoughts.

She had a lot to think about with her Academy orientation only five days away.

"Do you think it'll be like primary school?" she asked West.

"What's that?"

"The Academy."

Primary school made cabbage soup look like a spoonful of honey. Too many kids, too much noise, too much to remember to do so that she didn't come across like a freak. Knowing every minute of every day that she actually was a freak and there was no hiding it.

She'd learned a lot, but most of it was by fire.

"I don't think so, Clover. The students are older. I don't think there will be as much chaos."

"I hope my roommate isn't an idiot."

"They don't let idiots into the Academy."

Clover shrugged one shoulder. Her pack was starting to drag on it. "They let idiots in everywhere."

chapter 3

Popularity, I have always thought, may aptly be
compared to a coquette—the more you woo her, the
more apt is she to elude your embrace.

—JOHN TAYLOR,
MESSAGE TO THE HOUSE, DECEMBER 18, 1816

Clover smoothed her palms over the full skirt of her
pale yellow dress. The cotton was soft and warm under her fingers.
The dress had been her mother's and was Clover's good-luck charm.

West told her to wear the same Academy uniform the other girls
would be wearing. He'd picked up her gray pants and navy blazer
at the Bazaar. They didn't fit right and were made of itchy fabric
that felt like sandpaper against her skin.

Her mother's old clothes were mostly cotton, worn to a smooth
comfortable texture, and fit like they were made for her.

Still, maybe she should have taken her brother's advice. No one
younger than Mrs. Finch wore dresses anymore. Now that she was
in front of the Academy, Clover wondered if blending in was more
important than luck. But the truth was, she didn't blend, anyway,
no matter what she did.

She clutched Mango's lead in her hand and tried to breathe
through her anxiety. She'd made West stay at home. If she was old
enough, and smart enough, to be accepted into the Academy, she

was old enough and smart enough to go to orientation without a babysitter.

At least that had sounded like a good plan at home. Now she sort of wished her brother were with her. She looked down at Mango, who sat at her right side when she stopped walking. "Ready?"

He tilted his head, the folds of skin on his face jiggling slightly. She had a feeling she would need him even more than she needed her mom's ghost to get through today.

She took a deep breath and pushed open the heavy front door to the administration building before she could upset herself any more. Mango's toenails clicked along the floor as they walked to the huge desk at the far end of the front room.

A banner stretched across the ceiling that said, *Welcome, New Students!*

The woman behind the desk grinned, showing a mouth full of worn-down teeth that didn't quite fit the rest of her. Then she looked from Clover's face down to her feet. "My, what a pretty dress. And a dog, too."

"It was my mother's." Clover rubbed a damp palm against her hip. "The dress, I mean. The dog is mine."

The woman raised both dark eyebrows. They were plucked to barely visible curves that arched above brown eyes. "May I have your name, dear?"

It was on the tip of Clover's tongue to say, *Don't you have one of your own?* But she stopped herself. "Clover Jane Donovan."

"Well, welcome, Clover Jane." The woman handed her a card encased in plastic with a pin on the back. She'd written Clover's first and second name on it. Would everyone else have their second name, or had Clover managed to make a mistake already?

Clover took the pin, and then she and the woman stared at each other for a minute. The woman was waiting for her to pin the name tag to her mother's dress. Clover didn't want to put holes in the soft yellow cotton. Finally, the awkward moment was over when the woman cleared her throat.

"Okay, first things first, Miss Clover. No dogs allowed at the Academy."

Clover knelt and pulled Mango's paper from a pocket on his harness, then handed it to the receptionist. "He's a service dog."

"Oh," the woman said, looking the document over. "Oh, my."

She handed it back to Clover.

"Where do I go now?" she asked as she shoved the paper back into its pocket.

"Well, to the ballroom. But . . ."

Clover looked down the long hallways that stretched on either side of the front room. At the end of one were double doors with people milling around them. "Okay," she said. "Thanks."

The skirt of her mother's dress swished around her bare knees, and her feet felt weird in white leather shoes that forced her to walk on her toes. Her brother made her wear them. He said her sneakers were too informal for orientation, and if she was going to wear their mother's dress, she had to wear the shoes that went with it. She hated how her toes squished into the front of them and the back slipped up and down on her heels. Her feet were already raw and swollen from the walk to the Academy. She didn't want to think about how they would feel by the time she got home.

Intellectually, Clover knew what a ballroom was. Still, as she came to the door, she braced herself for a room filled with every kind of ball she'd ever heard of: rubber balls, giant beach balls, baseballs, basketballs, the kind of tiny balls that bounced like crazy when you threw them to the floor.

This ballroom was basically a big square with hardwood floors and elaborate, brightly lit chandeliers overhead. More electric light than she'd seen all at once in her whole life.

There was no furniture except for a table along one wall that had stacks of folders and two more in the middle with food on them. There were no chairs.

There were also no melon balls or Ping-Pong balls.

Clover walked in a straight line toward the food, her arms pulled in tight against her body. No tennis balls, but there were a lot of people. The room was big enough that none of them needed to touch her, but Clover knew from experience that space didn't matter to them like it did to her.

"Oh, my God, look. She brought her dog," an all-too-familiar voice behind her said. "They aren't going to let her have her dog here, are they?"

Mango stayed at her side, heeling perfectly. He didn't react when a slender hand reached down and petted his head.

"Please don't touch him, Wendy," Clover said.

"Don't be so lame. I'm just saying hello."

Wendy O'Malley. They'd been in primary school together. For the first time, Clover looked around. Her low-level anxiety ramped up when she realized that she recognized nearly all of the faces in the room.

The Academy was her reward for putting up with Wendy and her gang of mean girls for ten very long years. It was *hers*. Somehow, it hadn't occurred to her until now that it was theirs as well if they passed the exams.

Her hand shook around Mango's lead and the walls of the ballroom closed in some, but she tried not to let Wendy see that she was rattled as she walked away. There was chocolate on the table. West almost never won them any sweets or enough sugar to make their own. She could count on one hand how many times she'd had real chocolate.

"You don't have to be so rude," Wendy said.

Mango made a soft sound next to Clover. He knew better than

anyone what happened when Clover had to spend any time around Wendy. Especially when there were no adults around.

"Still wearing your mama's hand-me-downs, I see." That was Heather Sweeney. Wendy's evil minion.

"You *both* passed the entrance exams?" Clover asked as her weight shifted from one foot to the other, once and then again. It didn't seem possible that they were both here. They barely had a full brain between the two of them.

"Of course we did," Wendy said. "I can't believe you did, spaz. Do they have special ed here?"

Clover looked around, but didn't see any adults. She didn't realize her weight-shifting had turned into full-fledged rocking and the low hum in her head was coming out of her mouth until Mango pressed against her legs and stopped her.

"I guess you'd know," she said.

"Right." Heather knelt and petted Mango on the head. "'Cause we're the weird ones."

"Don't touch him."

"But he's so cute." Heather's brown eyes narrowed slightly, but her lips turned up into a wide grin. Clover looked from her eyes to her mouth and back again. *She's not my friend.* A smile didn't always mean friendship. Another difficult primary school lesson.

"He's working." She moved Mango away from Heather. "He's not a pet when he's working."

"Oh, he's *working*. Well, why didn't you say so?"

Heather reached over to the table and grabbed a piece of chocolate. Before Clover could stop either of them, Mango had gobbled it up. "Its your payday, boy."

"You're going to make him sick!" Clover's hands flapped at her waist, trying to get her head and her body on the same page. A thousand thoughts flew around her brain, like butterflies caught in a net, careening off her brain and shooting off orders to her body in a disorganized puke of neurons and synapses.

Just breathe. In, one, two, out, one, two. Breathe. She would not lose it here. Not here. She had to calm down.

She almost got there, too, before Heather pressed a chocolate into the front of her mother's dress and ground it in with the heel of her hand, squirting bright red glaze over the yellow fabric and bruising Clover's collarbone.

Anger flooded Clover, pushing out her attempts at self-restraint. "What the hell is *wrong* with you!"

Heather stood next to Wendy, who was laughing with another girl. She leaned close enough that her breath brushed Clover's cheek. Clover stumbled back a step, barely containing the urge to double her fist and put it *through* Heather's face.

"You don't belong here, Clover Donovan," Heather said. "We all know that. Why don't you just go home to your brother?"

"Send her brother to me," the third girl said. Clover's anger hid the girl's name, even though she'd gone all the way through primary school with her. Holly? Polly?

"Leave her alone," said a boy, one of the few Clover didn't recognize.

"Oh great, now the freak has a boyfriend." Heather rolled her eyes and started to walk away. The heels on her shoes were twice as high as Clover's, but she didn't wobble. Not even once. Wendy and the other girl followed like sheep.

"Molly," Clover mumbled, suddenly remembering who the other girl was. She was on the verge of tears but fought hard to keep them back. Never let them see you cry. Any sign of weakness put them into a feeding frenzy.

She rubbed at the stain on her dress with a paper napkin instead, and managed to make the mess considerably worse.

"Don't let them get to you," the boy said after Wendy and

Heather moved off to where their friends waited to congratulate them on their successful bullying.

"Yeah, right."

"I'm Jude," he said.

She tossed the soiled napkin on the table. "Clover."

He wasn't nearly as tall as West but still maybe five or six inches taller than her five foot nothing. He had dark hair and olive skin with a thick scar that ran from his left ear to the corner of his mouth.

He was the only other person in the room not wearing the Academy uniform. He wore the same red canvas pants and white shirt that every Foster City kid Clover had ever seen had on. The red made him stand out, like he had a beacon on him.

"What happened to your face?" she asked. His fingers went to the scar and Clover winced. Why couldn't she ever get things to come out the right way? "I'm sorry."

Jude put his hand down and held his fingers out for Mango to sniff. Clover hoped her dog wasn't going to be sick from the chocolate.

"It's okay," Jude said. "We almost all come out of Foster City with scars."

"That happened in Foster City?"

Jude shrugged. "My house father was a sick son of a bitch."

Clover looked at the scar again. It was deep and almost as thick as one of her fingers. West had the virus scars on his cheeks, but they were less startling. Lots of people had those. "Does it still hurt?"

"Not anymore."

"Did you get boarding?"

Jude smiled and nodded. "Did you?"

"Yes."

Jude looked at his green plastic watch, then leaned in closer to her. "They have ham sandwiches. Want one?"

Clover followed him. Mango walked obediently beside her, now that she wasn't giving him any reason to worry. The dog didn't seem sick yet, so maybe one chocolate wasn't going to do anything bad to him.

"Crowds are hard for you, aren't they?" Jude said.

Was it that obvious? She looked up at Jude—at his scar again—and shrugged the same way he had when she'd asked a too-personal question.

"Me?" he said. "I can't stand confined places. I'm glad this is a nice, big room."

She took a bite of a small, square sandwich. It did taste good. She couldn't remember the last time West brought home a ham from the Bazaar. A year ago, maybe. "Are there other Foster City kids here?"

"Not here, but there are a few already enrolled."

"I wasn't sure how many got through the exams," she said. The Foster City kids didn't study at the primary school, but they were all brought in when they were sixteen to test.

"Our house parents are supposed to teach us. We try to teach each other."

"I thought they gave you the same resources we get." She frowned for a minute, recalling what she'd read about Foster City in the newspapers.

"Yeah, well, in theory."

If Jude's house father did something that scarred his face as badly as it was, what were the chances that the man had made sure that his charges were ready for the exams? "You passed, though; that's good."

"You did, too. Sounds like those girls didn't expect you to."

Clover watched Heather and Wendy talking with a couple of other girls, their heads together. One girl's head popped up like the periscope on a submarine and dropped back down when she saw Clover watching them. "People underestimate me a lot."

Jude plucked a peach from a bowl and took a bite. "I wish I could fill my pockets with some of this stuff."

"I won't tell if you do."

Jude held the peach to his nose and inhaled. "I can't go into my interview with food squishing around in my pants."

Clover's stomach contracted at the thought of her interview. Maybe the only thing worse than a crowded room was a room with one adult who didn't understand her. Sometimes it was like she spoke a language no one else could decipher.

"Paulette Casey." A man as short and fat as Santa Claus stood in the doorway. His white hair was combed from one side of his nearly bald head to the other and tucked behind that ear.

Paulette was a girl who hadn't been awful to Clover in primary school. Not friendly, either, but at least not overtly cruel. Clover watched her curl her index finger into one of her tight, dark, corkscrew curls.

Clover turned back to Jude. "What do you think they'll ask us?"

"Who knows. You'd think with all the stuff they asked on the exams, they'd know more about us than we do."

The exams took three days and were designed to test not only knowledge, but aptitude, memory, honesty, and a slew of other characteristics.

The Academy was only for the best.

Clover was surprised all over again that Wendy and Heather made it in. They were still huddled together with a gaggle of other girls, looking over at Clover and Jude every once in a while. The hierarchy was already forming. Did they really have to be there? Maybe if Clover told Kingston how dimwitted they were, he'd kick them out.

They must have cheated on the exams. Clover was sure that Mr. Kingston would want to know that. The Academy wasn't the place for cheaters.

"Do your folks work for the Company?" Jude asked.

Clover picked up a chocolate from the tray on the table and shoved her thumb into the bottom. Something white and creamy oozed out. "My dad does. My mom died of the virus when I was a baby."

She put the candy back and wiped her thumb on a napkin before asking Jude, "What about your parents?"

"Um . . ."

"Jude Degas." The man with the weird hair moved away from the doorway to let Paulette Casey back into the room.

"That's me," Jude said. "Talk to you later, Clover."

"Yeah, sure." Clover watched Jude walk away, then knelt next to Mango and took his wrinkled face in her hands. "You aren't sick, are you?"

Mango woofed. Clover turned back to the food table. She wished she could bring some sandwiches home to West. She eyed Mango's harness—it had a pocket on each side—but decided against it. Too gross. She'd eat one for him, she decided, and picked up another sandwich.

"Aww, look, a dog and his pet miniature pig!"

Wendy, Heather, and another girl came up behind her. Clover turned to face them. "And a couple of trained monkeys. We're a regular zoo, right?"

Mango pressed his side against Clover's leg, and she offered him the rest of her sandwich before she tightened her hold on his leash and turned away from the food table.

"Love your retro look, Clover," Heather said behind her.

Clover sighed. Why couldn't they just leave her alone? "Thanks."

"Yeah, it's super sexy."

Clover felt cool air on the backs of her thighs when Wendy took a handful of the bottom of her dress and flipped it up.

Clover pushed Wendy away with one hand and her dress down with the other, still holding Mango's lead. "Don't touch me."

"Why not? I heard people like you let just about anyone *touch* them." Wendy bent at the waist and put her face close to Clover's. "You don't belong here, and you know it."

How could someone so stupid have gotten past the exams? Wendy and Heather both had fathers who were higher-ups in the Company. Maybe that was it. Wendy reached for Clover again and Mango moved between them, baring his teeth in a low growl.

"Call off the monster, Donovan. I was just playing."

"I told you not to touch me."

"Well, God. You didn't say you were going to sic your hound on me."

"Clover Donovan."

Clover sighed with relief. Jude came in past the man with the comb-over. Before she could take a step, Wendy grabbed her hand, crushing her finger bones together and making her yelp in pain.

"Good luck, *Clover.*"

Clover tried to yank her elbow back and pull her hand out of Wendy's, but the other girl held on tight. "Let me go."

"What's going on here?" the man demanded.

Mango barked as Clover finally pulled her hand free. Then Wendy screeched, "Her dog bit me!"

Oh, no. Wendy held one hand in the other, cradling it like a broken bird.

"He didn't bite you." Clover turned to the man who had called her name. "He didn't!"

Wendy tilted her head and then looked back at Heather with a barely perceptible smile. "You saw, didn't you, Heather?"

Heather nodded solemnly. "We know you need Mango, Clover. But if he's going to bite . . ."

"But he didn't. Mango doesn't bite. Make her show you her hand."

"He didn't break the skin," Wendy said, pulling her hand closer to her body. "It was more of a . . . pressure bite."

The man tugged his pants up nearly to his armpits. "Ladies. Miss O'Malley, go to the front desk and ask for directions to the health office. Miss Donovan, you come with me."

"But she's lying!"

"Can Heather come with me?" Wendy asked.

The man flipped one wrist in a dismissive gesture and the two girls headed for the door, Heather's arm around Wendy like she was afraid her friend might not make it.

Clover looked around for anyone who would back her up. Jude had moved closer to her, but he hadn't been in the room until it was too late.

"Mango doesn't bite," she said to the man.

"Mr. Kingston is waiting for your interview, Miss Donovan."

"But he didn't bite her. She's lying."

"Mr. Kingston is waiting."

Clover and Mango walked toward the door. Jude touched her arm as she passed, and she jerked away from him. It felt as though every one of her nerves was right on the surface of her skin. Mr. Kingston would hear about this. Wendy O'Malley and Heather Sweeney would not get away with blaming something on Mango that he didn't do.

The Academy wouldn't get her without Mango, and Kingston had written a *personal* note right on her acceptance letter about her high scores.

"Mango didn't bite Wendy," she said again, for good measure.

"Right through here." The man put his hand on the small of her back, and she arched sharply away from him.

Kingston's office had windows from floor to ceiling. Behind a huge wooden desk sat a small, trim man. "Hello, Miss Donovan."

"My dog doesn't bite." Clover looked back when the office door closed. "He doesn't bite anyone, ever."

"Oh." Adam Kingston was the headmaster of the Reno Academy.

He was the one who'd written the note on Clover's letter. And this was obviously the man himself. He had a big brass name tag on the edge of his desk. "Yes. Well, you brought a dog to your interview, that's . . . ah . . . I'm glad he doesn't bite."

"He's a service dog. And he's very well trained." *Make eye contact. Keep your voice low. Watch his face. Don't talk too much.* Clover ran through West's advice and clamped her mouth closed.

"I see. I wasn't aware that you had a . . . um . . . a disability."

Clover bristled against the word *disability* as Kingston ran a finger around his collar. She didn't suggest he loosen his tie before it strangled him. She was pretty sure that would be weird. "It's right in my application."

Kingston opened a file on his desk and flipped through it, running his finger down several pages. "There is no mention here of a physical problem. You do know that the Academy requires strenuous physical training, don't you, Miss Donovan?"

"I don't have a physical disability."

"I see. So, then the dog?"

Kingston was nervous. She didn't usually notice things like that, but he had sweat through his shirt and kept stumbling over his words. "I have autism."

"Oh, autism. I see, I see. I . . . um . . . and the dog?"

"Mango helps me."

"Helps you?"

"He knows when I'm getting overloaded. He makes it so I can go to class, just like everyone else. And he doesn't bite, Mr. Kingston. Wendy O'Malley is a huge liar. I can't believe she was accepted into the Academy in the first place."

"Well, yes. You did score exceedingly well on your exams, Miss Donovan. In some areas, close to the best I've seen."

Clover sat in a chair in front of the desk when Kingston extended his hand toward it. "Yes, sir."

"Your memory is extraordinary, in particular."

Clover dropped her hand to Mango's head. "I didn't cheat, if that's what you think. I'm sure Wendy and Heather did, though."

"Do you have a photographic memory, Miss Donovan?"

"An eidetic memory," she corrected, and then immediately wished she hadn't. "That's the right term. Anyway, I remember whatever I've read, and most of what I see. Less of what I hear."

Mr. Kingston nodded and looked down at her folder again. "That would explain the gaps in your scores. You need things in writing, then, to perform at this level."

"Yes, sir."

"There is the problem of the dog," Kingston said, without looking up. "You'll have to attend without the dog."

"You don't have to worry about him. Really. He won't get in the way."

Kingston hesitated, like he was thinking something over. Then he sighed and said, "Miss Donovan, you will have to attend school without your dog. You've been assigned to the research department at this time."

"That's good, but Mango—"

"Sometimes things change, as we become more aware of your strengths. Now, you've been roomed with a Miss Sweeney. Heather Sweeney. When you rejoin the group—"

Clover came out of her seat. "No! You can't do that!"

Kingston leaned back in his chair and looked up at her. "Miss Donovan, really."

"You can't do this." Clover tried to take a breath, in through her nose and out through her mouth, but her teeth were clenched so tight that her exhales came out in loud steam-train huffs.

"Miss Donovan, please calm down." Kingston looked from Clover to Mango and then to the door, yanking at his collar again. "Really, just sit down."

She sat on the very edge of the chair, the leather sole of one shoe tap-tapping on the wood floor, and hit the heel of her hand against her forehead a couple of times.

"I must insist that you stay calm."

She looked up at him and forced her hands into her lap. "I must insist that you don't discriminate against me."

"We are happy to—"

"I can't be here without Mango."

They looked at each other for a minute. He had beady eyes. And his forehead was sweaty. He kept brushing the palm of his right hand over it, pushing back a slippery patch of brown hair.

"And I can't room with Heather Sweeney," Clover said.

"Part of being at the Academy is following direction."

"You don't understand—"

Kingston closed her folder. "I'm afraid the Reno Academy might not be the best place for you after all, Miss Donovan."

"No. Wait, no. I already got my letter." Why hadn't she brought it? "You wrote me a note about my scores."

"Sometimes someone looks like a perfect candidate on paper, but in person they just—"

Clover kept from crying by sheer force of will. "You can't do this."

"You're already having problems with other students. And if you can't function without that animal—"

"He's a service dog."

"Please, let's not have a scene."

Not have a scene? Was he expecting her to just lie back and let him . . . "Steal my education. That's what you want me to let you do?"

"No one is stealing anything from you. Please, calm down."

"I'm calm!" She was sitting, wasn't she? She hadn't moved.

"I really must insist that you lower your voice."

"I'm not yelling."

"*When* you are calm, I would like to talk to you about your options."

She threw her hands up and the end of Mango's lead landed in her lap. She'd been clutching it so hard that the leather left an itchy impression across her palm. "I'm calm, Mr. Kingston."

Kingston looked over her shoulder at the door, like he thought he might need to call the old comb-over guy for backup. Clover waited to hear what he had to say. Not that it would matter. He couldn't take back her acceptance.

"My decision is final," he said, like he'd read her mind. He looked to her like he might have a heart attack any minute.

"Are you okay?"

He sat back in his chair and wiped his forehead again. "What? Yes, I'm fine."

"Because you look a little sick." Clover leaned forward and peered at him. "Do you always sweat that much?"

"Really, Miss Donovan. I'm perfectly fine." Kingston opened a desk drawer and pulled out another folder. This one was deep blue with white piping around the edges. The Company colors. "Your exam scores were extraordinary, as I told you."

"But you don't want me here."

"Getting along socially is an important part of the Academy experience. Autistics have a history of difficulty fitting in and being successful."

"Then maybe you need to change the way things are done here. Starting with not letting in cheating—"

Kingston inhaled, slowly, through his nose. His grip on the blue and white folder bent the edges. "I would like you to go see Mr. Langston Bennett this afternoon."

"Who is Mr. Langston Bennett?"

"You can find him at the Waverly-Stead building. He'll make you aware of the situation when you arrive."

"You're sending me to the Company? Now?"

Kingston darted his shifty gaze around the room, landing on the closed door more than once. Clover looked back there, too, but didn't see what he found so interesting. "The Company has laxer rules than the Academy, Miss Donovan. They are better equipped to handle differences."

Differences. "But I'm not being discriminated against?"

"You're being offered an opportunity that, I promise you, nearly every student in that ballroom would jump at."

"So offer it to Heather Sweeney. That way I won't have to room with her."

"You're making this difficult."

He was taking away her education. Was she supposed to make it easy? "Do I have a choice?"

"If you don't attend training, you have to work, Miss Donovan. That's how we maintain order in our city. And people have an obligation to do the work they are best suited for."

"Then let me come to school. I'll do my best to get along with Heather, as long as she leaves me alone and I don't have to share a room with her. And I can have Mango with me."

Kingston took an envelope from the folder. The same kind of rich envelope her acceptance letter had come in. He reached across his desk to hand it to her. "This is for the best."

"The best for who?" The envelope had *Langston Bennett* written across the front.

"The best for all concerned, Miss Donovan."

"I don't want to do this."

Kingston pushed his hair back and settled his hyperactive eyes on the door for a moment before he looked at her. "Your brother is a day laborer on the cantaloupe farm, isn't he?"

Clover nodded slowly.

"I'm sure you could go pick with him. Every job's important."

Clover took the letter and barely resisted the urge to crumple it into a ball and bounce it off Kingston's sweaty forehead. "This isn't fair."

"Life isn't fair, Miss Donovan. Ask your brother. West Donovan scored nearly as well as you did on his exams."

"That isn't true. He didn't pass."

Kingston looked at her another long moment, then reached under his desk with one hand. Within seconds, the office door opened and the man with the comb-over was standing there. "Ms. Donovan needs an escort to the Company building."

"I don't need an escort," she said. The man who'd walked her into Kingston's office had seemed kind of feeble. Now his eyes had gone steely and his jaw was set in a hard line. Clover shrank back from him a little bit.

"I'm glad to hear that." Kingston reached to shake her hand. She pulled away from the visibly moist palm and walked out of his office, Mango following at her side. "You're expected within the hour."

chapter 4

Clover weighed her options.

She could walk the remaining mile or so down Virginia Street
to the Waverly-Stead building in the toe-pinching torture shoes.
Or she could take them off and walk barefoot, the soles of her feet
touching God only knew what as the concrete scrubbed against
her skin.

She left her shoes on and promised herself she was setting them
on fire when she got home. Her sneakers went everywhere with her
from now on.

Angry wouldn't cover West's reaction when he found out she
went to the Company alone. Or that she'd been sent there at all.
Not voluntarily, either, even though Kingston let her walk out by
herself.

She should go home and wait to talk to West, but she didn't
want to. He'd go all big brother on the situation. He'd insist on
confronting Kingston, for one thing. And Clover wasn't sure she
wanted that.

Now that she'd caught her breath, she wasn't sure being sent to the Company was so bad. She hadn't anticipated the Academy would be a replay of primary school. Besides, if she was expected within the hour, then she was supposed to go without her brother, who still had three more hours of work.

In the end she decided it would be best to have all the information before she talked to West. And to follow the rules. Anyway, she was annoyed with her brother and embarrassed that it never even crossed her mind to question his test scores. She needed time to figure this all out before she talked to him.

The one thing she did know was that whoever Langston Bennett was, he'd better let her keep her dog with her. Her father gave Mango to her when she was eleven. He'd been trained at the prison. It helped for the detainees to have worthwhile work, her father said. It gave them a purpose and helped them remember how to be good citizens.

She wasn't going to do this without her dog.

Mango stopped when Clover did, at the front door to the Waverly-Stead building. Doors weren't exactly Clover's thing. Especially if she didn't know what was on the other side. She closed her eyes and steeled herself against the possibility that it would be loud in there, or that it might smell bad. Or have the same flickering, garish overhead lights as the primary school building.

Thousands of people worked for the Company. If a lot of them were on the other side of this door, it was going to be bad. Very bad. Clover already felt the crush of them like a tightness in her chest that kept her lungs from fully expanding.

She pushed the door open, slowly, and inhaled when she saw a softly lit room with a very tall ceiling. Two women and a man sat together in plush chairs off to one side of the cavernous lobby, talking quietly to each other. Otherwise, the only sounds as she entered were her leather-soled shoes and Mango's toes clicking on the marble floor as they approached the big receptionist desk.

The receptionist was maybe as old as West and had dark hair with a bleached streak in the front. White like Mrs. Finch's. She was considerably prettier than Mrs. Finch, though. Mostly because she was so much younger and young people were usually considered prettier just by virtue of their youth. Mrs. Finch might have been as pretty as she was when she was twenty. In fact, for an old lady, before her stroke Mrs. Finch wasn't bad-looking. After her stroke, Mrs. Finch's eyes—

The receptionist was staring at Clover's chest. When Clover looked down, she saw the sticky chocolate-and-cherry stain and covered it with her hand. "Heather Sweeney did that," she said.

The receptionist raised her eyebrows delicately. "May I help you?"

"Yes, you may help me."

There was a moment of silence, and then, "*How* may I help you?"

Clover cleared her throat and held up the envelope Kingston had given her. "I have this letter."

She pulled the envelope back before it could be taken from her. The girl tilted her head and read the name on the envelope without reaching for it again. "Mr. Bennett. Is he expecting you?"

What if he wasn't? She wouldn't have the Academy or the Company, then. "I think he is."

"Okay. Well, why don't I check?"

She smiled, but her face looked frozen that way, so Clover wasn't sure whether she would call Bennett or security.

Turned out she didn't say anything into the phone except for "Yes, sir," twice, before she hung up.

"Mr. Bennett will meet you at the elevator bank to the left." She pointed at Mango with her chin. "He said to keep the leash on the dog, okay?"

Clover tightened her hold on the envelope as she turned to her left, toward a wall of brass double doors. She'd read about elevators, and West told her that the Bazaar had some and had told her about riding them, but she'd never even seen one in person before. She looked back down the hall at the receptionist, who waggled her fingers before turning her attention back to her computer.

Clover watched a digital counter above the elevator door start at eighteen and count down to one, her hands clenching and unclenching at her sides. Finally, one of the sets of double doors opened and a tall man in navy blue pinstriped slacks and a white button-up shirt stepped out.

Langston Bennett was about the same age as Clover's father. Maybe forty, then. His hair was dark on top, going gray on the sides, and cut very short. His most distinctive feature, though, was a series of deep virus scars on either side of his face. Much worse than West's, or any others that Clover had seen. She couldn't imagine the kind of sores that left scars like that.

His eyes drifted to her stained dress, but he didn't say anything about it. "You must be Miss Donovan."

His voice ricocheted down the cold, marble hallway. Clover took a step back from it. Mango picked up on her anxiety and pressed against her legs. The pressure helped. The man came toward her and Clover forced a breath through her nose.

"Miss Donovan?" He reached for her, and she stepped back again.

"Yes," she said. This had to be Langston Bennett. And he was looking at her like she was crazy. "It's nice to meet you, Mr. Bennett."

His tight posture relaxed when she said his name. Her brain insisted that she step closer and offer to shake his hand, but her body would not obey. He closed the gap instead and put a hand on her shoulder, to turn her toward the elevator. She barely held back the instinct to yank away from him.

"Right this way," he said, sweeping his other hand toward the open elevator door.

Clover exhaled slowly through her nose and peered through the open doors. So, an elevator was a box swinging by cables over dead air. So what? She could do this.

"How high are we going?" she asked, after Bennett was in the elevator, while she still stood outside it.

Bennett put a hand out to stop the door from closing and leaving her behind. "What's that?"

"Which floor is your office on?"

"The eighteenth floor," Bennett said. "You can see the whole city from my window. Even beyond the wall."

Eighteen floors. At twelve feet a floor, that was more than two hundred feet above ground level. She stepped into the box.

The elevator wasn't as bad as she was afraid it would be. The car was big enough to hold fifteen or twenty people. The walls were mirrored, even on the backs of the doors. Dozens of Clovers in yellow dresses with gory red stains and Langston Bennetts in pinstripes stood in infinite rows, riding more than two hundred feet up a narrow shaft, pulled by cables.

What were the chances that the virus had spared someone properly trained to maintain the intricate system of pulleys and brakes that kept them from plummeting to their deaths?

The red digital numbers above the panel of buttons registered each floor. It took less than a minute to reach eighteen. And then the door opened again and it was over. Mango walked beside her as she followed Bennett into a long, silent hallway.

She'd never been higher up than the third floor of the primary school building. Until she stood on solid ground, Clover didn't realize that she expected to feel a swaying or some kind of instability at this elevation.

On either side of the hallway, large windows looked into offices that in another lifetime had been hotel rooms. The hallway was lit from above and nearly all the offices had lamps and overhead lights blazing.

"You use a lot of energy in this place," she said. She and West got only two hours a day. And even that was just enough to run the water heater and a couple of lamps.

Bennett kept moving as he answered. "We do important work at Waverly-Stead. Energy is precious; we have to allocate it to the places it will do the most good."

"All work is important," she said, mostly to herself. Bennett stopped walking, but when Clover turned back to him he just started up again and didn't say anything.

The wall to Clover's left opened to another elevator bank. She glanced up at a chandelier, bigger than she was with at least a hundred lit bulbs. Bennett followed her gaze.

"How much do you know about Waverly-Stead, Miss Donovan?" Bennett asked as he guided her through the door into office 1812.

Clover guessed she knew as much as anyone did about the Company. They'd taught her some in primary school. She'd studied in the library for the entrance exams. "Edward Waverly and Jonathon Stead started the Company to manufacture and distribute the suppressant."

May eighth was a day of celebration for the whole country. That day, Waverly and Stead released the suppressant. Three weeks earlier, on Clover's birthday, Ned Waverly stumbled into a portal deep in the ancient waters of Lake Tahoe—a doorway between present day and exactly two years in the future. When Waverly came through it, he found that a drug had been developed that cured the virus and kept healthy people from being infected. He got his hands on a sample, brought it back to his own time, and found the chemist, Jon Stead, who had developed it. With Waverly's help, the suppressant was discovered two years early and ended the Bad Times eighteen months ahead of schedule.

They saved millions of lives. According to the histories, fewer than twenty thousand people were left in the United States when the suppressant was developed in the original time line. Waverly and Stead were able to save almost that many just in Nevada by developing it early.

They won the last Nobel Prize in medicine, or any discipline, ever granted. People all over the world practically worshipped them. They were heroes. After the Bad Times, once the virus was controlled, their Company privatized nearly every part of what remained of the United States of America.

They worked with the government to build a wall around a single city in each state to create safe places for survivors to grieve and start to live again. Clover had no idea what was outside the walls of Reno now. When she thought about it, she pictured a jungle, growing wild and overtaking whatever human-made things might have gotten in their way over the past sixteen years.

She knew from reading the classified ads that some of the walled cities thrived; others struggled. But it had never occurred to her to want to venture outside her city. The idea that she'd see beyond the walls today erased any last bits of guilt she felt over not going home before meeting with Bennett. If she'd waited for West to come home and then argued with him, there might not have been enough light to really see.

"Well, you do know something about Waverly-Stead," Bennett said, stopping her in the middle of wondering out loud how the absence of people had affected the black bear population in the Sierra Nevada. He held out his hand and Clover hesitated before letting go of Mango's leash to shake it.

Bennett pulled his hand back and wiped it on his slacks. "I believe that letter is for me?"

"Oh." She passed the envelope, now hopelessly crushed, to Bennett. "It's from Mr. Kingston at the Academy."

"Yes." Bennett led her into his office, already lit with three lamps even though it was empty before they walked in, and offered her a seat before he opened the letter and read it. Took his time, too, making Clover sit, squirming in her chair, for what felt like an hour but was probably only five minutes. Too bad his curtains were drawn. What a waste of energy, using electric lights when the sun was shining. And leaving those lights on when no one was even in the room?

"Very interesting, Clover," Bennett said as he set the letter on his desk.

The switch from *Miss Donovan* to her first name probably meant something. "What's interesting?"

"Your entrance exams were extraordinary."

"I know. You'd think Kingston would want me there, wouldn't you?" Clover rested her hand on Mango's head, and he propped his chin on her knee. "My dog does *not* bite, by the way. Mango is very well behaved. And no one would want to room with Heather Sweeney. Have you ever met her? She's really awful. I mean—"

"No. No, I haven't met her. I may know her father, though." Bennett leaned back in his seat. "And unlike the Academy, we work with service dogs quite often here at Waverly-Stead."

"You do?"

"Absolutely. There are skills we need to continue to ensure the health and safety of this country's citizens, Clover. We don't let anything get in the way of developing and making use of those skills."

"You mean those people," Clover said.

"Excuse me?"

"The skills belong to people."

"Well, yes. Yes, of course." Bennett tapped his right forefinger against his temple. "Your mind is a gift, Clover. At Waverly-Stead, it is an asset that will allow you to help your fellow citizens."

"Help them how?"

"As a Time Mariner."

Clover choked on her next breath, and Mango lifted his head. "Kids aren't Mariners. No one is, until after they graduate the Academy."

"You're right. But some lucky children—children with skills the Company depends on—are on the Mariner track. They start as Messengers. Do you know what a Messenger is?"

Clover recited a primary school textbook definition. "Messengers travel forward and gather the news from two years in the future, then bring it back to be analyzed so that problems can be solved before they occur. Messengers are the front line in the defense against a return of the Bad Times and essential to the operation of the world's most effective justice system."

Bennett smiled, showing a mouth full of very white, very straight teeth. "Exactly. Messengers protect us against another civil war or outbreak of disease. They are a big part of making sure that we can all live without fear. Waverly-Stead is dedicated to making sure that the Bad Times never happen again."

Clover pulled up whatever information she had about Messengers. Since the scope of what they did was so narrow, there weren't very many of them. Being a Messenger usually led to becoming a Time Mariner, traveling forward through the portal under Lake Tahoe and working with the information the Messengers collected. There were more Static Mariners, those who didn't travel through the portal, than Time Mariners. Everyone on the Mariner track, including Messengers, made up the Company's military ranks.

Clover didn't exactly know how those on the Mariner track were chosen, mostly because it wasn't described very well in her schoolbooks or lessons, and it had never occurred to her that she'd ever need to care.

Apparently, they randomly swooped kids up from the Academy. Not exactly something they bragged about.

"How can I be on the Mariner track if I don't graduate from the Academy?" she asked.

"You'll learn here. Starting today with your first mission." She waited for him to elaborate, but he didn't. Instead, he said, "Your guardian will continue to receive your rations and extras, of course, since Messengers don't live in the barracks."

"My guardian?"

Bennett raised a dark eyebrow and leaned back in his seat. "That's your brother, isn't it?"

Right. Her brother, who had no idea where she was. "Can I talk to him about it first?"

Bennett gave her a tight little frown and shook his head. "There isn't really anything to talk about, is there?"

"My brother will be really worried if I'm not there when he gets home from work."

"He'll be made aware of the situation." Bennett leaned back in his chair and watched her, like he was trying to gauge something. She couldn't figure out what, and that made her nervous.

"I'd really like to go home before I make any decisions. I can come back tomorrow." Clover came to her feet. A tight knot gathered in her belly, and she clenched Mango's lead in both hands to keep from flapping them as excess energy surged down her arms. "I have to talk to my brother. And my father."

Bennett walked toward her. "Your father. James Donovan. He's an executioner, isn't he? Such important work. And I'm certain he'll be pleased when he learns of your important role."

Clover held her ground on shaky legs, and for a minute she was sure she felt the whole tall building sway under her. "I need to go home now."

Bennett didn't move. "Did you study the Vietnam War in primary school?"

"Yes."

"Then you've heard of the draft?"

This was absurd. "Are you saying I've been drafted?"

"We don't call it *drafted*, sweetheart."

"My name is Clover."

"Yes. And you have a certain set of skills that makes you invaluable to your country."

"What skills?"

"The important thing is that we recognize them, and we are equipped to help you learn to use them."

Clover didn't know how to answer that, so she changed the subject to give herself time to think. "Can I look out your windows?"

Bennett froze, as if she'd shocked him with her request, then shrugged. "Of course."

Mango followed her closely to the closed curtains. She figured out how to open them while Bennett sat down in his chair, watching her. The view was startling. Like nothing Clover had ever seen before. She could see over the tops of all the trees and buildings and houses below. The gray concave curve of the wall cut a line between the relatively manicured occupied part of Reno and the wilder area beyond.

If the window were on the other side of the building, Clover would have been able to see the farms. As it was, she could just make out the gate, standing wide open. Two people, as small as ants, milled near it. "Are there just two guards at the gate?"

Bennett came to stand beside her. She felt his breath blow over her head and took a giant side step away from him.

"Yes," he said.

"All this work, to build the wall, and the gate is left open with just two guards?"

Bennett smiled slowly when she looked at him. She tried to place the look that swept over his scarred face. Irritation? Maybe pride. She couldn't be sure. "Waverly-Stead has helped build America into a country where the virus and violent crime, are a thing of the past. Who would want to leave their city?"

Clover's brow furrowed as she thought about what she knew of the walls. "They weren't built to keep people in."

"That's right. And there is no one to keep out anymore."

"I really have to go home," Clover said.

"After your first trip through the portal, you will. I'll make sure your brother gets word."

"Mr. Kingston said I could work at the farm with West."

Kingston's forehead wrinkled. "I would be personally offended if you were wasted with the dirt slingers."

chapter 5

Bennett led Clover and Mango outside, across a
courtyard, and behind the main building to a tower so tall that
Clover had to lean back and crane her neck to see the top.

They entered a small lobby on the first floor, at the end of which
was another bank of elevators. Overhead, Clover saw a giant chandelier that matched the one she'd seen in the main building. At least
on this one, the bulbs were unlit. Gas lamps attached to the walls
cast a soft, flickering glow instead.

"What is this place?" Clover asked.

"The first three floors hold the offices for the Mariner and guard
units," Bennett said. "The next two are our physical training facil-
ities, and then the barracks up to the top."

This elevator didn't have any mirrors. Just brass handrails and
cream and muted pink candy-striped wallpaper that looked to be
about as old as the building itself.

Bennett pushed the number seven button and then let his hand
fall on her shoulder.

"Please don't do that," she said, sidestepping away.

Bennett dropped his hand to his side but continued to stand a little too close as the elevator took them up.

Bennett led Clover to room 745. It looked like the hotel rooms she'd seen in movies and books. That made sense, since the building had once been part of a resort casino.

Clover wondered if every room in the barracks had the same dark, pressed-wood dresser and table and chairs. The same bed, made up with a white comforter and two pillows. Heavy, dark red drapes were parted and allowed a breeze through the half-opened window, billowing the lighter curtains into the room.

"There's a uniform hanging in the closet. You'll need to hurry if you're going to make the lake in time for the next mission."

Clover stood watching Bennett watch her. "Are you staying in here while I change?"

For the first time, Bennett seemed flustered. "I'll wait in the hall."

He closed the door, and Clover locked it behind him. She found a brown jumpsuit and a leather belt with a hip pocket attached to it hanging in the closet. A pair of heavy black boots sat on the floor beneath it.

West was never going to believe this, she thought as she pulled off her mother's dress and stepped into her Messenger uniform. She barely believed it herself. Sure, she belonged in the Academy, and she was positive Adam Kingston would regret his decision someday, but in the mean time she was getting ready to dive in the *Veronica*. The *Veronica*!

Clover had to roll up the uniform's arms and legs and cinch the belt so it wrapped nearly twice around her waist. The jumpsuit was marked size small but was still too big for her. The boots fit. She had no idea what she would have done if they hadn't, since her only other choice was her mother's torture shoes, and even she knew that would look ridiculous.

Clover tied the boots on and her feet immediately felt as though she'd encased them in blocks of concrete. She would kill for her sneakers.

When she looked at herself in the full-length mirror on the back of the bathroom door, Clover thought she looked like a child playing dress-up in her father's uniform. Which reminded her of her mother's dress. She started cold water running into the sink with the stopper in place and picked the yellow dress up off the bedroom floor. The stain seemed beyond removal, but Clover turned off the water and shoved the dress into the basin, making sure the stain was submerged.

Bennett stood across the hall from her door when she opened it. He looked her up and down when she and Mango came out.

"It doesn't fit," she said.

"We'll find you a smaller uniform," he said. "You're fine for today."

They took the elevator back down to the lobby. Another man waited for them. He wore a navy blue uniform that fit him perfectly.

"Officer Usher," Bennett said. "This is Clover Donovan. She's assigned to tonight's mission as a Messenger Trainee. She's only to observe. Officer Usher is a Static Mariner, Clover."

The Company had Time Mariners, who traveled through the portal, and Static Mariners, who didn't. They came through the guard track into military service. While every Time Mariner lived in Reno, every city in the country had Static Mariners.

Usher seemed to be in his early twenties, although Clover wasn't great at judging age. His hair was nearly white-blond, with a reddish tint that made it look almost pink. His face was covered in virus scars that made her think about West.

"Are you sure I can't talk to my brother first?" she asked.

"Come on, sweetheart," Usher said, moving toward the door without waiting to see if she would follow. "We're in a hurry."

"My name is Clover."

He turned back. "What?"

"My name is Clover, not *sweetheart*."

Usher looked to Bennett with eyes so light blue they were almost colorless. "Really?"

"Clover, I'm sure Officer Usher didn't mean any disrespect. And, like I've already told you, as soon as you're gone, I'll notify your brother of your whereabouts."

She hesitated, but neither man did. They walked together down the hall without looking to see that she followed. Clover hurried to catch up, clomping in her heavy boots with Mango's leash wrapped around her hand maybe a little tighter than was necessary. She didn't want to be left behind.

"Does the dog have a name, too?" Usher asked as they walked into the elevator.

"He's Mango." Bennett told her they wouldn't try to make her leave Mango behind, but she wanted to be sure. "He's a service dog."

"I know." She looked up at him in surprise. He tilted his head toward Mango. "He's wearing a vest."

Right.

"Have a good mission," Bennett said after they'd stepped off the elevator into the lobby. "I'll debrief you myself when you return."

For some reason, that promise didn't fill Clover with happy thoughts as she followed Usher through the building to a large lot out back filled with Company cars, trucks, and vans.

She'd learned in primary school about the time before the Bad Times. Cars everywhere, causing noise, pollution, and accidents. The need for foreign oil to keep them running caused wars, and keeping them running changed the weather, if you believed the environmentalists. Clover thought she might.

Now there were only official vehicles. Ambulances and guard cars, big trucks that carried goods to the trains, and Company cars, like the one Clover was about to ride in.

With a hugely diminished population, there was plenty of domestic oil now. Enough to allow for the use of vehicles without looking to other countries. But when the walls were built, all personal vehicles were taken out of the cities. The blacktopped roads that were designed for cars and trucks were mostly traveled by bicycle now.

Every New Year's Eve one person won a Whole New Life at the Bazaar. The winner received an electric cart, the kind old men used to drive around golf courses. They got a key to the charging station downtown, where they could replenish their cart's battery once a week. There were so few of the vehicles around, though, that whenever a participant drove one they attracted a crowd. Like a one-person parade.

Usher brought her to a white van with the blue Company logo emblazoned on the side. She looked back toward the buildings. "Where is everyone else?"

"They're already at the lake, preparing to launch," Usher said as he opened the van's door for her. "We need to hurry."

She hadn't been in a car since she was a baby. Maybe she should have been nervous, but she was fascinated. Her parents owned a huge orange Jeep before the city was walled and personal cars were banned. She had a picture of the four of them in front of it, taken the day she was brought home from the hospital. West's toddler cheeks were smooth and plump. Her mother didn't know yet that she'd been infected by the virus.

Clover watched movies at the library, and the recorded chaos of roads filled with cars, trucks, buses, and motorcycles made Clover wonder how anyone survived the experience of being in the middle of it all.

The noise alone was more than Clover could imagine.

She let up on Mango's leash so he could hop into the van first, then climbed into the seat.

"You'll only observe this time," Usher said once they were inside.

"Okay."

Usher looked at her for a few seconds, then reached across her body and pulled a dark gray woven belt from near her ear across her lap and hooked it at her hip.

"Oh, a seat belt!"

"Yes, a seat belt. We buckle up for safety." That last bit made him chuckle. She didn't get the joke.

It took about ten seconds for the novelty of the belt to turn into irritation that felt like a thousand ants crawling across her skin. The belt's rough texture hit her across the neck and tickled her ear; the sharp edge bit into her collarbone. Usher hadn't even put the van into gear.

"Can I take this thing off? It's trying to strangle me."

"No." Usher glanced at her, then reached over and pushed a button that lowered the shoulder belt four or five inches. "Better?"

The irritation lessened immediately. She still didn't like it, but it was livable at least. "Yes. Much."

"Good." He pulled on a lever on the side of the steering wheel, and the van moved backward. "Now, this is an observation run for you. You'll ride along with your trainer. The two of you will pick up the disc and bring it back."

"That sounds easy enough."

"It does, doesn't it? Your number one rule is to avoid accidentally changing the future. You don't talk to anyone except your trainer. Your uniform lets people know better than to talk to you."

He stopped the van and looked at her until she nodded that she understood. Then he pulled up on the lever again, and they moved forward. Clover had never actually seen a Time Mariner but had been taught from childhood that if she ever did, she was to pretend they weren't there. They even practiced STI, Stop-Turn-Ignore.

"Messengers have a half-hour window to get in and get out. That's an absolute, do you understand?"

"Yes."

"Good. Your trainer will have a van at the lake on the other side. You'll drive it—"

"I don't know how to drive."

Usher blew out a breath. "Your trainer will drive you to the pickup box where you'll find the info disc."

He reached into one of his uniform pockets and pulled out something about the length of her thumb, pale and curled, wrapped in clear plastic, and handed it to her.

"What is that?" she asked, without reaching for it.

He shoved it into her hand. "A fortune cookie, in case your trainer doesn't have an extra."

"A fortune cookie?" Clover started to open the plastic, but Usher stopped her.

"It's not for now. You open it on the other side. There's a piece of paper inside, with a sentence printed on it. Read it out loud."

"Out loud to who?"

"The trees, honey. It doesn't matter."

"My name is Clover. Why do I have to eat a cookie?"

"No. You don't eat it. That thing is older than you. It'll make you sick."

She frowned and turned it over in her hand. It looked okay to her. "I don't understand."

"You don't have to. It's a ritual. Just do it. The most important thing is not to talk to anyone, other than your trainer. Even the Mariners. Do you understand?"

She didn't need to be convinced. Changing the future, when her whole job was to bring back reports about the way it stood without her influence, didn't make sense.

The idea of talking to someone outside her own time line was upsetting, anyway. It was too strange to wrap her head around, so she didn't even consider it.

"Don't you wish you were a Time Mariner, so you could travel in the *Veronica*?" Clover asked.

Usher didn't give any outward sign that he'd heard her question. She was going to ask again, but they came to a stop at the huge metal gate in the wall that she'd seen from Bennett's window.

"We're leaving the city?" she asked. Mango had laid down in the space between the van's front seats, but something in her voice caught his attention and he sat up. Probably the panic. "I've never been outside the city."

"Clover, you know the portal is in Lake Tahoe. And you know that Lake Tahoe is outside the city walls."

Of course, she knew all that. Knowing didn't help much. Clover jumped when she heard a crunch and saw that she'd cracked her cookie. A narrow slip of paper showed through the shell. She shoved the whole thing into her pocket. "What's it like? Out there, I mean."

"The road to the lake has been cleared. You won't see anything too out of the ordinary. Some empty neighborhoods, then a lot of trees."

Usher drove through the open gate, flicking his hand twice, once at each of two guards.

He was right. The outside was a lot like the inside, except even without people it was so crowded. There were houses, all squished up next to each other, on both sides of the street for the first few miles. Cars parked everywhere. But everything fell away as they drove farther from the city.

When the road changed from a wide, flat highway to a winding mountain road, Clover saw the trees. Nothing like the parks in

Reno. These pine trees looked a thousand feet high and were probably that many years old. She turned in her seat and tried to see to their tops.

That was when things went off the rails. Clover's stomach flopped over as the landscape flew past. She groaned and squeezed her eyes closed.

"Look out the front window," Usher said. "You're just carsick."

Clover cracked her eyelids and then covered them with her hands. She burped and moaned. "I'm really sick."

"It's the mountain road. No horizon." Usher reached into another pocket in his uniform and pulled out something that he put in her palm. "Suck on this, it'll help."

He'd given her a peppermint candy. His jumpsuit was as good as the Bazaar. She unwrapped the candy and put it in her mouth, against her cheek. It did settle her stomach. The novelty of the sugar distracted her for a few minutes anyway. It did *not* let her watch out the car windows, though.

"There's medicine," Usher said. "Make sure you ask your trainer for some, or you'll never make it through the trip."

When Clover peeked again, the lake had opened on her side of the road. It was massive and brilliantly blue. Watching it gave her something stable to look at, and her stomach didn't protest too much. Clover's breath caught as she watched small waves crash against the rock cliffs.

She'd spent time at the Truckee River, of course. It ran just a half mile from her house. But this was something different.

Usher drove the van down a long, winding road to the water's edge. More vans were already parked in the small lot. Clover barely noticed them and even forgot to worry about her stomach. She was too busy gaping at the gigantic structure at the end of the long dock.

"That's the *Veronica*," Clover said. It was magnificent. Usher started toward the dock. Clover and Mango followed. "It's a submarine. Named after Ned Waverly's dead wife."

"That's right. A steam-powered submarine. Electronics don't travel through the portal."

Clover walked ahead of Usher. "Where is everyone?"

"Inside. They're waiting on you."

The *Veronica* ran on hydrogen peroxide, which produced heat to power a steam engine. The hull was narrow and sleek, made of dark, polished wood, the most beautiful thing Clover had ever seen.

She'd studied it, of course. She knew it was fashioned after a World War I model, and there had been fear initially that none of the survivors had the skills to build it.

And she got to see the *Veronica* in person. To actually ride in it. West wasn't going to believe this. She barely believed it herself.

She and Mango walked across a gangplank to the entrance at the top of the ship. At first Clover was worried about getting her dog down into it, but there was a small lift to her left. It was open, with just a rail rather than walls and no ceiling at all.

Mango went into the lift without a problem, and there was just enough room for the two of them to ride it down together. She closed the gate behind her and turned to look around for some kind of control panel.

"Na—No electricity on the *Veronica*."

Clover looked up and over her right shoulder at a man in a black jumpsuit, staring down at them. His right arm jumped in what almost seemed like a greeting, but not quite. "Are you my trainer?"

He shook his head, first normally, and then with several hard, quick jerks to the right. "No, no, no, no—" He exhaled forcefully through his nose. "No. I'm not."

Clover blinked up at him for a minute, then asked. "How do I work this thing?"

He pointed toward the ropes in front of her. "It's like a dumb—idiot!—waiter. Pull the rope on the right to go down. Idiot! Idiot!"

Clover bunched her hands into fists at her sides, the leather lead cutting into her palm. "I'm not an idiot."

"Idiot! Moron! I know that."

"Well, then why did you . . ."

The man stepped back, out of her line of vision. He called back, "Have a good mission."

A hot flush rose up her cheeks. She reached for the ropes and pulled. It was surprisingly easy to lower herself and Mango into the hold. When she got to the bottom, she looked back up. The man who'd called her an idiot peered down at her. "That one's yours."

He pointed to a door to her left, and then his whole body jerked that way and she cringed back, sure he'd fall in on her. After he was gone, she opened the door into a room that was larger than she expected and lit with some kind of recessed lighting that gave a warm, even tone with no flicker of fluorescent or too-bright glare.

A woman in a brown jumpsuit similar to Clover's, only better-fitting, sat in a chair against a curved wall. It had a rounded back and a small step under it that the woman had her feet on. Best of all, each chair along the wall was at least three feet from the next. Clover had been afraid that the ship would be crowded, but apparently the Messengers had their own cabin, and it was very well designed.

"You must be my new trainee," the woman said. She had light virus scars over her cheeks, as though the cure came just too late to save her from them. "I'm Leanne Wood. Bennett radioed ahead to expect you. We don't have long, at least not on this end, but I wanted to meet you and make sure you were prepared for the trip."

"I'm Clover," she said, looking around. The room was made entirely of highly polished dark wood. She pulled a folding seat down from the wall and sat in it. It was padded, the cushion covered in a soft fabric that didn't itch or have a weird texture. Mango sat at her feet, pressing against her shins. "Bennett told me to expect you, too."

The *Veronica* rolled forward and then back, making Clover nearly come out of her seat.

"Don't worry," Leanne said. "It's weird the first time, but you get used to it. Buckle up."

Clover looked over her right shoulder, where the strap in the car had been, but didn't see one. Leanne stood and pulled a harness over Clover's head and clipped it into the buckle between her legs. The straps were snug, but soft, and they didn't dig into her skin or put pressure anywhere on her body.

"Have you been doing this a long time?" she asked Leanne.

"Almost ten years."

"Why aren't you a Mariner then?" Leanne's eyebrows shot into her blunt-cut chestnut-colored bangs and Clover winced. "I'm sorry."

Leanne bent and rolled up the leg of her jumpsuit. She had a metal prosthetic where her right leg should have been. Clover wanted to get on her knees and look at it more closely but stopped herself.

"I can run, jump, do just about anything any of the Static Mariners do. But rules are rules. Mariners can't have a physical disability."

Rules were rules, of course. But sometimes they weren't fair. "It must make you angry."

Leanne didn't respond to that, and Clover didn't push it. She'd be angry if she were Leanne. She was already angry enough that having autism kept her out of the Academy, and that ended with her on the Mariner track and riding the *Veronica*.

"What did you mean, we don't have much time?" Clover asked. "Aren't you going with me?"

The submarine jerked awake. The floor vibrated under Clover's feet and up through her body, leaving her with the unpleasant feeling that she couldn't get away from the sensation. Before she could react, a loud clanking forced her to press her hands to her ears.

"Shoot." Leanne raised her voice above the noise just as it settled into something less horrible. She reached over Clover's head for a pair of headphones with a microphone extending from the left side and handed them to her. "Those will help. Also, put your feet on the riser. This part will be over soon. I promise."

Clover lifted her feet, and as soon as they were off the ground the vibration settled to just a slight hum. The earphones blocked out what sounded like a swarm of bees trying to get into her head. It blocked out everything else, too.

Leanne put on a second pair of headphones, then pushed a button on the left side and Clover heard her voice through her own. "They can't take off while I'm still on board. You're going to do just fine, and I'll see you on the other side."

"Wait, what?" Clover said, but knew immediately that her voice wasn't being transmitted. She pushed the button over her own left ear and spoke again. "What do you mean on the other side?"

"I don't travel," she said. "You get to meet the thirty-five-year-old me. Lucky girl."

"Wait!" Leanne did, but Clover couldn't think of anything to say, except, "What happened to your leg?"

"The virus took too much of it." There was a sensation of shifting under Clover then, and Leanne headed for the door. "You'll be fine, I promise. Do you have a cookie?"

Clover pulled it out of her pocket and held it up for Leanne to see.

"Perfect. Don't forget to read the fortune out loud. Even if it feels silly."

"But why . . ."

"See you soon." Leanne left, and despite Clover's barely contained anxiety, the trip through Waverly's time portal was anticlimactic. The *Veronica* dove first, just long enough for Clover to think about the millions of gallons of water surrounding her, pressing against the polished wood walls. And then it came back up. Clover felt the movement like a pressure in her head.

She waited until the ship had finished its ascent and she felt it dock, then lifted the headphones off one ear. When there was no hum, she took them off, then set one foot on the floor. No vibration either. She unbuckled herself and stood up, hung up her headphones, and left the Messenger cabin.

When she pulled herself and Mango back up in the dumbwaiter lift, Leanne was on the dock. Except that her thick, straight hair was cut to chin-length and she'd grown out her bangs, she didn't look much different two years older.

"Hey! Told you it wouldn't be so bad. Two minutes for you, two years for me. Ain't that a kick?"

Clover bit at her bottom lip, thinking about what Usher said about talking to people from the future.

"We're going to drive out and get the disc, come back, and you'll carry it through. Easy peasy." When Clover still didn't say anything, Leanne said, "It's okay to talk to me. Just no one else from this time line, okay? That's important. Not even any of the Static Mariners."

"Officer Usher said you could give me something," she said as she lowered herself on wobbly legs to the dock and felt for a second like her stomach was a step or two behind the rest of her body. "To keep me from getting carsick."

"Right, right. It's in the van. I'll give you some. We'll get the disc and you'll be home before you know it."

"This is so weird." Clover looked at the group of uniformed Mariners waiting at the other end of the deck. Some in the black

Time Mariner jumpsuits and others in navy blue Static Mariner uniforms. Only Leanne and Clover wore brown. "Why don't the Mariners just have the disc waiting for us?"

"It's in a lockbox. Chain of custody is important when you're dealing with future information. The fewer people who have access to the disc, the better."

They made their way to the van, which was similar to the one that Usher had driven her outside the city in an hour ago. Maybe the exact same van, only two years older. Clover shook her head. "This is so weird."

"Just be grateful that the whole Messenger program is designed to keep us from seeing anyone. Imagine running into yourself."

"That would be . . ." Clover couldn't find the right word.

"Yeah. It was hard enough to get used to my trainees seeing me age two years in a few minutes."

An hour later, Clover was in the first van again, in her own time with thirty-three-year-old Leanne and Bennett, who'd come to drive them back to the tower.

"What did you think, Clover?" Bennett asked.

"It's pretty strange. But you already know that, right?"

"I'll have to take your word for it."

"You've never done it?"

Bennett didn't look away from the road. "I rely on people like you to fill me in on what's happening over there."

"Well, you should try it," she said. He didn't say anything else about it, so she didn't either.

The three of them rode in silence up the elevator in the tower next to the Waverly-Stead building. Clover was getting used to the hanging-box part, at least. On the seventh floor, Bennett got off with her. Leanne stayed on. Her room was on ten.

"My dad must live in this building," Clover said as Bennett walked with her toward her room. He still stood too close to her. Not enough so that he was actually touching her, but just inside her personal zone. She fought down the same skin crawl she'd felt earlier.

"No. Executioners have their own barracks."

He followed her into her room and closed the door behind him. For no reason that she could put her finger on, her throat closed up and she gripped Mango's lead more tightly.

"Leanne has the disc," she said.

"I know." Bennett smiled at her. He sat on the edge of the mattress and patted a spot next to him. "We're going to debrief now. It won't take long."

"Okay." She sat on the chair, which wasn't nearly far enough away. She wanted to go home. *Trust your instincts*, West had told her. Bennett gave her the creeps. She glanced at the door and decided she had a pretty clear route out of the room if she needed it.

"Who did you talk to on your trip, Clover?"

"Leanne," she said. "And a Time Mariner who helped me figure out the lift."

"Okay. What was the Mariner's name?"

"I don't know."

Bennett frowned, his scarred face wrinkled, and he looked ten years older. "Always ask, Clover. Anytime someone talks to you on a trip, you take their name."

Something else that would have been good to know ahead of time. She didn't say it. Or ask what the big deal was, since they obviously knew who was traveling at the same time as her. She just wanted him to leave. "I'm sorry."

"Don't forget again."

"You have to be told something to forget it," she said. And then apparently she did care, because she said, "He didn't take my name, either."

Bennett wrote something in a small notebook he took from his pocket. "Was Leanne with you the entire time you were on the other side of the portal?"

"Yes."

"She was never outside your view?"

Clover bit at her thumbnail. She didn't want to get Leanne in trouble by accidentally saying the wrong thing. "What's this about?"

"Standard questions, that's all."

"She was with me the whole time."

"Did you read your fortune?"

"Yes."

"Do you have anything unusual to report?"

Seriously? "I went to orientation at the Academy and ended up time-traveling in a submarine."

Bennett stood and stretched his back, which Clover was happy to see took him closer to the door and away from her. "Don't worry, Clover. This will all be second nature before you know it. Someone will come with your suppressant soon, and a doctor will clear you to go home, after you've been quarantined for twenty-four hours."

"Home to my house?"

"Yes. Home to your house. You travel only twice a week. As long as there is no threat of you not returning for your next mission, you can go home. There isn't that threat, is there?"

She shook her head. She wasn't lying either. She wanted to go back into the *Veronica* and see Leanne again and go beyond the walls. And drive. "Is this my room, then? Like a permanent room?"

"It's yours. Feel free to bring some things to keep in it, if you like."

Bennett left and closed the door behind him. Clover heard a click. When she tried the knob, she found the door locked.

Mango was at her side, pressing his bulky body against her legs.

For the first time, she realized she was rocking from foot to foot, and she wondered if she'd done that in front of Bennett.

She pulled the little slip of paper she'd saved from the fortune cookie from her pocket. *You are on the verge of a life change.*

She slid the edge of the paper into the edge of the frame around the mirror above the dresser. Her face was pale, and she still looked silly in the far-too-big uniform.

She sat on the floor, her legs going out from under her so that she landed hard on her rear end. Mango pressed his head into her lap and she methodically petted him. "We're Messengers, Mango."

West's scalp ached from yanking his hands through his hair so often in the last couple of hours. What was he thinking, letting Clover go to the Academy alone?

Was she lost? It was nearly inconceivable that anything worse than that had happened to her. Knowing that she was probably just wandering around somewhere didn't stop a chill up his spine. He couldn't remember the last time he didn't know exactly where his sister was.

Yes, it was almost inconceivable that any of the terrible thoughts in his head were actually happening. Except here he was, conceiving.

He knew that no real, violent crime had been allowed to happen since the walls went up. He had faith in that. Faith enough that he'd sent his sister alone to a viper's nest of primary school bullies who'd gone all summer without their favorite target.

She trusted too easily. Even people it was obvious she should be permanently wary of. They apologized when it suited their needs, and she believed them when they said they were her friends.

Usually just before they made her the butt of some miserable joke.

West stalked back into the kitchen, opened a drawer, and picked up the blue folder holding his Company application. Less than three weeks from now, his little sister would be someone else's worry. Someone else would freak out when she took off.

West sank down into a chair.

Clover never took off. She just wasn't that girl.

So where was she?

He couldn't call the guard. That would open a file in his sister's name. His, too, for that matter. No good, all around. They'd treat Clover like a runaway and him like the guardian who couldn't control her. The best they could hope for was that Clover would be allowed to keep her place at the Academy, under extra scrutiny. In the worst-case scenario, Clover would be sent to Foster City as soon as she was found.

And West? He didn't know, but it wouldn't be good. He'd involve the guard if he had to, but it hadn't gotten there yet.

West put the folder back in the drawer, grabbed his jacket, and headed out of the house. He had maybe ninety minutes of light before sundown, when the curfew bells would ring and he'd better be indoors. Being caught out after the bells was to bring a lot of unnecessary trouble on a person. If he didn't make it home on time, and the guard caught him, he'd be taken in for questioning and his chances of ever getting in at the Company would be close to zero.

It took twenty minutes to walk to the Kingston Estate, and then he wasted another ten pacing back and forth in front of the gate trying to make up his mind to knock on the door.

This was the delicate part, where he had to ask after his sister without making it obvious she was missing.

The front door opened as soon as his knuckles touched it. West stepped back, then squared his shoulders, trying to look like he belonged on the headmaster's front porch even though his heart beat in his throat.

And then he saw Bridget, standing there with her hand on her hip and her head tilted so the end of her ponytail touched her bare shoulder.

He'd been nervous about talking to Kingston. This was worse.

"West? What are you doing here?"

"I'm looking for my sister."

Her smile faded. "You think your sister is here?"

"No, I don't think she's here." And then he peered past Bridget into the entrance of the house. An oil lamp on the table behind her gave everything a sort of warm glow and reminded West it was nearly dusk. "She isn't, is she?"

"Why would she be here?"

"Bridget?" a male voice called from somewhere in the house. "Who's at the door at this hour?"

Bridget lifted her pale eyebrows, as though she were wondering the same thing.

"My sister was at orientation today." He hesitated, then decided to go with the truth. He wasn't positive he'd be able to lie to her anyway. His words stuck in his throat as it was. "She never came home."

"It isn't dark yet. Clover probably got home while you were out looking for her."

"You don't understand. Clover—"

"Bridget?" Adam Kingston appeared behind his daughter, and West straightened again. "West Donovan. You shouldn't be here."

"My sister—"

Kingston held a hand up to stop him. "I'm sorry, but as I explained to Miss Donovan earlier today, we do not allow animals at the Academy."

Although he had no idea what he expected Kingston to say, this was so far from it that it took West a minute to form a response. "Mango's a service dog."

It wasn't like she'd hidden him. He went to her exams with her.

He'd been at primary school with her since their father gave him to her.

"It doesn't matter," Kingston said. "A rule is a rule."

Bridget's mouth opened, but when Kingston darted a look at her, she didn't speak.

"You don't understand—" West started to say, pulling himself back to the real problem, his missing sister, but Kingston cut him off again.

"She will be fine. I wouldn't have sent her if I didn't believe that. Miss Donovan is an extraordinary young woman, and the Company is better equipped to handle her special needs than the Academy is."

The silence between them drew on long enough to become awkward before West broke it. "You sent my sister to the Company?"

Kingston pulled a cloth from his pocket and mopped his face. His pasty complexion went even paler. "She's been accepted into the Mariner training track. That's more than what most of our graduates can say, Mr. Donovan. Now, we wish you a good evening."

"You sent my sister to be a Mariner?" That couldn't be right. Even saying it out loud sounded ridiculous.

Bridget started to speak again and actually managed a squeak before her father pushed her farther into the house and slammed the door shut.

West stood rooted to their porch, feeling more than a little queasy. Clover was sent to the Company to join the Mariner track?

Clover *went* to the Company without telling him?

They couldn't make her a Mariner. Could they? She was just a kid, barely out of primary school.

He backed away from the door and then walked toward the gate.

What the hell just happened?

The house door opened again and when West turned, he saw

Bridget flying down the steps. He caught her to keep her from plowing right into him.

He looked at the house, expecting her father next, but didn't see him. "What's wrong?"

"Nothing. I just . . . just tell your sister to be careful, okay?"

He held her away from him by the shoulders. "Be careful of what?"

Bridget bit her bottom lip. Her eyes were Company blue. She had the kind of soft, fair skin that pinked up easily. "She's different, right? I mean, she's got the dog and the—"

Bridget flapped her hands, almost delicately, two or three times at her waist. West took her hands to stop her, then let them go when she froze. "Yes, but I don't understand—"

"Bridget!" Her father yelled her name from the front porch.

West registered each second of the next moment like a still frame. Before he could insist that Bridget explain her warning, she rose to her toes and leaned toward him. His hands slid up her arms and around her back as she pressed her mouth against his.

She tasted like the strawberries that grew along the Kingston Estate fence. Her mouth slipped around to his ear and she whispered, "We need to talk."

West nodded. He probably couldn't have spoken if he tried. Not even to ask what they needed to talk about or where. He'd figure that out, somehow. And then time snapped back like a rubber band and she left him with more questions than answers.

chapter 6

Far and away the best prize that life has to offer
is the chance to work hard at work worth doing.

—THEODORE ROOSEVELT,
"SQUARE DEAL" SPEECH, SEPTEMBER 7, 1903

Clover was still missing when West went to work at
dawn the next day.

He didn't want to go. He needed to figure out where his sister
was. But if he was missed at the farm, the guard would come look
for him. They'd better find him on his deathbed, too, or there would
be hell to pay. A missing sister was not an acceptable excuse for
making someone else do his work.

What would he do, anyway? March into the Company offices
and demand they turn her over?

All he could do was hope she'd be home when he returned.

He spent eight hours weeding and fertilizing cantaloupe on the
verge of ripeness and trying not to think of all the things that could
be happening *right that minute* to Clover. Inconceivable or not.
Bridget's warning the night before didn't help. He still had to figure
out a way to talk to her privately. At the moment, that seemed like
an insurmountable task.

When he got home, he was filthy and exhausted. Worry and
railing against his own imagination and the frustration of being

completely unable to help or protect Clover had drained him. When he opened the door, he knew immediately she wasn't there. The house was too empty. Too exactly how he had left it. Clover was a force unto herself, and he knew immediately that she had not been here.

He sat at the kitchen table and tried to sort out what he knew. Kingston sent Clover to the Company. The bastard. Maybe they put her right to work. It didn't make much sense that they wouldn't let her come home first, especially because she was a minor, but where else could she be?

Maybe someone had told their father, but no one had thought to let West know what was going on. James was an executioner doing Company work. It was possible that whoever Clover had been in contact with at the Company recognized her as his daughter. But West was her guardian. Someone should have let him know what was happening, instead of making him worry about the implications of trying to find out on his own.

What if something happened to Clover because West was too afraid that checking on her would ruin his own chances at the Company?

"I have to get out of here," he said out loud to the empty house. Maybe Bridget was on her porch, waiting for him to come find out what she wanted to talk to him about.

And then the front door opened, and Clover was home.

Relief flooded West first, strong enough to make his knees weak. That was followed by a wave of rage that threatened to drown him. He sat without moving, trying to get control of himself before he spoke.

Clover stayed by the door. She let Mango off his leash and the dog remained at her side, looking up at West with a curiously tilted head. Clover looked as shaken as West felt as she kicked their mother's white leather shoes across the living room.

"You're mad at me," Clover said.

Clover Jane Donovan, Queen of the Understatement. "You think?"

"Didn't they tell you? They were supposed to. And it's not like I had a choice."

He stayed still in his chair, mostly because he didn't feel he had control of his limbs and needed something stable under him. "No one told me anything. Including you."

"They took back my acceptance, West. The headmaster sent me to the Company. It just happened really fast."

"You couldn't come home?"

"I was drafted. Mr. Bennett told me he was going to tell you."

"Wait a minute. You were what?"

"Drafted." Clover sat in a chair across from him. "You shouldn't be so mad, anyway. It isn't like you tell me everything that goes on in your life."

"What are you talking about?" Did she know he'd signed up to start his Company training? He hadn't kept that from her, exactly. He just hadn't told her yet.

"You told me you failed your entrance exams."

Oh. Damn.

"Why would you lie to me about that?"

"I didn't think you'd understand," he said.

"Understand what? That you couldn't join the Academy and still take care of me?"

West exhaled. "Yeah. That."

"You aren't my father," she reminded him.

Their father would have sent her to Foster City. "I know that."

"But you constantly underestimate me, just the way he does." She sat back in her chair and crossed her arms over her chest. "I can take care of myself."

"No. You can't."

"I'm not a baby, West! I'm a Messenger now."

"You're sixteen. It doesn't matter what you're capable of; they won't let you stay here alone. You'll be sent to live in Foster City, even if you do have a job."

"Why would I have to go to Foster City?"

West opened his mouth to tell her about his application, but the words wouldn't come out. This was a nightmare.

"I don't know what the big deal is," Clover said.

West closed his eyes and forced a slow, deep breath. "You don't understand."

"Yes, I do."

"No, you don't!" He went to the kitchen drawer where he'd stashed his Company folder and pulled it out.

"What is it?"

Christ. This was a flat-out tragedy. "I have an interview with the Company."

"Since when?"

"Since the day you got your acceptance letter."

"Why didn't you say something?"

"I don't know. I should have." Mango hadn't left Clover's side. Not to eat or drink. Not to curl up in his favorite chair. He picked up on the tension in the room and stayed on duty. "Are they going to let you keep Mango with you?"

"Yes. The Academy wouldn't. And they were going to make me room with Heather Sweeney! She's—"

"I know who she is." A spoiled officer's daughter who made a career out of torturing Clover.

"Maybe this is for the best," Clover said. "I mean, the Mariner track. I never even considered it. And it was so cool, West. I got to ride in the *Veronica*, and I had to read a fortune cookie, and—"

He held a hand up to stop her. "You'll end up in Foster City while I'm in training."

She hadn't thought about that. It showed on her face. "I can stay home. Bennett said I could."

"He doesn't know that I'm headed for training. And you can't stay here alone, even if you were allowed to. How will you eat? The food is in the Bazaar. Remember the Bazaar? It wouldn't matter if they gave your ration tickets directly to you; you aren't old enough to collect on them."

She couldn't even if she were old enough. He doubted she'd make it through the door and into the chaos inside. He didn't say that. Or that there was no way he'd let her go there, even if her sensory issues didn't stop her.

"Mr. Kingston wouldn't let me into the Academy. And they didn't exactly ask me if I wanted to be a Messenger. Drafted, remember?"

A meltdown was imminent. West felt it. Mango felt it, too. The dog pressed his weight against Clover's legs and the top of his head against her hand, trying to calm her.

"We'll work this out," West said.

She shifted her weight from her left foot to her right and did the thing with her hands she did sometimes when she was upset, rubbing her knuckles together like she thought she might light a fire with them. "When do you go to training?"

"September seventh."

"The day after school starts." Clover's face crumbled, and tears fell down her cheeks.

"Oh, hell. Don't cry, Clover. Come on."

West came around the table and knelt next to her. He waited until she leaned against him, then wrapped his arms around her. It was rare that Clover allowed herself to be touched, but when she was in this space she needed it. She sobbed against his shoulder. "I really wanted to go to the Academy, you know?"

"We'll change Kingston's mind. We'll go to the Academy tomorrow. If the Mariners want you, they'll still want you in four years. They'd be stupid not to."

"He won't change his mind."

He had to, West thought. The alternatives—Clover in Foster City or him waiting two more years to join the Company—were unthinkable. He still hadn't wrapped his head around the idea that his little sister had somehow been conscripted into the Company ranks.

"Why don't you go for a run while I make supper?"

"Okay," she said. As quickly as her meltdown had come, it was over. "I had a ham sandwich at the Academy before they kicked me out. I wanted to bring you one, but I had to eat it instead."

"Was it good?"

"Really good. Maybe you can get us a ham next week."

"I have to ask you to leave," Kingston said.

West concentrated on not letting his irritation show. He and Clover sat in Kingston's office in matching reddish leather chairs. Kingston had some kind of little man, big desk complex. He looked absurd sitting behind the outsized oak monstrosity.

"All we want is an explanation," West said.

"I have told you, and I told Clover when I sent her to the Company, sometimes someone looks like a perfect candidate for the Academy on paper but in reality is not a good fit."

"She's smarter than any three students here put together."

Clover looked tiny in her chair, holding herself stiff and very controlled. She looked at her knees and gripped her hands together in her lap. She didn't move. Not even when Kingston said, "I'm sure that's not true. But even if it were, it doesn't matter. She is not right for the Academy."

Her attempt to control her behavior only highlighted how different she really was from other girls her age.

"She's exactly right for the Academy. Or aren't you in the business of training the best minds in Reno anymore?"

"Please, don't make me send for the guard."

Clover stood up. Her green eyes were red-rimmed, but no tears fell. "I want to go home."

West scrubbed his hand through his hair and finally stood, too. "You're making a mistake, Mr. Kingston. A huge mistake."

Kingston didn't answer, except to raise one shoulder as if to say *maybe*.

"I can't believe he didn't budge an inch," West said after they'd left the campus and made their way down Virginia Street and up California Avenue back home on their bicycles. "Not a damn inch."

"Did you really expect him to?"

Maybe he shouldn't have, but he did. In what world did it make sense that Clover was pulled out of school and dumped into the Mariner track before she was even old enough to feed herself? "We'll appeal."

"I'll be as old as you before it's even looked at," Clover said.

God, he hated that she was right. "Maybe Bennett can help."

"He seemed pretty excited to have me at the Company. He's the one who kept telling me I was drafted."

"This doesn't make sense. Mariners are trained at the Academy. If they wanted you there, why would they take you right out of primary school?"

"I don't know," Clover said. "Kingston was going to put me in research, anyway. He said so, before he decided I didn't belong at the Academy at all. I wasn't headed for the Mariners."

West sat quietly for a minute while Clover ate salad greens and tomatoes from their garden, tossed in a little of their precious oil and some vinegar she had made herself from a recipe she'd found at the library and juice pressed from Mrs. Finch's apples. "So, I'll cancel my training."

"You can't." She didn't even pause as she brought her fork to her mouth. They couldn't afford to lose their appetites just because they were upset.

"Yes, I can. It's only two more years. No, less than that. Once you're eighteen, you won't need a guardian."

"You've wanted this your whole life."

"What am I supposed to do, Clover? Do you want to go to Foster City?"

"We'll find Dad," she said. "He'll know what to do."

Sure he would. "He'd have you in Foster City before you even knew what hit you."

"Maybe it's not as bad as it seems. I have to go to the Waverly-Stead building tomorrow for a driving lesson," Clover said. "I'll try to find out what happens in situations like this. They can't really have employees living in Foster City."

They were going to teach her to drive? West heard Bridget's voice telling him to be careful. He needed to find a way to talk to her. Clover took another bite and chewed slowly. West could practically see her wheels turning.

chapter 7

Families is where our nation finds hope, where
wings take dream.

-GEORGE W. BUSH,
SPEECH, OCTOBER 18, 2000

"Turn the wheel the way you want the van to go. That's
it. Now, sharper."

Clover pulled the steering wheel harder to the left and the van
made a tight turn.

"You're a natural," Leanne said. "It took me forever to learn."

Clover's cheeks actually ached from smiling so hard. She turned
the wheel to the right and the van followed in a wider, spiraling
turn. "It's pretty fun."

Two deep dimples formed when Leanne smiled back at Clover.
"Ready to try the street?"

The van's engine rumbled under Clover when she gave it a little
gas. She loved how she could hold a picture in her head of the way
the wheel turned the axis, which turned the tires. She didn't fully
understand how stepping on the gas pedal or brake worked, but
she would find out. She could hardly wait to get to the library on
Wednesday.

Driving was like running, only more. More free. More fast. More
everything.

Clover turned onto the street and then sped down back roads, staying away from the main avenue with all its bicycles. Leanne lowered the passenger window and wind blew through Clover's hair and over her face. She didn't dare look away from the road to see whether Mango, who was sitting in the space between the front seats, was enjoying himself. She bet he was.

"You really like this, don't you?" Leanne asked.

"I love it. Who wouldn't?"

"I remember when people still drove personal cars. Can you imagine hundreds of other cars all flying around you?"

"I've seen it in movies."

"Not the same at all."

Clover had spent the last half hour trying to figure out how to ask Leanne about kids working for the Company. Finally, she blurted it out. "What happens to kids who get drafted but don't have a guardian at home?"

Leanne shot her a look. "The Company doesn't *draft* kids. Who wouldn't want on the Mariner track?"

Clover imagined that some people might not, but for some reason it seemed best not to say so. Instead, she filed away Leanne's insistence that what had happened to Clover didn't happen to anyone and said, "I wish we could pick up my brother."

Leanne shook her head. "Bennett would kill us both."

The rule was no unauthorized passengers. Still, West would love this. She tried to remember every detail to tell him later.

He'd like Leanne, too, she thought. Clover wondered how long it would take to grow her hair out long enough to put it in two pigtails like her trainer's. She couldn't wait to get home and tell West everything.

Only, when she and Mango met West later at the suppressant bar, he didn't even ask about driving or Leanne.

"Don't you want to know?" she finally asked him.

"Know what?"

"About driving! About what Leanne said. What's wrong with you?"

"How was it?" West asked.

"The driving was amazing." She still felt the miles racing under her. They'd stayed inside the city walls, but after a few hours, Clover could drive forward and backward, make turns, and park. "I wish you could have been there."

"Yeah."

West didn't even look at her. Maybe she'd said something wrong. It was hard to tell, sometimes. "I didn't even get sick this time," she said.

"That's great, Clover."

The suppressant bar was about a half mile from their house. West and Clover went there at five o'clock every afternoon, without exception. It didn't matter if she had the flu, or homework, or if it was five degrees outside with two feet of snow on the ground.

The room had two long, waist-high counters that divided it into thirds. A tall, bald man with skin the color of the caramel candies Mrs. Finch sometimes made them stood at the registration station just inside the door.

Years ago, the word *caramel* had crossed with *camel* in her head and Clover imagined the thick muscle at the back of the man's neck growing into a water-filled camel hump.

West elbowed her, and she pulled her ID card from her pocket and handed it over. The caramel-camel man looked at it, then at her and back at the card. Without a word, he found her name on the computer in front of him and checked it off.

Being dosed was clinical and very impersonal. Despite seeing him nearly every day for as long as she could remember, Clover didn't know Caramel-Camel Man's name. He had never spoken to her.

Their doser tonight was a woman with a riot of dark curly hair held back from her face with a wide pink headband. A couple dozen other people sat at stools along either counter. Some of them talked to each other while they waited for their doses.

This was the worst part of Clover's day, but she'd been doing it since she was an infant, and if she'd ever complained, she couldn't remember it. The suppressant kept her healthy. It saved her brother and kept him alive. It kept the virus from coming back and killing them all. The suppressant was their miracle.

Her upper thighs still had a faint collection of scars from the first year, when they gave the suppressant with hypodermic needles. West had faint pockmarks on his upper arms as well. The suppressant was thick and delivered cold. The needle they had to use back then to push it was as thick as a spaghetti noodle. Clover was glad she didn't remember the old days.

For as long as her memory stretched, she, West, and the rest of Reno had small ports implanted at the back of their necks. The medicine was still as congealed as jelly and stung like fire ants eating toward your brain, but at least the long, thick needles were a thing of the past.

Clover rubbed around her port after the doser was done, helping the medication move through so it would stop stinging. "I wish I could take you driving," she said to West as they started back to their house.

He walked with his head down and his hands in his pockets, deep in thought. "Me, too."

"Leanne said that kids aren't drafted into the Mariner track."

West stopped walking and turned to look at her. She waited for him to respond to that. When she said it out loud to him, it sounded a whole lot more ominous than it had just in her head.

"Can you make it home on your own?" he asked.

"Of course, I can practically see the house from here," she said. "Why, where are you going?"

"I won't be long."

"West."

"I promise. Go on."

He waited until she started walking toward home. In fact, he stood there longer than that. She looked over her shoulder twice and saw him still rooted to his spot on the sidewalk, watching until she walked the last few hundred yards home and went inside.

As soon as Clover and Mango were inside the house, West turned and walked toward Bridget's house. It was iffy, showing up so close to dinnertime. Kingston could be home, or he could still be at the Academy getting ready for the next semester to start. Maybe West should have waited until the next day, but he really didn't want to. Bridget had something to tell him, and after hearing that Clover's trainer didn't know that kids were being drafted by Bennett, it suddenly seemed vital that he find out what it was. The sooner, the better.

Be careful, she'd told him. He needed to find out what exactly he needed to be careful of.

He was afraid he'd have to knock, so as he walked he tried to come up with some story in case Kingston answered the door. All he could come up with was an apology for his response to Clover's being sent to the Company. It was weak, because he wasn't really sorry at all, but nothing better came to him. He had no legitimate reason to knock on the headmaster's door.

He didn't need an excuse in the end. When he reached the Kingston Estate, Bridget was in the front pasture, working with her horses. Jesus, she took his breath away. Corny, but true.

"What do we need to talk about?" he asked when she saw him and came close enough that he didn't have to shout.

"Not here." She leaned over the fence and looked both ways

down the road that ran in front of her house. Then she opened the gate for him. "Come with me."

She led him through the pasture, which was planted with alfalfa. The sweet scent of the grass wafted up into West's nose as he crushed it under his feet. She looked back again, then took his hand and pulled him into the stables.

West wanted to trust her. He had once; when they were in primary school, they were friends. Maybe more than friends. But then her father was promoted and she moved out of West's orbit. He didn't know how to trust her now, no matter how badly he wanted to. "What do I need to be careful of, Bridget?"

She let go of his hand and, despite his reservations, West had to fight to keep from taking hers back. "I don't know."

"What do you mean, you don't know?"

"I—" She stopped and took a breath. "I overheard something I shouldn't have."

"Something about Clover?" What could she have possibly overheard about his little sister? The Donovans didn't matter to anyone, except that they were as much a part of keeping the mechanics of the city running as any other citizens.

"Not her specifically. But they look at the test scores to find them."

"Who does? Them who?"

"My dad and Langston Bennett. They look for kids with certain test scores." She looked at the dirt at her feet. "Kids like Clover, you know?"

Langston Bennett was the man to whom Kingston had sent Clover. The director of the Mariner program. "Why do they want them?"

Before she could answer, her father's small white Academy car pulled into the driveway a few feet from where they hid.

"Oh, no," Bridget said. "Oh, God. Stay here until we're inside."

She started to leave the stables, but West caught her arm. "Why do they want them?"

Bridget looked over her shoulder. "He can't find you here."

"When can we talk again?"

"Soon," she said. "I promise."

It was two more days before Clover had another mission. She hadn't been able to get any information from Leanne about underage Messengers and where they lived. Despite thinking and talking about little else, she and West weren't able to come up with any plan other than for her to show up and keep her eyes and ears open.

"Be careful, Clover," West said, before he left for the farm that morning.

Clover took a bite of her oatmeal. "If you knew how easy the job was, you wouldn't be worried."

"Just promise me you'll be careful."

There was something odd in his tone that she couldn't quite put her finger on. "I promise."

After he left, she filled her pack with a water bowl for Mango, a couple of books, a pair of pajamas, and a change of clothes before heading out herself with Mango's lead in her hand.

"They might let us move into the barracks," Clover said to her dog as they walked, the sun warming his pale fur and her upturned face. "West isn't always right, even if he thinks he is."

Mango made a small sound and Clover picked up her pace to a gentle jog. Maybe Leanne would let her drive to the launch site. The idea of driving outside the city walls sent a small shiver of anticipation down Clover's back, and goose bumps covered her arms as she moved into a run.

Mango ran beside her, his wide, strong body easily keeping up.

After a few minutes she made herself slow down. Arriving at the Waverly-Stead building sweaty and pulsing with adrenaline was a bad idea.

"Your mission is canceled," Bennett said when she saw him half an hour later. His eyes darted to Mango and then back to Clover's face. "I'm sorry you came all this way."

"It's not that far."

He nodded slowly. "Well, that's good, then."

They stood and looked at each other for a few awkward seconds before Clover asked, "Should I go home?"

Bennett cleared his throat. "Yes, I suppose so."

Clover turned to go back upstairs to change, but stopped when she realized she'd responded to the wrong part of Bennett's statement. She came back and asked, "Why is the mission canceled?"

Bennett looked relieved that she'd put them both back on the same page. "Leanne was in an accident and broke her good leg. We're going to have to get another team to make the run tomorrow. We'll have to find you another trainer, since you don't know how to drive."

"I know how to drive."

"You said you didn't."

"Leanne taught me."

"In two days?"

"I don't want another trainer," Clover said. "Can't I go alone and meet the future Leanne on the other side?"

"That's where she broke her leg." Bennett ran his palm over his mouth and down his chin. He looked at Clover for a long moment. Clover was about to ask why Leanne couldn't drive with her on this side and another trainer meet her on the other side, but Bennett kept talking. "Show me you can drive. Take me to the launch site."

Bennett made her skin crawl and she didn't like the idea of being trapped in the van with just him. But she was sure driving would make it worth it. Besides, maybe he'd drop his guard and she'd be able to get some information from him.

Clover and Bennett walked together to the van. When she got behind the wheel, her black boots under the rolled cuffs of her brown uniform hung inches from the pedals. She reached between her legs and pulled on the lever to slide her seat forward.

"She taught you that, at least," Bennett said.

"She's a great teacher. She's been doing it for ten years, right? She must have taught a lot of kids to drive."

Clover looked sideways at Bennett, but he didn't take the bait. Yet.

Cerebral things came naturally to Clover. Math, science, reading. Except for running, most physical things did not. She was clumsy and awkward and often felt out of place in her own body. For some reason, being behind the wheel of the van, feeling the engine roar to life, then purr as it waited for her to put it in gear, felt as normal as breathing to her.

She put the van into drive and pulled out of the parking lot, onto the avenue toward the wall gate. Bennett watched silently as she passed through it and started toward the mountain. He seemed relaxed when she sneaked a glance at him.

"You're doing well, Clover," he said.

"I told you, it's not that hard." She turned away from the road for just a second, a few miles after the highway turned into a winding road. A heartbeat. Instead of a nod of approval or some other sign that she was doing all right, Bennett stiffened, both hands white-knuckled on the dashboard, and the color drained from his face. Clover looked back to the road and screamed.

A black bear, hulking and unruffled, reared up on his hind legs, twenty-five feet in front of the van, and froze there staring at them as they barreled toward him.

"Oh, God. Oh, God!" Clover put her weight on the brakes and

wrenched the wheel to the left. The van skidded past the bear so close Bennett could have petted its coarse dark fur through the window. On the driver's side, they nearly scraped the sheer cliff side. Clover overcorrected and the tires ground in the rocks inches from the dropoff on Bennett's side. The brakes locked and they skidded to a stop in the center of the narrow mountain road.

Clover gasped as she yanked at the belt that had tightened across her chest, then fought panic when it wouldn't loosen at first. Finally it did, and at least she could breathe again. Shaking, she watched through the rearview mirror as the bear climbed into the trees at the top of the ravine.

Bennett put his hand on her shoulder and Clover barely bit back a yelp as she tore away from him. Mango, who had been thrown against the front of the van, scrambled to his feet and pressed his head against Clover's thigh. She lifted his face by the chin and looked into his eyes. He seemed okay.

"Clover, are you all right?" Bennett asked.

"I think Mango peed."

Bennett blinked at her and then looked at the growing dark circle in the gray carpet under her dog.

"I'm sorry. I shouldn't have looked away," Clover said.

"Carpets can be cleaned. I'm not sure I could have avoided hitting that animal."

Clover breathed slowly, through her nose, trying hard to control the nausea that sat like an iron cantaloupe in her belly. "That was an American black bear."

Bennett pulled himself up straighter in his chair. "Yes, I think you're right."

"Probably four hundred pounds. They aren't in hibernation yet. Not until October, or maybe November," Clover said, talking as much to herself as she was to Bennett. Six feet from Bennett's seat, the ravine waited to eat them alive. She wrapped her arms around her body and shook, adrenaline working its way through her system. She had come so close to driving them into it. "No one would have ever found us."

"Oh, they would have eventually." Bennett's voice had lost its confident swagger. It squeaked and sounded hoarse, like he had a sore throat.

"Do you want to drive now?" she asked, suddenly sure that she'd never be allowed behind the wheel again.

"No," he said. As upset as she was, he was worse off. His face was a strange shade of pale. If he drove, they'd both have to get out of the car, and there was no telling where the bear was now. "Not unless you want me to."

She did, but she wanted him to know she could still drive. "Should we go back?"

"No." He sat back in his seat and adjusted his belt. "No, let's continue."

Clover tightened her hands around the steering wheel for a moment and then shifted into drive again. She forgot to ask any more questions about kid Messengers.

"Do you remember how to get to the pickup spot?" Bennett asked when they were at the launch site.

"Yes." It was just a straight shot, maybe two miles around the lake.

"And you remember the rules?"

Clover stood near the van with Mango, adjusting her jumpsuit in a futile effort to make it look like she belonged in it. Her dog seemed to have recovered from their unexpected adventure. "I remember."

"I have no doubt that you're going to make me proud, Clover."

She certainly hoped so. She needed the Company to consider her mature enough to live in the barracks full time so her brother

could finally stop having to take care of her. Maybe avoiding the
bear without killing herself, Mango, or Bennett, and then complet-
ing this mission perfectly would do the trick. At least she didn't get
carsick on the windy roads this time. Maybe being behind the wheel
made a difference. Driving had concrete rules. It made sense, even
when it almost killed her.

The Messenger room in the submarine was all hers today. A
Time Mariner named Casey Danner helped her get Mango into the
hold. It wasn't easy, since the man did everything he could to avoid
actually touching the dog. She leaned against the curved wall and
Mango settled close by. The *Veronica*'s engine started, sending a
low rumble through the floor into her feet. She lifted them onto the
little stoop that protruded from under her chair. She didn't know
how it worked, but somehow her chair itself was insulated from the
worst of the vibration, which would have made this part of her job
almost unbearable. Mango's ears twitched as he felt what she didn't.
She took the big headphones from their hook to her right and settled
them over her ears, blocking out the engine noise before it got worse.

The submarine submerged and then a few minutes later
reemerged. The whole experience was as anticlimactic as it had
been the first time, except today she had the rush of knowing she'd
be able to drive alone for the first time in a few minutes.

When she came out, she was the only person in the hold. She
stood near the dumbwaiter lift and looked up through the opening
to the outside of the *Veronica* in time to see a man standing at the
opening. He flapped the hand that was visible to her once, then
twice at his waist, like a bird. Then he reached into a pocket with
that hand and pulled out his fortune cookie before stepping out of
her line of sight.

Not far out of it, though, because she heard the plastic wrapping
as he opened the package, and the crack of the stale cookie. And
then: "There is always sunshine after a downpour."

Clover waited until she heard the Mariner walk away to leave the hold. After she got Mango up and out, she looked toward the dock and saw the Mariner walking alone toward a group near the parked vans. He'd read his fortune out loud, even though he thought he was alone. Clover patted her pocket, to be sure she still had hers.

She made Mango get into the passenger seat of their van and buckled the belt around him. He tilted his big head and looked at her like she'd lost her mind, but she wasn't taking any chances after the whole bear thing. When she settled herself behind the wheel, she looked between the seats. A faint stain, in the same shape as the considerably fresher stain Mango had just caused, was still visible. This was the same van, then.

Driving to the pickup spot was a lot less eventful than driving to the launch site had been. No bears. No deer. Not even a coyote or a jackrabbit. She did see a blue jay, which was pretty cool.

She left Mango in the car before she started toward the box. She thought about the bear, though, as soon as she got a good look at the dense forest, and went back for him.

"Come on, boy. I'm not doing this alone." He wagged his whole body, and Clover had to set her keys in the footwell and use both hands to unbuckle him.

Mango jumped out of the van just as a soft, male voice from behind her said, "Mango."

Clover spun and then jumped when the door slammed shut.

"No!" She yanked on the door handle, which didn't do anything. She peered into the window, at her keys on the footwell, and then glared at the source of the problem. "Look what you did! I'm locked out."

It took a minute for her to realize what was happening. She was talking to someone she shouldn't. And she knew who he was. She might not have recognized Jude Degas, except for his scar. Once she did, though, it was very clearly him. In the two years that had passed while she was in the submarine, Jude had shot up to almost as tall as West. He'd been nearly as skinny as she was at the Academy orientation, but had managed to put on some weight between then and now. His face had hardened; the leftover boyishness at sixteen was gone at eighteen.

Mango tilted his head to one side, as if analyzing the boy who knew his name. Maybe remembering him from the Academy orientation.

"Clover, do you remember me?"

Bennett had told her not to speak to anyone. Not even people she knew. One word could change the course of the future, and she must avoid that at all costs. She'd already said more than one word, but that didn't mean she had to make it worse.

Bennett also told her it wouldn't happen. No one was allowed outside the city walls except Company and government employees on a specific mission. Jude should still be in school. He shouldn't be here.

Stop-Turn-Ignore. She'd practiced it a hundred times in primary school. Teachers took turns walking through the classrooms in a black jumpsuit, giving students a chance to stop what they were doing, turn their backs, and ignore the pretend Mariner.

Clover lowered her eyes and walked the three or four yards to the pickup box without acknowledging Jude. As if pretending he wasn't there would make it so.

The box looked something like a metal mailbox, maybe a foot square, attached to a post that was embedded into the ground. She punched the code into the number pad on the front and the door sprung open. She had the disc in her hand before it occurred to her that she maybe shouldn't have retrieved it with Jude standing there watching her.

She didn't mean to look at him again, but she couldn't help it. He hadn't moved. Maybe she should be scared of him, but just a few days ago he'd been nice to her. Mango was good at sensing danger, which wasn't one of her strong suits. The dog wasn't upset.

"Clover," Jude said. His voice had deepened.

"You shouldn't be here," she said, then clapped a hand over her mouth.

Maybe Bennett had sent him to see if she would break the rules.

She never broke the rules.

Except she just had.

Clover shoved the disc into the pouch attached to her belt and turned toward the van.

"Please," Jude called. "Wait a minute."

No. No. No. Stop-Turn-Ignore. She glanced at her watch. Twelve minutes gone. She had eighteen left, or she'd be left here overnight and would have to face the consequences the next day. It occurred to her that she didn't even know what the consequences were.

She yanked on the van's door handle and nearly took her own arm off when the door didn't open. She tried again. And again, even though she already knew she'd been locked out. Then she ran around the vehicle, trying each door. When she came back to the passenger side, Jude waited patiently.

"Clover."

She glared at Jude, her fingers so tightly clenched around Mango's leather lead that her knuckles were white and fingers cramped. "What? What do you want?"

"I'm not going to hurt you. I'm your friend."

"Do you know how much trouble I'm in? Do you? I'm going to be—well, I don't even know what I'm going to be. Except in big trouble."

He unlocked the door with a single key on a silver ring, then backed away from her immediately. As if he knew that being too close would overwhelm her now. He didn't try to pet Mango, didn't even acknowledge the dog beyond saying his name the one time.

"What are you doing here?" she asked him. "How did you get that key?"

"I have something for you. We don't have a lot of time for me to talk you into taking it. You're barely going to make it back as it is."

"I can't take anything from you."

"Yes, you can." He pulled something from his back pocket and thrust it toward her. "You have to."

"Are you crazy?"

He didn't answer. Which could have meant yes, or could have meant no. The thing he was trying to give her was a stack of paper, folded into the shape of a book.

He just held it there, until Clover took it and turned it over in her hand. A booklet made of stapled-together sheets of the same flimsy recycled paper she used at home, with a grayish cover made from thicker handmade stock.

"What is this?"

His dark eyes swept across her face. "I forgot we were ever so young," he said, instead of answering her question.

"I'm not that young," she said. "And you aren't that old."

He shook himself. "You better run. You can't be late."

"But—" Clover looked at the little rough-made book in her hand.

"Read it, Clover. And then make your choice."

"What choice?"

He stepped forward and slid one hand along the side of her face and into her hair. He wrapped his other arm around her waist to pull her to him, then kissed her on the mouth. She was so shocked by the gesture, by being touched, that she couldn't get herself together in time to pull away. He had already moved away by the time her nervous system kicked in with the message that he was too close. And *kissing* her. She jerked back anyway.

He went into the woods. "There are bears in there," she called. But it was too late.

She should have thrown the booklet into the woods and forgotten about it. But for some reason, she shoved it inside her jumpsuit, between her T-shirt and her belly. It didn't feel good there—the handmade paper was rough and its corners poked into her skin—but she didn't know where else it could go that no one might accidentally find it.

She was standing with Mango in the lift before she remembered her fortune cookie. She pulled it out, opened the package, and cracked the cookie to get the small paper out.

"Do the thing you fear, and the death of fear is certain." She pushed the plastic back into her pocket, along with the fortune paper, and pitched the cookie over the *Veronica*'s side for the fish or the birds, or whatever might want to eat it.

She was the last person back, and a Mariner waiting inside to close the hatch glared at her as she slid into the Messenger cabin. He didn't speak to her, so she didn't bother with his name.

After the *Veronica* docked in her own time, she found the van parked nearby with a single key hanging from a silver ring in the ignition. Her heart went into her throat as she ran a finger along the ring's smooth edge.

The whole drive back to the barracks building, she told herself, out loud, that she should toss the booklet. For all she knew, Bennett had sent Jude to see if she would take it. In the end, she wanted to know. Her curiosity trumped her natural tendency to follow the rules, and she couldn't make herself destroy what Jude had given her before she knew what it was.

Bennett wasn't waiting to walk her into the barracks and debrief her, which was a huge relief. A Static Mariner walked her up to her room instead. She'd have to wait and see if that was any worse.

"Did you speak to anyone during your mission?" he asked after taking the disc from her and locking it into a square, flat box attached to his belt.

"A Time Mariner named Casey Danner."

The guard asked about the specifics of their conversation and took notes on a clipboard without looking at her. "Did you see anyone other than Mariners from the future timeline during your mission?"

Clover's mouth went dry, but she managed to say, "No."

"Do you have anything to report?" He did look at her then, and she was sure he could see through her, into the truth behind her lie.

"No."

He stood and left, locking her into her room for her quarantine, without another word.

Clover locked the door from her side as well and took off her boots and her jumpsuit. She pulled the booklet from under the hem of her T-shirt and sat on the edge of the bed. She'd be left alone until the doser came with her suppressant. Then a guard would bring food for her and Mango. She tried not to let herself draw too many similarities between being locked in her room and being in prison.

She ran her fingers over the cover of the booklet. It had been printed somehow. It almost looked like someone had carved a stamp and inked the front that way.

Freaks for Freedom, it said. What did that mean? The inside pages were covered with print. She flipped through, reading headlines, until she got to the middle and something fell out into her lap.

Jude had stuck a folded paper into the pages of the booklet.

Clover's fingers shook slightly as she opened it. The air seemed to leave the room when she saw her brother's face looking up at her.

She knew what she was looking at as soon as she saw it. She closed her eyes and wished it away, but when she opened them again, she still held a dispatch flyer with West's face on it.

Was it a joke? Some kind of elaborate, awful prank? The picture of West was current; it looked like it had been taken from above as he was leaving the Bazaar.

> **West James Donovan, age 19**
> **Height: 6 feet**
> **Weight: 165 pounds**
> **Dark brown hair, green eyes. Virus scars on the face**
> **and thighs.**
> **Subject is wanted for the murder of Bridget Hannah**
> **Kingston.**

Murder? The absurdity of it made her wonder again if this was some kind of prank.

She stood and paced the small room in her underwear and T-shirt, her socked feet padding on the carpet. Mango hadn't settled since they got back to the room, and now he did what he was trained to do, moving in front of her to stop her repetitive motion. She nearly tripped over him.

"Mango!" He pressed against her and she sank to the floor, wrapping her arms around him. The idea that West would kill the headmaster's daughter was so impossible, she couldn't imagine it.

Until it struck her that of course he wouldn't kill her or anyone else. The report of Bridget's death would show up in the databases before it happened. A dispatch flyer would be distributed—this dispatch flyer—and stop the crime before it was committed.

They'd stop it by putting her brother in front of a firing squad.

Not their father's squad, of course; that would be too cruel. But West would be executed.

Clover reached for the booklet. *Freaks for Freedom*, it said on the cover. And under that, *A Zine for Truth*.

She flipped through the pages again and saw an article about the prevalence of child abuse in Foster City. Another about the need for citizens to "cry out as one against the tyranny of the suppressant."

A little cheesy. A lot of typos. But what she read put her heart in her throat.

Jude would lose his mind sometime in the next two years. That much was clear. Everyone knew you don't talk to Travelers. Not Mariners, not Messengers. Not ever. Even Foster City kids knew that, surely.

He must have made up these stories and the dispatch flyer. Because there was no way West would even think about killing Bridget Kingston. He wasn't very good at hiding that he liked her. A lot.

She turned more pages of the zine until she reached the back two pages.

READ ME CLOVER was written in big, bold letters in purple crayon across the top with arrows pointing to an article torn from the sanctioned city newspaper, neatly trimmed and pasted to the pages. "Kidnap and Murder of Headmaster's Daughter Averted by Arrest of Local Farmer."

Clover threw the zine away from her and went to the dresser where she'd stored her clothes. She pulled out her jeans. She couldn't do this half naked.

chapter 8

The mission of the United States is one of
benevolent assimilation.

—WILLIAM MCKINLEY,
LETTER, DECEMBER 21, 1898

West drew his hands through his hair and tried to
ease his heart rate to something that didn't make him feel like he
was about to keel over. "Tell me again."

"This kid I met at the orientation was at the pickup box." Clover sat on a kitchen chair with her feet tucked under her, rocking
and orchestrating with her hands as her words tumbled over each
other on their way out. "Only, you know, he was older."

"And?"

"And he gave me this." She waved the booklet at him. He hadn't
built up the courage to look through it yet. "I've told you this
already."

"And you were there alone, because?" West could kill Bennett
for letting her drive by herself. Worse, for putting her alone on that
submarine full of Mariners and sending her into the future with
no training.

"I told you, Leanne broke her leg in the future. Her real leg,
not the fake one." She adjusted herself, so that she was sitting with
her feet on the floor and looked at the booklet. *Zine*, it said on the

cover. "Jude knew me, West. Way more than I knew him. He acted like we were friends."

She hesitated over the last word, and a deep flush rose up over her neck and cheeks. Friends, huh?

And who was this kid? The idiot had talked to her while she was in her Messenger uniform. While she was two years in the future. Whoever he was, he would have been arrested at best, and shot at worst, if someone *had* been with Clover.

Did that mean that he knew she'd be alone? He seemed to know her, she'd said. So maybe sometime in the next two years she'd tell him. "How do you know he was your friend?"

Clover reached into her pocket and pulled out a key on a silver ring. "He used this to unlock the van when I couldn't get in. Only I hadn't given it to him yet. I didn't even get it until I got back through the portal."

"Why do you have it?"

"Bennett said I can drive myself until Leanne is better. It's the same key as Jude had at the box. I would have missed the return trip if he hadn't been there."

The ring was very simple, with no distinguishing features at all. Maybe it wasn't the same one. West looked at the dispatch flyer again. He felt disconnected from the guy in the picture, even though it was himself, without a doubt. Someone was setting him up, and they weren't doing a very good job of it. Of all the people in Reno, Bridget Kingston was on a very short list of those he'd risk himself to protect.

"Well, I'm obviously not going to kill her," he said to the picture, then looked at his sister. She met his gaze with cool, dispassionate eyes that were the same bottle-green as their mother's had been. West could just remember, like an eerie sense of déjà vu, his mother looking at him the same way when he drew a road for his toy cars on her kitchen floor with a permanent marker. The faint remains of his artwork were still imprinted on the tiles.

"That isn't the point," Clover said.

He wanted it to be the point. But she was right. If the newspaper article was genuine, then whether he would commit the crime was irrelevant. He would be punished to save Bridget's life.

He was certain the dispatch Clover had brought back from the future was generated after his name was run through the violent crime database during his Company interview. That wasn't scheduled to take place for two weeks.

The fact was, he would be arrested as soon as his name showed up in the database, and the next thing, he'd have a bullet in his head. But not until he'd spent a week or so in prison. He'd heard that they didn't bother to waste food and clean water on prisoners accused of violent crimes, and that some didn't even make it to their own executions.

"Let me see," he finally said to Clover. She gave him the zine, and he read the article pasted into the back. It was cut from the *Reno Gazette-Journal*. The dispatch flyer as well. Neither was dated.

The Company, headquartered in the west, and the government, headquartered in the east, ran the justice system in all of the cities with a one-two punch that was so effective, West was unaware of any major crime that had happened since he was five or six years old.

In their city, the *Reno Gazette-Journal*—once a big daily newspaper, it was an eight-page weekly now—reported the murders, robberies, and rapes that the Mariners stopped before they happened. There weren't many, but enough that the citizens never forgot what they were being protected from. The contrast between the world the newspapers suggested was constantly a near-miss, and their own safe, secure city was stark.

It had never occurred to West to question the system of prosecuting crimes that had not yet happened. He had a sudden, painful change in attitude now, and there was nothing he could do about it.

A walled city didn't leave too many places to hide. Flyers went out a few weeks before the date the crime was to take place, and the community did the job of finding the wanted person for the guards.

Someone would turn West in and be rewarded with a Whole New Life, the same as if they'd hit the New Year's Eve megajackpot at the Bazaar. A house with a big garden, enough to eat, a choice job, twelve hours of power a day, an electric cart to get around in. There were people who studied the dispatch flyers and searched for the criminals, like old-fashioned bounty hunters.

Did the flyer mean he would kill Bridget if he wasn't stopped? It was supposed to mean that. Whenever West saw a dispatch, he always knew that someone would be saved.

"Maybe this is fake," he said.

Clover pointed to the bottom of the newspaper clipping. Stuck on with a piece of masking tape was a note. *Help is in the Dinosaur, fifteenth floor.* "We can find out."

West tapped the note with his index finger. "We aren't going there."

"What else can we do?"

The Dinosaur was the last casino, on the far end of downtown from the Waverly-Stead building and the Academy. The only former resort casino in Reno that wasn't being used for some other purpose now, it hulked, dark and broken down, like the decomposing remains of the last brontosaurus.

"I'm serious, Clover. We aren't going there."

"They'll kill you. You get that, don't you?"

Clover was rocking again, hard enough that she looked like she might take flight. She ground her knuckles together in her lap until Mango pushed his head against them, and she started to pet him instead.

West knelt on her other side, but not too close. It was a balancing act with her, but one he'd been doing for a long time. Close enough to get and keep her attention, not so close that she pushed him away. She was so small that they were nearly eye to eye with him on one knee.

"Jude seemed like a friend?" he asked her. "Tell me why."

It was a loaded question. She had to think to answer it, which redirected her energy and slowed her rocking.

"He said he forgot we were ever so young," she said. "That sounds like he knows me now, right?"

"What else?"

"He had the key to the van."

How would he know she'd need it, if she didn't tell him? How would he get it, if she didn't give it to him? "Is there more?"

She looked up at him. "He kissed me."

Christ.

"Okay," he said, finally. "We'll go."

The Dinosaur was nearly five miles from their house, so Clover and West biked there. Clover didn't love biking, mostly because she had to leave Mango behind. Ten miles round-trip was too far for him to run beside them.

Riding her bike also gathered up all her physical awkwardness and bundled it into one neat package. It took all her attention and then some. One moment of distraction and she was careening into a light post or falling off a curb.

She didn't like anything about this. Downtown was dead beyond the Waverly-Stead building and the Academy. Like some kind of graveyard with elephantiasis, each building a gargantuan tombstone. Even those used for storage were devoid of life.

They traveled the service road behind the casinos instead of down the avenue. They didn't see anyone once they left Virginia Street. This was the worst idea ever.

"What if it's a setup?" she asked West when they pulled into the Dinosaur's back parking lot.

Time travel made Clover feel like her brain was running on a hamster wheel, trying to figure things out, but going nowhere fast. Bennett might already know that West was supposed to kill Bridget. He could have arranged for her to be alone at the pickup box in two years. Could have engineered her bringing West here, where he could be arrested.

"Try to breathe, Clover."

Try to breathe. Why didn't she think of that?

They made it to the Dinosaur without any broken bones. West pushed and pulled against several doors until he found one he could force open. He reached for her hand, and for once she didn't mind at all. He held a crank-powered flashlight in the other and flicked it on as they entered the pitch-black space.

The flashlight made a weak, yellowish circle in the perfect dark that was so thick and complete, it seemed to actually suck in the light. It felt like they were walking into the giant mouth of some hungry beast that might eat them whole.

"I'm not going in there," she whispered, and yanked her hand back.

"This was your idea," West answered, in a matching whisper. "It'll be okay."

She wasn't so sure. But West went in, still holding her hand so that their arms stretched between them. Him inside and her out. She didn't want to be left behind, so she went after him, tripped over a step up into the lobby of the casino, and would have landed on her face if West hadn't caught her.

She walked closer to her brother than she would have normally, the hand he'd been holding tightened around a fistful of the back of his T-shirt, as they made their slow way out of the lobby and passed dead slot machines and moved toward the big pit of game tables in the center of the casino. Clover had only a bare-bones idea of how a casino was laid out, from old newspaper photographs and books that she'd seen in the library. West went to the Bazaar every week and seemed to know what he was doing.

As far as Clover could tell in the dim light, it was as if the Dinosaur were just waiting for someone to send it some juice and let the players stream in. The machines stood in rows, like soldiers. A few times, she nearly tripped on the high stools set at each machine, but West kept her upright and it wasn't as bad to walk through the yawning dark as Clover feared.

Getting to the fifteenth floor was going to take some effort, though. Without energy, the elevators were dead, empty crates. West found a wall and started to follow it, looking for a door that would open to stairs.

Clover had looked at pictures of the Dinosaur in its glory days, but she couldn't bring up any memory of seeing a diagram of stairways. She wished now that she'd come across an exit map or . . . and then she remembered. There was a framed map of stairways and emergency exits mounted on the wall next to the elevator in the Company building.

"Go back to the elevators," she said.

"They aren't going to work."

She sighed, because how stupid did he think she was? And then she pulled him back to where they'd passed a hallway with four elevators a few minutes before.

Just like at the Waverly-Stead building, there was a framed map over the call buttons. "See," she said as West directed their light to the map.

"Okay. I see." He studied the map for a minute, then moved her to the side and said, "Hang on."

He drove the butt of their flashlight into the glass. Clover jumped and covered her ears; the sharp noise echoed around her brain.

"What's wrong with you?"

West took the map gingerly out of the frame. "We need this. The stairs are just over here."

"You could have warned me at least."

The stairwell, when they finally found it, was narrow and painted white. The light reflected and bounced around it, making the flashlight far more effective here. West folded the map and put it in his pocket, then started up.

"Wait, West," she said as she looked into the darkness above. "What if guards are waiting for us?"

West hesitated, too. "Do you think he'd work with the guard?"

A thousand scenarios had rushed through her head since Jude had handed her the zine. In two years, he would be only halfway through his Academy training. It was possible, she thought, that just like she was snapped out of the Academy and put into the Mariner program, he was put early into the guard. Maybe that was what they did with Foster City kids and she just didn't know it.

But then she remembered that he'd kissed her. Like it wasn't the first time. He knew how to get around her instinct to pull away from being touched. He knew her. And he knew her well.

"No," she finally said. "Let's go."

The first few floors, Clover's heart jerked at each landing, sure the door would open and guards would be there ready to arrest them both. By the tenth floor, she didn't care. It took all of her energy to take one stair after the other. There were two dozen to each floor, twelve and then a ninety-degree turn with a small landing before twelve more and a big door to the next floor.

"You okay?" West asked her at the landing on the fourteenth floor.

"Yeah, you?"

He grunted and they climbed the last flight.

They stopped in front of the door marked with the number 15

painted in red. It was hard for Clover to imagine a time when there were enough people to fill hotels like this. She thought all the residents of Reno could probably fit inside the Dinosaur with room to spare.

She reached for the door and West grabbed her forearm. "What do you think you're doing? You can't just rush in there. We need a plan."

"We can't just stand here."

West put his back against the door.

"Just give me a second. I need to think."

"If we're doing this, let's just do it," she answered. "What is there to think about?"

"I don't know. What if—"

The door opened and West fell backward into the hall, pushing Clover away from him at the same time. She cried out and stumbled back until the edge of the metal step behind her bit her calves and forced her to sit down hard on the third stair.

"West!"

He steadied himself and stepped back through the doorway to her. As soon as he was out of the doorway, she saw Jude standing there, looking as scared as she felt.

"What are you doing here?" Jude asked. "You shouldn't be here."

"Neither should you," she said.

"What are you doing here?" he asked again.

"You invited us." West pulled Clover up by the arm and pushed her ahead of him out of the stairwell.

"Wait, where are you going?" Jude held the door open. "Just leave before you get us all in trouble."

"Jude," Clover said. "I have to show you something."

"Just leave. Please."

"We can't leave," West said.

Jude was afraid of someone. No. *For* someone. He stood between them and the hallway, keeping them from moving away from the door, in the same protective way West stood between her and Jude.

He would change a lot in the next two years. More, even, than she had realized when she saw him at the pickup box. Physically, of course. But there was also a confidence about him then that hadn't fully developed yet in this time line.

"We're friends," she said. "Well, we will be friends."

His jaw relaxed as his eyes moved from West to Clover. "Where's your dog?"

"He's at home."

"What do you have to show me?"

She pulled the flyer with West's picture on it out of her pack and handed it to Jude.

He held his flashlight on it so he could see, and then looked back at them. "Is this supposed to make me feel better?"

"You gave it to me."

"What? I didn't—"

"Two years from now."

It took another minute. Clover stayed where she was and watched him think it out.

"Okay," he finally said, and let them into the hallway.

West followed Jude as he led them down the long dark hallway. He had Clover by one hand and his flashlight in the other, adding to Jude's to illuminate the crayon blue carpet and dirty yellow walls. He stopped at a door marked 1534 and knocked on it three times in quick succession.

A girl opened the door. She was about Clover's size, but West thought she was no older than fourteen. She looked from Jude to West.

"Jude? What're you bringing in here?"

Jude got her to let them in. Sunlight filled the room through an open window. Inside another girl, identical to the first, sat on one of two huge beds.

"Clover and . . ." Jude looked to West.

"West."

Jude pointed to one girl and then the other. "Geena, Marta."

"Are you crazy, bringing these hoodies in here?" Marta asked. She shot a look at West and Clover that dripped hostility.

"I might be," Jude said. "They're friends. I think."

Marta shrugged her narrow shoulders and went to stand by the window. The twins were not as young as West first thought. Once he'd heard the one girl speak and gotten a good look at them, he adjusted his assessment of their age closer to Clover's. While his sister inherited her small stature from their mother, West got the impression that Geena and Marta were stunted somehow. Their too-large heads were perfectly round and both covered in a fine fuzz of brown hair, like the crew cuts his dad used to give him. It was as if their heads had kept on growing, expecting their bodies to catch up.

"They really friends of yours, Jude?" Geena asked.

"I think so," Jude answered. "Gather everyone in my room. I'll be right there."

"You live here?" Clover asked. Marta gave her a narrow-eyed glance before following her sister out into the hallway. "How can you live here? How do you eat? What about water? Power? I thought you were from Foster City."

"Clover," West said.

"Sorry."

"It's okay," Jude said. But he didn't answer any of her questions.

"Look," West said to Jude. "We don't mean you, or them, any harm."

"How did you know I was here?"

She pulled the zine out of her pack. "You gave this to me."

Jude reached for it and Clover pulled it back. He lifted his eyebrows, and she hesitated just another second before thrusting it at him.

"I want that back," she said.

He took it from her and asked, "What happened to you the other day anyway? You just disappeared."

"I was drafted," Clover said.

"Drafted? What do you mean, drafted?"

"I'm a Messenger. Don't ask," she said when he opened his mouth. "I don't know why. It just happened. Something about my test scores. And Kingston said I wasn't a good fit for the Academy after all."

"He put me in the engineering track," Jude said with some pride in his voice. Deserved pride. The engineering track was one of the most difficult to get into. He'd work, after graduation, building things or designing them. Or helping to run the complicated systems that gave them fresh water and electric power.

"Really?" she asked. She inflected wrong, her question sounding incredulous instead of interested, and West saw her wince as soon as the word hit her own ears. Her face colored, and she added, "I'm impressed."

Jude thumbed through the zine, changing the subject. "I didn't give this to you. What is it anyway?"

"We aren't sure," West answered. "It looks like you're going to write it, or some of it, a couple of years from now. And me, too."

"Huh." Jude went back to the front of the zine and looked more closely at the pages. Finally he pointed with his chin toward West's dispatch flyer, sitting on top of the dresser. "And that?"

"It was inside. And damned good question." He pointed to the zine. "How am I going to write that, if I'm executed in a couple of weeks?"

"So who you mean to off?"

"What?"

"Who are you planning to kill?" Jude said, more slowly. "Bridget Kingston. She related to the headmaster?"

Jude was considerably smaller than West and three years younger, but he had a way of holding himself that made West think they were more evenly matched than anyone might think.

"I don't plan to kill anyone." West took the zine from Jude, flipped to the back pages, and handed it back, his finger on the small picture of Bridget. "Especially not the headmaster's daughter."

Jude studied the newspaper article pasted over the last pages of the zine, then looked from Clover to West. "You have to go."

chapter 9

Determine that the thing can and shall be done, and
then we shall find the way.

—ABRAHAM LINCOLN,
ADDRESS TO HOUSE OF REPRESENTATIVES, JUNE 20, 1848

Jude's lack of curiosity baffled Clover. He'd sent
for her, or would send for her, and he didn't even want to know why.

Now she and West rode home in silence. Clover's fear for her
brother was a lump of ice in the pit of her stomach. Maybe she
wasn't great at reading people, but she knew West wouldn't kill
anyone. But that didn't matter. No one would listen to her, and if
they did, they wouldn't care what she had to say.

She watched West riding ahead of her. If they didn't think of
something, and fast, he would be dead by the end of the next month.

Clover was able to call up anything she'd ever read or seen,
because her brain filed it all away as pictures. She could flip through
them, make connections between them, figure things out. She had
no point of reference for what the dispatch flyer and newspaper
article suggested. Her brother a murderer. Her brother writing
subversive articles.

Her name not showing up in the zine at all.

"I'm sure we can figure out some way to make this okay," she said.
"If you really write those articles in two years, we have to, right?"

There were two with West's name on them. One talked about calorie crops and how the Company restricted them to keep the citizens of the cities under its thumb. The other was about using honey as an antibiotic.

That last one caught her eye, because she'd just started reading about beekeeping. Maybe that meant something. Clover couldn't figure out what, and her brain was starting to throb from trying.

They pulled into their yard and put their bikes inside the garage.

"What are we going to do, West?" Clover asked quietly as they made their way to the front door.

"I don't know."

"But, West—"

"I don't know!" He opened the door and tossed his pack in the hall. It slid across the wood floor and smacked into the leg of a table, knocking a stack of Clover's books over. "I need to think."

"But they're going to—" West stopped short and Clover plowed into his back. "Hey!"

"Shut up," he whispered.

"We have to talk about this." She tried to move around him, but he shifted his weight to block her. She saw around his shoulder, though, into the living room. "Oh."

Their father stood there, tall and lean, an older, colder version of West. He held a book he'd taken from the low, overstuffed shelf that ran along one wall, under the big windows that looked out over the backyard. The book was a novel. A mystery that belonged to him.

He didn't look at the book, though. He looked at West. "There you are."

"What are you doing here?"

Clover pushed her way around her brother. "Hi, Dad."

"Hi, baby." He didn't make eye contact with her. He never did. As much as West looked like him, she looked like their mother.

They would have made a perfect storybook family, Clover had often thought. Jane was just over five feet tall, like Clover, with black hair and green eyes.

Clover had cut her waist-length hair when she was ten, leaving herself with an inch-long stubble, in an effort to stop reminding her father that she was the reason her mother was dead. It didn't work.

It startled her to realize that their father had been crying. His eyes were puffy and bloodshot. He looked old and tired. "West, I—"

"You know. How do you know already?"

Clover froze, her legs and arms going stiff and unmovable, while James sank into a chair, still holding the book in one hand.

"You think I'm going to kill that girl?" West's voice cracked over the word *kill*.

"The database is never wrong." That was what the newspaper said every time it reported an averted crime. Said it with resolve, though. With pride. Their father said it like the words hurt him.

"They didn't run your name yet," Clover said to her brother. "They couldn't have. Not yet."

West exhaled slowly. "Did they really send my own father to bring me in?"

James shook his head, his gaze fixed on the floor between his knees. "I heard you had an interview. I ran your name myself."

"Why would you do that?" Clover asked. It was illegal, and totally unnecessary. Then she remembered the dispatch and struggled to take another breath, like oxygen had thickened to syrup in her lungs.

"You thought you'd find something." Even Clover could hear the anger and bitterness in West's tone. She looked at her father, and he must have heard it, too, because he looked wounded. "You ran my name, because you thought you might find something like this."

James shook his head.

"Don't lie to me!" West slammed the heel of one hand into the wall.

The thud reverberated through Clover, and she caught her breath as tears started to fall down her cheeks. She felt hot. Almost feverish. "West."

"I'm sorry," he said, under his breath. "I'm sorry."

"I came to warn you," James said. "I came to help you."

"You shouldn't have done it. If you get caught, Clover—"

"Where have you been?" Clover asked, cutting her brother off. She didn't want to hear the end of his sentence. Irritation prickled her too-hot skin like she'd fallen into a cactus. "If you were here, this wouldn't be happening!"

James finally looked at her. "You know I can't be here."

"You can!"

He looked back at his son. "I came to warn you, West. No one else knows. Not yet, anyway."

"How long?" West asked.

"A few days."

"What if he doesn't go to the interview?" Clover asked, even though she knew better.

"You know it doesn't matter," West said quietly.

The discs that Messengers like Clover brought back from the future were analyzed. The information gleaned from them was put into a computerized database. The database. Even if West's name wasn't specifically searched for, a week before Bridget's death date, it would come up anyway. Bridget would be put under protection by the guard until West was arrested.

That meant they had until Tuesday. Two days. West would never make it to his interview. Clover wondered if anyone had ever had advance notice of a dispatch before.

"You have to stay with her, Dad."

A lump of ice slid from Clover's throat to her stomach, sending a shiver through her even though she still felt too hot.

"She'll be fine in Foster City." He looked at Clover again. The whites of his eyes were shot through with red. They looked wet, too, like he was about to cry. That shook her, more than anything else that had happened since she saw Jude in the future.

"She'll be eaten alive there, and you know it."

"It's not that bad," James said. "Hundreds of kids—"

"I'm not going there." She had a job; she could take care of herself if it came to that. But it wouldn't. It couldn't. "And West isn't going to kill anyone."

"It doesn't matter," West and James said together.

"Yes, it does!"

"Clover, he'll be accused and there is proof."

"Proof? Bridget Kingston is probably sitting on her own front porch right this minute!"

"It's not premeditated," James said quietly. As if that mattered. "You hit her with a marble mantel clock. The database says it's a crime of passion."

Passion? "He barely even knows her. Where would he even get a marble mantel clock?"

"It belongs to her father. She's killed in her own living room a week from Tuesday."

"West wouldn't be in the Kingston Estate. What would be—"

"It's okay, Clover," West said.

She flapped her hands hard enough to make her wrists ache and rocked back and forth from foot to foot. Poor Mango circled around her, trying to get her attention so he could do his job and calm her. "No, it's not."

James stood up, returned the book to its shelf, and picked up a framed picture of himself and their mother. "Hide until the date has passed."

"He can't hide." Clover's stomach ached. "He needs the suppressant."

James looked at her like she was breaking his heart. Then she realized she was thumping her forehead with the heel of her hand and forced herself to stop.

"I have to get back," James said. "Hide, West. At least long enough for her death date to pass. I'm not sure how much good it will do, but it's something."

"He'll get sick," Clover said. "The virus will come back. They won't let him back in if he's sick. Do you want him to die? Do you?"

West caught her by the arms before she could launch herself at her father with her fists flying, and when she started to panic, Mango pressed his heavy body against her legs. She yanked away from both of them and threw herself at her father, making him look at her. "You can stop this!"

"No. I can't." He looked from her to West. "I can't. I wish I could."

He handed the photograph to West, kissed Clover on top of her head, and then he was gone.

"You shouldn't have yelled at him," West said. Clover sat in a corner of the sofa, curled into a ball, her arms wrapped around her drawn-up legs. West hated when she was like this, on the verge of getting lost inside herself.

"He doesn't even care," she said against her knees.

"There isn't anything he can do."

"He could try! How does he know what he can do if he doesn't even try?"

James had given him a heads-up, and even that was more than West expected. More than James should have done, because West was pretty sure that running his own son's name through the database was a crime that came with severe punishment. Interfering with the justice system was a capital offense. Their father risked leaving Clover with no one.

West sometimes wished he could either love their father fully or really hate him, like Clover did in turn. James had never recovered from their mother's death. He'd loved her in a way that West wasn't sure he'd ever have the chance to love a woman. She loved him back, too. Anyone could see it in the pictures of the two of them together and read it in the letters Clover kept in her trunk.

He couldn't bring himself to blame their father for leaving them. Maybe because he had a few shreds of memory of his parents together. Clover's looks and his scars were too much for James to live with. Besides, the Company wouldn't accept dependent children as an excuse not to accept a promotion.

"I have to get out of here," West said. "I have to—"

"What? You have to what?"

"I have to *go*. What else can I do?"

"You'll be killed." Clover looked scared. Really scared.

"I'm going to be killed anyway."

"The virus will come back without the suppressant."

"What else can I do? You tell me, you're the genius."

Clover rocked, her small body tightening around itself. West was tempted to try that himself, to see if it would ease some of the sharp tension that was squeezing the life out of him. Someone was going to kill Bridget. It wasn't him, but that meant it could be just about anyone else. He might survive if he hid, but she wouldn't.

West sat next to Clover and she went limp, sliding into his arms. Almost catatonic. He and Mango both worked to calm her. She used to do this when she was a little girl, collapse into a shell of herself when their father left. As if her body couldn't contain her grief.

Mango pushed his weight against Clover and West spoke softly to her, not really saying anything, until she could sit up on her own again.

"We have to save her," Clover said. She looked up at him and echoed his earlier thought: "It's the only way. If you hide, she'll die anyway and you'll be blamed regardless."

"How can I save her? I don't even know how I'm going to save myself."

"Think about it. You can't be executed for a crime that doesn't happen."

"You know better." Murderers were executed in the city every year. Not many, because violent crime had become rare. But they all had one thing in common. None of them had ever actually killed anyone. They were executed before it could happen.

"*Someone* kills her, West. If it isn't you, then who? If we can find out—"

"It won't matter."

"It'll keep her alive."

West picked up the picture of their parents from the sofa next to him. They stood together on a beach, sometime before he was born. Jane was beautiful, laughing, her dark hair caught in the wind. She smiled up at James, his arms wrapped around her waist.

They looked so happy.

Maybe West wouldn't ever have the chance to look at a girl that way. But if he could keep himself and Bridget alive long enough, maybe he'd get to find out what it was like.

West waited until Kingston pulled out of his long driveway in the small white car with the Reno Academy logo on the doors. It took another minute to gather his courage, and then he went up the walk and knocked.

Bridget answered, wearing a pair of fitted black pants, rolled to midcalf, and the same kind of white T-shirt West wore to work every day. She'd knotted it at her side so that it hugged her body. She was barefoot and had her dark blond hair pulled back in a loose, low ponytail. Flour dusted her hands and arms and clothes, and she'd wiped her cheek with some as well. The smell of baking bread filled his nose.

"I need you to come with me, Bridget," West said. "It's important."

The plan was simple enough. Convince Bridget that, for her own safety, she had to come with him. They'd think of step two later.

"Come with you where?"

Good question. "I'm not sure yet. Somewhere."

"We can go to the stables."

This was going to be so hard. How could he persuade her to go away with him? He wouldn't do it, if he were her. "We have to get away from here."

"Why?"

"I wouldn't ask if this wasn't important. Life-or-death important."

"What are you talking about?"

Bridget looked concerned, but more about his acting like a jerk on her doorstep than by what he was telling her. How could he blame her? He didn't even know what the real threat was. This was taking too long.

She was five foot seven or eight and had the solid build of a girl who always had enough to eat. West could carry her off if she fought him, but he was less convinced that no one would notice.

She had to come on her own. The words just slipped out. "Someone is going to kill you."

Bridget took a step back into her house. Wrong direction. When he started to follow her, she put a hand out to stop him. "You're freaking me out."

"I know. I know, but I need you to trust me." She tried to close the door, but West was faster. He slipped in, pushing her ahead of him, and closed the door.

"My dad will be home soon."

That was a lie, but West didn't blame her for it. She was terri-fied. He saw it in her blue eyes, the pupils dilated wide open, and heard it in her quick, short breaths. She pressed her back to the stair rail. "I'm not going to hurt you. I promise."

"What do you want?"

"I want to save you from whoever is going to kill you a week from Tuesday."

Bridget sidled farther from him. "Oh, God. You're crazy, aren't you? My dad said so, when you came here looking for your sister. I didn't believe him, but it's true."

"I'm not crazy." She fought away from him, and he grabbed her by the arms. "Look at me, Bridget! You know me. You know I'm not crazy."

For a second, he thought he'd gotten through to her. She tilted her head and took one deep breath as she looked up at him. But just when he let his guard down, she twisted to get away from him and moved toward the open hallway that led to the kitchen.

He caught her arm again and hated when he felt her stiffen under his palm. "Can't you see I'm trying to help—"

The front door opened behind him and West dropped Bridget's arm. His first worry was for himself, because he expected to see that she had been telling the truth and her father was home. Bridget tried to get around him, probably expecting her father as well. He grabbed her again and held her tightly in place behind him.

"Let me go!"

"It's not your father."

She wrenched away from him and looked around his shoulder.

"Let the girl pass, son," the man said.

West nearly complied. It was a good bet the man was someone who had more right to be here than he did. But Bridget didn't try to get away from him now. She shrank back, suddenly hiding behind him instead of being kept there against her will, so he stayed put.

The man came all the way into the house, carefully closing the door behind him, then clicking the deadbolt into place. "Who's your friend, Bridget?"

"My father is still at work," she said from behind West. Her voice, usually sweet and slightly high-pitched, sounded raw with fear.

"I know where your father is." The man came closer. He didn't have any kind of visible weapon, and there wasn't any threat in his voice. If he was here to do either of them any real harm, he wouldn't be here at all. He would have already been arrested. Still, the hairs on West's arms stood on end and when he looked back at Bridget, her face had lost its color.

"I asked you a question, Bridget," the man said. "Who is your friend?"

Bridget shook against West's back. She was really scared. West didn't think he could have been any more on edge than he was when he knocked on her door a few minutes ago, but he was wrong. He straightened to his full height and tried to keep his voice steady. "We'll be sure to tell Mr. Kingston that you stopped by, Mr. . . ."

The man didn't fill in his name. And he didn't take his eyes off Bridget over West's shoulder. "Whoever your friend is, I'm afraid I'll have to ask him to leave. Your father wouldn't like me leaving you alone with a dirt slinger."

He knows who I am. West had that thought just as Bridget's breath caught and she grabbed a handful of his T-shirt. Something was wrong. He didn't know what, but he went with his instincts and pulled her with him, up the hall. She jerked forward, landed against his back, and then took the stairs with him.

"Where?" he asked Bridget. The man followed, but slowly. As if there were no question that they might get away. "Where!"

She tugged on his hand and took him through a doorway into what must have been her father's bedroom. West closed the door, hit the thumb lock, and then shouldered a tall pine dresser in front of it with Bridget's help. The room was gigantic, with an enormous four-poster bed and a fireplace. On the mantel, West saw a marble clock. "We have to get out of here."

"What's happening?" she kept asking. "What's happening?"

"Who is that man?"

"Why is this happening?"

West had no idea. They could sort that out later. "Bridget, I need you to focus. Do you understand me? We have to get out of the house."

If they could get out onto the street, they could disappear. At least long enough to get away. Whoever that man was, West was fairly certain he wouldn't kill them or try to grab Bridget in the open. If that was his plan, then this wouldn't be happening at all. West held on tight to that, even though a stubborn insistence that the system worked didn't make much sense for him right now.

West went to a floor-to-ceiling sliding glass door that opened onto a small porch. When he opened it, he saw a wooden table and chair, painted white, where Mr. Kingston likely took his coffee in the morning in the shade of a big old oak tree. The branches hung over, thick and sturdy.

"Have you gone out this way before?" West asked.

The door rattled. "I just want to speak to you, Bridget," the man said.

"What's happening?" she asked West again.

"Bridget!" The dresser rocked, then settled back on its feet.

She crowded onto the patio with him, and he yanked the curtain closed and then the door, hopeful the man would check the bathroom first and give them time to get down the tree.

Bridget went ahead of him, shimmying out onto the nearest branch. As soon as she put her weight on the next limb, West followed. Somehow they managed to scramble down the tree without more than skinned palms.

West took Bridget's hand and they ran, without waiting to see if the man looked down over the railing.

"What the hell just happened?" Bridget asked when they finally slowed. She walked close enough to him that he felt her shaking with exertion or fear.

If he knew, he would tell her. He would tell her what he did know, in a minute, but right now he needed her to answer a question. "Who was that man?"

She hiccuped and didn't answer at first. When he waited her out, she finally said, "Langston Bennett."

James hated what it said about him that he wished, hard, he'd never run his son's name through the Company database. He should have just done his job that morning. Just his job, nothing more.

The guilt that had permanent residence in his gut pissed him off. He was in the protection business. He might not spend as much time as he'd like with Clover and West, but he kept the city safe for his kids. James sat on the edge of his barracks bed and held his head in his hands, wishing he could reach in and tear out the part of his brain that made things so hard.

He'd gone into the office that morning, as he had dozens of times, expecting an administrator to hand him the stack of folders with his crew's jobs for their monthly on-week. Instead, he found the room empty. The folders were on the edge of the desk, topped by a note with his name on it.

He should have taken them and gone. Would have, too, except that his crew mate Coal's brother-in-law worked in the training office. He'd heard that West had an interview scheduled and passed the information along. Lots of congratulations from the whole crew.

James was maybe a little hurt that West hadn't told him about his interview himself, but he understood. He might be able to kid himself into believing that he'd had no choice but to accept a promotion that required him to live in the barracks with his crew, but his boy was smarter than that.

Understanding why his son hadn't shared his news didn't make it feel any better.

James told himself he stayed away because it upset his kids to see him. Especially West, who had a pit of anger always brewing under the surface. A more selfish reality was that it upset James to be in the house he'd shared with Jane. The house where she died. Where he'd killed her.

He never stopped hurting, not even after more than sixteen years. And he never stopped remembering what he'd done.

His kids didn't know. No one did. The truth, that he had murdered his wife, lived inside him. It ate away at his ability to function like a normal, rational person. Eventually, it stole his ability to live with his children.

He knew that Clover thought he'd left because she looked so much like her mother. And that West believed his scars reminded James of Jane, too. The truth was worse, and so much more self-serving. The pair of them reminded him of his failure as a husband and a father. Losing Jane had left him raw, and being near Clover and West was like pouring acid into his wounds.

He was a coward. If he'd been brave enough to withstand Jane's pain, she'd be alive. If he'd been brave enough to be the father Clover and West deserved, instead of hiding in his work, he'd still have a family. Instead, he lived alone and told himself that keeping the city safe for his children was more important than being present in their lives.

And then he found himself alone with a computer that connected to the Company database. He wanted to see for himself that he'd managed to raise his son to be a *good* man, even though he knew in his heart that everything good about West was despite James, not because of him.

It wasn't until he was faced with the proof of his son's violent crime that he realized what he'd been afraid of all along. That he would find a warning that his son's anger—an anger he helped create—would finally boil over.

Screw Coal for putting the idea in his head. Screw Jane for getting sick and making him kill her—oh, God, he hated himself for even having that thought. And, most of all, screw himself for not just letting the system do what it was designed to do.

Now, because he was vain enough to think that he could predict what he would find, he knew something he wished he could scrub away. And he'd told West, which was just as bad in the eyes of the law as the murder his son would commit if he wasn't stopped.

The system wasn't broken. No. James had lifted his rifle, pointed it through the gun hole in the execution room, and fired it at a human being with a red X over his heart once or twice a month for three years. The system could not be broken.

Which meant the database couldn't lie. James had to believe that West would kill the Kingston girl if he wasn't stopped. He'd given him forewarning, anyway.

James lay back, fully clothed, on his hard mattress and stared at the ceiling. Every protective layer he'd wrapped so carefully around himself was unraveling, thread by thread.

chapter 10

The freedom of speech may be taken away and,
dumb and silent, we may be led like sheep to the
slaughter.

—GEORGE WASHINGTON,
NEWBURGH ADDRESS, MARCH 15, 1783

Clover sat on the library steps, watching for West.
At this point, she didn't even care if he had Bridget with him. She
was pretty pissed off at the headmaster's daughter for getting her
future self killed and putting West in this position.

"Please, please, please," she whispered, holding on as tight as she
could to her knees, forcing herself not to rock or do anything that
would draw attention. *Please* let West come walking down the street.

Clover didn't know exactly who she was praying to, but she
prayed hard.

It must have worked, because he was there. And not bleeding
or even running. He had Bridget by the hand and they moved at a
good clip, but not like they were being chased.

"Let's go," he said as he passed. He slowed long enough to slip
Clover's overstuffed pack onto his own shoulders.

"What happened?"

West stopped and turned to look at her. "It was Langston Bennett, wasn't it? The man Bridget's father sent you to?"

Clover hesitated, her heart beating in her throat. "Yes. Why?"

"Later," West said, and took off again, pulling Bridget with him. Clover had to jog to catch up with them.

"We have to go back to the Dinosaur." She was prepared to argue with him about it if necessary. They needed a safe place to make a plan, and their house wasn't it. The Dinosaur was the only choice. No one would look for West there.

"I've been thinking the same thing," West said.

"Our house is the first place they'll look. And those kids in the Dinosaur seem to know how to hide."

"I said I agree already."

"The Dinosaur?" Bridget looked and sounded a little lost. Maybe more than a little.

"Yeah," Clover said. "The Dinosaur."

"There are people in the Dinosaur?"

Clover let that go. She would have been surprised herself, if she didn't know better.

"Maybe we should go to the Academy instead and talk to my dad," Bridget said. Clover snorted. West glared at her, and Bridget just looked even more confused. "What? He'll at least know why Mr. Bennett was at our house acting so weird."

"Langston Bennett was at your house?" Clover stopped walking again, and this time, when West didn't stop as well, she raised her voice. "Langston Bennett was at her house?"

West looked around, then came back to Clover, with Bridget still following in his wake. "Yes."

"Why?"

"He—" Bridget started to say.

West put a hand on her arm and interrupted her. "He works with her dad, okay? You already knew that. But we don't know why he was at her house."

"Do you think he's the one? I mean, I thought we had some time."

"So did I. And I think we probably still do. Let's go, okay?"

There was more. Clover felt it. But West was right; they needed to get moving. If Jude and the others didn't let them stay, they'd need time to find somewhere else before the curfew bells rang.

When they reached a suppressant bar two or three miles from the Dinosaur, at the edge of the residential part of the city, West came to a stop.

"What are we doing?" Bridget asked. Her voice sounded funny. Too high-pitched. And her blue eyes darted all around, like she couldn't find anything to focus them on. "Shouldn't we keep moving?"

"Clover and I need our doses."

That took Clover by surprise, even though it shouldn't have. It was the right time of day. But this wasn't their regular bar, and there was some risk involved in stopping somewhere unfamiliar. They wouldn't blend.

There was no law that said you had to go to a certain bar, but it was what people did. Not just West and Clover, or some people or even most people. As far as Clover knew, all people chose a bar and stuck with it. Changing because of a move or a job switch that made another location more convenient was a big deal. The dosers, and anyone inside being dosed, would remember the strangers who came in today.

"Oh," Bridget said. "Oh, okay."

She didn't let go of West, though, and when he took a step toward the bar's door, she held on to him. "Bridget, you better wait out here. We'll be right back."

Even Clover could see that Bridget was wound tight enough to break.

Bridget dropped West's hand and fidgeted her fingers at her sides as she looked up and down the street, nodding. "Yeah. What if he comes by here?"

"He won't," West said, firmly. "But if he does, you come inside. Everything will be okay."

"West's the one who needs to worry," Clover said. West shot her the evil eye. "Come on. The faster we get in, the faster we can get back out."

Bridget looked up at West. Her black pants were dusted with white flour, and her hair was falling out of its ponytail. "It's just, I've never been to a bar without my dad."

"Everything will be okay," West said. "I promise."

Just when Clover's irritation felt on the verge of spilling over, Bridget straightened and said, "Right. I'll be fine."

Finally. Clover pushed open the door to the bar and walked in with Mango. West followed on her heels. Their father said they had several days before West had to worry. That was before West took Bridget. Could Mr. Kingston have reported his daughter missing already? Watching West go in and give his ID was nerve-racking. She could only imagine how scared West must have been that his ID would trigger a call to the guard.

The only thing scarier was the idea of not being dosed and the virus that was dormant in his body coming back to life. She was too young to have any memories of the virus. She knew that people like West and Leanne, who were scarred from their battles with it, still carried it in them. It crouched in their bodies, waiting for the opportunity to burst out again and eat them alive like miniature cannibals. Zombie cells.

Clover was so nervous, she was sure she'd draw attention to herself. But nothing happened. They gave their identification cards to a woman who was nothing at all like the Caramel-Camel Man, and someone they'd never seen before inserted the suppressant delivery tubes into their ports. The whole experience was unnerving but happened without incident.

After it was over, they went back outside and found Bridget just where they left her.

"She's still here. You did a good job scaring her," Clover said.

West glared at her, and Bridget made a weird little sound. "What? You did."

"Wouldn't you be scared if someone told you that you were about to be killed?" Bridget asked.

"I said he did a *good* job. It was a compliment."

They walked in a row, Clover on one side of West and Bridget holding his other hand. The sky was just turning shades of yellow and pink when they made it to the huge, tumbledown casino.

Now what?

"I'll go in and talk to Jude," West said. "You two wait here."

"I don't think so," Bridget said.

"I don't either." Clover scratched Mango's ears when he pressed his broad head against her hand. "I'm less threatening, and he knows me."

"No," West said. She hated when he got unmovable like that. Especially when the stand he took had to do with underestimating her.

She stood nearest the big glass door and Bridget was between them, so there wasn't much West could do when she grabbed a light from the side pocket of her pack, pushed the door open, and slipped into the Dinosaur with Mango.

Jude wouldn't hurt her. She knew that, somehow. She didn't pick up on things like that very often. Or at least, not in any reliable way. Usually, she thought someone was her friend when they very much weren't and managed to completely put off everyone else. But Jude was her friend in the future, and somehow, she trusted that.

She stopped before she'd gone far and cranked up her flashlight, releasing some of her excess energy, then flicked it on.

She trusted Jude, but she still wanted to see him coming.

"Clover!" West called for her, and she saw another light illuminate the space to her right.

"Come on," she said, slowing to wait for him and Bridget.

"I don't want to be here," Bridget said.

"Oh, my God. Stop whining." Clover pushed ahead and walked toward the stairwell.

"Clover!"

She slowed a little but didn't look back at West. "What? It's annoying. You'd never let *me* get away with it."

They made their way up, again, to the fifteenth floor. Slower this time, because West had to help Bridget. Clover kept moving at a pace that was maybe faster than she really wanted it to be. She was at least as tired as Bridget. This was the second time she'd done this climb today, plus a ten-mile round-trip bike ride that morning.

Jude didn't surprise them on the fifteenth-floor landing this time. Instead, they walked to room 1534 on their own.

West knocked three times, like Jude had, and the door opened casually. Not thrown open in anger or cracked open so someone could peek through. A girl, one of the twins, froze and looked out at them with brown eyes that went as perfectly round as her face. Marta, Clover thought.

She held the door in one hand, as if she might slam it closed again. But she didn't. "What's this, then?"

"We need to talk to Jude," West said.

Marta looked West over with a bald, obvious appreciation that made Bridget look almost as uncomfortable as West did. Clover covered her mouth to capture a snort of laughter before it came out.

Marta made a disgusted sound and shooed them away with one hand. "He made you go once, and you come back with another hoodie?"

None of them answered or moved. After what felt like an eternity, the girl sighed and said with exaggerated enunciation, "You shouldn't be here. Especially not with her."

"We need to talk to Jude," West said again.

Marta shrugged and pulled a flashlight from her belt. She

pushed between Bridget and Clover into the hallway. When the three of them stood there watching her, she turned back and threw up her hands. "You want the man, let's find him."

They walked—single file except for Bridget, who stayed next to West—down the dim hallway to a room four away from 1534. Marta knocked on the door.

Jude looked out, saw her, then them, and opened the door the rest of the way. "Are you kidding me?"

Marta gave Jude a look that said *They're all yours* and went back down the hallway.

"You can't just bring people here. Are you insane?"

"Probably," West said. "Jude Degas, meet Bridget Kingston."

Jude muttered a rude word under his breath. "Come in, then."

His room had a bed pushed lengthwise against the wall across from the bathroom door. A round table and four chairs sat in front of the window. A cheap-looking brown laminate dresser and matching nightstands at the foot and head of the bed rounded things out. The space reminded her of her barrack. Except placing all the heavy furniture against the wall left a lot of open space in the center of the room.

Jude was claustrophobic, Clover remembered. The Dinosaur was big, but this room was isolated, hundreds of feet in the air. He wouldn't like to feel closed into it.

A doorless closet held four shirts and two pairs of red pants, and two Academy uniforms, all neatly hung. A pair of boots sat on the floor next to a stack of red and blue plastic storage bins.

Jude stayed standing and didn't offer any of them seats. Clover sat in a chair anyway. She was so tired her legs felt limp. West sat Bridget in one, too. The girl looked like she might fall over at any moment.

That left the two boys facing each other down.

"I can't do anything for you," Jude said. "And if you keep coming here, you're going to get us in trouble."

"Actually, you *can* do something for us." West used his quiet, adult tone. The one he used on Clover when he thought he was right and she was wrong. He used it a lot. "We need to stay here for a while."

"You have to leave. Now," Jude said.

"We aren't going anywhere."

"You sure about that?" Jude said, his voice low. He didn't back down an inch, even though he had to tilt his head back to look West in the face. Clover's heart thudded and she felt the beats on her eardrums. She shook her head to clear that, and started to move closer to them, but they both put a hand out to stop her.

"I don't want a problem," West said to Jude.

"Then don't cause one, hoodie."

"We need to figure out what's going on."

"I agree, you do," Jude said. "But what does that have to do with us?"

"You need to know, too." Clover pushed West's hand away when he held it out again. "You gave me that zine. You had the keys to the Company van."

"Clover," Jude said. He looked sorry for her.

"You kissed me!" Clover wrapped her arms around her body. This was so *stupid*. Mango was tense, sitting close to Clover and panting.

"Jesus, Clover," West said. Jude just stared at her.

"Wait in the hall," she said to West. "And see if you can find some water for my dog."

Both boys said, "What?" at the same time.

"Take Bridget. And get Mango some water."

West grunted and shook his head. "No way."

"Jude will listen to me. Tell him you'll listen to me, Jude. Otherwise, we're just going to stand here all night going back and forth."

West looked at Jude, who lifted his shoulders. "I'll listen."

West didn't look happy, but he took Bridget out into the hall.

Clover sat again, with Mango so close to her he was nearly in her lap. "Do you have any water in here?"

Jude walked to his bathroom and came back with a little plastic bucket filled with water that he put on the floor in front of the dog. He scratched Mango's ears once, then stood without making a huge deal about it.

"I want to help you, Clover," Jude said. "I do. But—"

"You saved West's life and Bridget's, too."

"That wasn't me."

Two years would change him. But this was still him. They had—would have—some kind of relationship then that she didn't fully understand yet. But this was where it started, and she was surprised to find that she wanted it to start. Whatever it was.

"It was you. You knew Mango's name. You had a key that you wouldn't have, or even know you needed, unless I told you. And you warned me that my brother is going to be executed for Bridget Kingston's murder."

"And I kissed you?"

"Yes."

"I don't know what I'm supposed to do," he said.

"What are you and those girls doing here, anyway?" Clover was genuinely curious. He'd obviously set himself up here, and those girls seemed like they had as well. "How many are there of you? How long have you been here?"

"Since I heard that I'd been accepted into the Academy. About two weeks after the kids from Foster City were given the entrance exams." He didn't say how many there were, and she decided not to ask again, even though she had to actually bite the question back. "All we're trying to do is keep the guard from sending us back to Foster City. That's all. As long as they don't know we're here, we're fine. No one is looking for us. They're looking for you."

"No, they're not."

"They will be. You think Adam Kingston isn't going to raise the alarm for his missing daughter?"

That question had buzzed around her head enough that she had an answer. "I think even if he does, they aren't going to cause a scene about it. Not yet, anyway. People aren't supposed to be able to be kidnapped anymore, remember?"

"Yeah. But he's not just going to let his little girl go missing forever."

"How do you live here? What about food? Water? How do you—" She glanced toward the bathroom.

Jude ran an index finger over the scar on his face. "Do you remember how I told you I got this?"

"Yes," she said.

"We do what we have to. So far, we haven't had to do anything that comes close to being as bad as living in Foster City."

"But *how* can you live like this?"

"We manage."

Clover pulled her pack to her and dug around until she found the zine, opened it to the back page, and showed him the note that told her to come here. "Tell me the truth, Jude. Would you have written this if it weren't true?"

He took the zine from her. "I can't imagine why I would do this at all."

"Because we're friends, and you know I'll be alone at the pickup box. In two years you know, because I'm telling you now." She pulled her van key on its silver ring from her bag as well, and swung it in front of him. "You have this with you. How do you think you got it?"

"Friends?" He tilted his head and looked at her so frankly that she shifted her gaze to over his left shoulder. "Sounds like we're more than friends."

She didn't know what to say to that. Her hands flapped against her upper thighs while she tried to figure it out.

Jude sat on the edge of the mattress. "We all work. That's how we do it. Every day, we work. You can't just come here and take our rations and use our—"

"We have a house full of things that might be useful here."

"Will it be hard to get back into your house?"

She couldn't lie. Not now. He'd know it in a heartbeat, and doing this right was important. Maybe the most important thing she'd ever done. "It might be, but I think it can be done."

Jude looked at her another minute, then stood and went to the door to let West and Bridget back in.

"You can stay, at least for now." Jude glanced at Bridget. "At least until we get the whole story."

"Thank you," Clover said. She gave West a hard look, and he echoed her thanks.

"You can stay as far as I'm concerned, anyway. I can't promise that the others will give you a pass," Jude said. "But they'll be happy for whatever rations you got at your house, if they get past the rest of your trash. You can't convince them, you have to go. That's the rule."

West swung his gaze back to Clover. "Those rations are all we have."

"We share here," Jude said. "If you aren't down with that, you can go now and save us all some trouble."

West pinched his lips together into a thin, bloodless line. "Fine," he finally said.

"Dinner's in an hour. You can meet everyone then."

Everyone turned out to be the twins; another girl, Emmy, who looked no older than seven or eight; her older brother, Phire, who was maybe twelve or thirteen; and Christopher, who looked old enough to be out of Foster City without having to run away.

Faced with them, Clover guessed it made sense that there were homeless children, refugees from Foster City, in Reno. Probably even more than just this half dozen. But it had never occurred to her before. She'd read books about runaways, about children living on the streets back in a time when the streets were a lot scarier than they are now. When people were allowed out at night, when the bad guys weren't executed before their crimes could be committed.

She looked at Jude, her eyes tracing his scar. Except, it turned out, not all the bad guys were executed. And Foster City kids obviously weren't kept track of as closely as kids from the neighborhoods, like Clover, West, and Bridget.

"How do you get your doses?" Clover pointed at Christopher. "Where do you work? How do you get your rations?"

"Clover." West said her name under his breath. She was all too familiar with his tone.

"What? He looks old enough to work."

West shook his head once, and she closed her mouth. But God, she wanted to know. How did Jude pass the exams with no one to teach him? How did they eat? None of them were old enough to work, except maybe Christopher, and he might or might not be old enough to get into the Bazaar to collect his own rations. Jude was sixteen like Clover—old enough to work, but he was going into the Academy instead. He was two years from being able to live, legally, without a guardian or to get into the Bazaar to pick up his own rations.

Clover and Bridget sat on either side of West at a long table in what Jude called the boiler room. Christopher sat in a chair near the open window so that he could hear and join in the conversation while keeping watch for anyone coming into the courtyard. He was a tall, broad-shouldered black boy with a lopsided smile and soft voice. He walked with a limp. Like half of his body was an inch or two shorter than the other half.

"I work, my foster father gets my rations," Christopher said. "Would do it if the other kids got my share, but they don't even get all of their own."

"You don't have to explain yourself to her." Geena didn't glance toward them. Her focus stayed tight on Jude. "We're supposed to take in hoodies, right? Now we're just hooking them in off the damn street."

Geena and Marta both looked like they'd done everything possible to avoid looking like girls. Anything soft or pretty was hidden or destroyed. Their chopped hair and hard, black make-up around their brown eyes were the most obvious examples. They wore oversized T-shirts and baggy pants that looked like they'd never been washed.

Geena had a crude metal ring looped through the left side of her bottom lip and Marta had a similar one through her right nostril, providing an easy way to tell them apart. Clover had a hard time not staring.

"They're here," Jude said. "There isn't a lot we can do about that now."

"He got a point." Christopher kept his eyes on the window as he talked. "We keep them here, we know they don't go to the guard."

West made a dismissive sound but didn't say anything. There was a difference between wanting to stay somewhere safe and being unable to leave that place when they were ready.

"Makes no sense they're here at all," Geena said. "I vote no. We ain't got enough to worry about?"

Clover pointed at Jude. "He invited us."

"Not exactly," Jude said when all of the Foster City kids turned their eyes to him.

"Yes, exactly." She pulled the zine out of her back pocket and put it on the table in front of Geena, who didn't even look down at it. Jude took the zine and read out loud the invitation to come to the Dinosaur's fifteenth floor.

"I carried in the hoodies," Jude said when he was done reading.

West pushed his chair back from the table, just a little. "We're here. I'm not willing to die, or let Bridget die, for your convenience. So we need to figure out what to do about it."

"What you're willing or not willing to do isn't our concern," Jude said.

"It is now."

"Like hell," Geena said.

"You should read the zine." Clover pushed the little book closer to Geena, who still didn't look down at it, and then it hit Clover. "You can't read."

"Clover," West warned quietly when Geena's glare turned colder.

Jude picked up the zine and flipped through it. The soft pages made a *thwap, thwap* sound as they slapped together.

"Jesus, Geena," he muttered under his breath. "This article says the dope's a crock."

"Yeah," the girl shot back. "So that proves they're all crazy, yeah? Dope's a crock. Whatever."

"You wrote it."

Her eyes went wide for a moment, and then she shrugged and closed down again. "Who says she didn't make it up herself?"

"Your name's on it. You meet her before this morning?"

"What does that mean, dope's a crock? Don't even make sense."

"Says the suppressant doesn't suppress anything," Jude said. "That we were all cured and protected with the first dose."

That silenced the room for a few heartbeats, and then everyone spoke at once. Clover covered her ears with her hands. She leaned back against her chair, then bent forward closer to the table, back and forth as the voices rose around her.

"The Dinosaur is big enough to house every kid in Reno," West said. "What are there, a thousand rooms in this place? More? How many can the six of you use, anyway? We won't be a problem for you."

"You think it's about space?" Jude asked. "You go live in Foster City, and come back to talk about space."

"What's wrong with his sister?" Emmy asked, pointing at Clover, who had started to hum out loud, despite her efforts not to.

"I don't know," Phire said. "She's some kind of freak."

"That's enough," Jude said.

"We're all freaks!" Clover stood up and tore the zine out of Jude's grip. "It says *Freaks for Freedom.* Freaks! That's us."

West put a hand out and stopped Jude from touching her. Every inch of her skin felt pulled tight, like it might pop at any minute.

"Who you calling a freak?" Geena said.

"You." Bridget waved Geena off when the other girl started to deny it. "Oh, yes you are. Don't you know that no one is supposed to live like this? That's the whole point of . . . well, of everything."

"Bridget's right." Jude put a hand on Marta's shoulder. "You think the hoodies know what happens to us? We're the Company's dirty little secret."

Clover desperately tried not to lose the death grip she had on her behavior. Pacing would help. Rocking. Humming to drown the others out. She covered her ears again and repeated *calm, calm, calm* in her head.

It worked. Maybe not the way she wanted it to, but the room went quiet. Clover felt them stare at her but couldn't stop herself from humming under her breath as she tried to bring herself all the way down. Mango pressed his body against her legs, lending her the pressure that helped her focus. She finally sat back in her chair and let Mango put his head in her lap.

"She calls *us* freaks?" Geena said. "Damn."

chapter 11

A friend is one who has the same enemies
as you have.

—ABRAHAM LINCOLN

"We go to the bar in the morning," Jude told Clover
and West after the meeting ended with the somewhat grudging
consensus that they could stay. For now. "Early, when we can get
lost in the crowd. We leave the Dinosaur as a group, but we don't
go in all at once; we take it in pairs."

"I go in the morning, too," Bridget said. "With my dad before
school."

Clover sat on the floor in Jude's room. Everyone else had left.

"Maybe it would be safer if we were all on the same schedule,"
West said.

Jude shook his head. "You ain't going to be here long enough
to adjust."

"I'd rather just stay on the same schedule I've always been on,"
Clover said. She felt like someone had tossed up all the parts of her
life and let them come crashing down in a chaotic mess. Why
couldn't she hold on to this one thing?

"The less often someone leaves the Dinosaur, the safer we are,"
Jude said.

"How have they not caught you already?" The harder Clover thought about it, the less reasonable it seemed that there was a whole group of unaccounted-for kids running around outside their placement in Foster City.

"We aren't watched as closely as you. We don't count as much," Jude said.

"You can keep your regular time for now, Clover," West said.

"You mean *we* can."

West looked pale. A little sick, even. "I can't. I shouldn't have gone tonight."

"Well, you have to be dosed." Bridget looked around the room for some support.

Clover was only too happy to give it. "She's right, West. You can't just not get dosed."

"I'll be okay." West picked up the zine with his free hand and flipped to an article about the antibiotic qualities of honey that had his name on it. "This says so."

"That girl can't even read," Bridget said. "How do you know that article—any of those articles—even mean anything?"

West flipped the zine to the article Geena had written and read out loud. " 'The suppressant's only purpose is to let a few people control the rest of us.' "

"She can barely speak English. You can't do this!"

West continued. " 'The Company is keeping us addicted.' We have no idea if I'll actually get sick."

Bridget stood. "If your big plan is to make me watch you kill yourself, I want to go home. Right now."

She went to the door, twisting away when West reached for her.

"Maybe we should let her go home," Jude said.

West was gone then, too, without a word.

Clover hugged her knees to her chest and rocked. Not much,

just enough to keep hold of herself. Jude moved to the seat West had left, closer to Clover, and picked up the zine. "I don't blame her for being upset. It's hard to believe this is true. I mean, Bridget's right. Geena can't even read."

It had occurred to Clover that the future Jude, knowing that she would respond to his friendship, might be setting them up. He might want her brother dead for some reason that he didn't even know right now. "You wouldn't make this up, would you?"

He thought about it, instead of jumping to deny that he'd do such a thing. Clover wasn't sure if that was good or bad. "I don't have any reason to believe I would."

"Promise me, right now, that you won't give me this zine in two years unless it's true."

Would it matter, if he did promise? He'd already given her the zine. The reason the Company was so uptight about travelers not speaking to anyone from the future was that once something was done, it couldn't be undone. Even if Jude had given her the zine as a trick of some kind, and she changed his mind now, it was too late. She couldn't unread the zine.

"You got my word," he said, then made a cross over his heart with his right index finger.

They were stuck in a time loop. Living in a present perpetrated by the future. "This is giving me a headache. I don't know how much we should depend on the zine," Clover said.

"What? You're the one who brought it to us."

"I know, but—"

The door opened again, and West came in with a calmer, but still visibly upset, Bridget. They sat next to each other on the edge of Jude's bed.

"Bridget can already dose with the rest of you. Clover can keep

our regular time for now. I'm going to stop taking the suppressant."
West put a hand up to stop her when Clover started to protest.
"Everything will work out."

"How can you know that?" Clover asked. "How can you possibly
know that?"

"I don't. We need to figure out why Langston Bennett tried to
do whatever he was going to do to Bridget."

"None of this makes any sense, West. You should have already
been arrested," Clover said. "They should have taken you weeks
ago, before you could kidnap Bridget. And if Mr. Bennett planned
to hurt Bridget, he should have been arrested already, too."

"Obviously there are things we don't know yet." West took
Bridget's hand again. Whatever else was going on, they were getting
along just fine. "There's still the possibility that Bennett being there
was a coincidence."

"Is there any doubt in your mind that the man who came into
your house wanted to hurt you?" Jude asked Bridget.

Bridget snapped her mouth closed and tears spilled down her
flushed cheeks.

"Is there?" Clover asked.

"No."

Clover couldn't have cared less about why Langston Bennett
was at the Kingston Estate, except that she and her brother had
been sucked into the aftermath. And now West's big plan was to
commit suicide for Bridget. She brought the topic back around to
what was really important. "You have to be dosed, West."

"I agree," Bridget said.

West sat back in his chair. "I'd rather die here than on the firing
line."

"I'd rather you keep breathing," Clover said. "And keep all your
skin."

"She's right." Jude scratched his temple, contemplating West.

"I mean, how the hell would we get your carcass down all those stairs?"

Bridget let loose a strangled sob that Clover might have thought was silly, if she didn't have a matching one caught in her throat.

Jude grimaced and muttered, "Sorry. But you can't die up here. If that's the real plan, it does suck."

"I need to get to the library." Clover couldn't keep thinking about questions that had no rational answer. "There has to be some information, somewhere. I need to get on the nets."

"I have a wireless laptop," Jude said. When the room went silent, he added, "I liberated it from my house father when I left Foster City."

"Liberated?" Bridget asked.

"Stole," West said.

"He took enough from me. It was the least he could give." Jude went to his dresser, opened a bottom drawer, and pulled out a laptop computer. It was old and clunky, and if it worked, Clover would be duly impressed.

"You can connect to the nets on that thing?" she asked.

"Yes."

Not long after the walls went up, wireless Internet was banned. Computers had to be plugged directly into the nets, at a library or through a sanctioned home connection for the few who had energy to waste on that sort of thing.

The new modems gave limited access. For safety. Censorship, so that the Bad Times wouldn't ever come back. It was one more thing that Clover had not only never questioned, but never even considered questioning. Until today.

Clover moved closer to the computer. "What was he doing with it?"

"You don't want to know," Jude said, and then, "Trust me," when Clover started to say she did.

"How do you get power here?" Clover asked instead.

"No one has used the Dinosaur, even for storage, since the virus. They didn't do much to turn off the electricity. All we had to do was hit the breakers until we found one that gives us a little juice where we want it."

"Unbelievable." Mango settled back on the floor under the table, now that Clover was totally focused on the laptop and no longer rocking. "Show me."

Jude opened the computer and touched a button in the upper left corner of the keyboard until the screen lit bright blue. A few minutes later, Jude had the computer connected to the nets. Wirelessly.

"Are you sure they don't have some way to track when someone is connected like this?" West asked Jude.

"My house father spent all his time on this thing and they never came after him." Jude slid out of the way and let Clover sit in front of the computer. "There's no way they knew what he was doing on it."

"How do you know?" Bridget asked.

"Because if they did, I wouldn't have had to live with him for four years."

"Oh."

"Yeah." Jude sat near Clover and watched her as she went into the classified ads.

"Look at this one," Clover said. "This guy in Iowa wants to trade his Whole New Life for a kidney. How sad is that?"

" 'We must adjust to changing times and still hold to unchanging principles,' " West read from over her shoulder. "Jimmy Carter. What's with the presidential quotes? Didn't you see one the other day, Clover?"

A small communication box opened in the center of the screen before she could answer.

Hello, Clover.

The words, black letters on a white field, popped up one by one. No one spoke. Clover asked Jude, "How did you do that?"

"Me? I didn't do anything."

"Well someone did."

"Hey! Don't answer," West said when Clover put her fingers on the keyboard. "It must be the guard. Jesus, how did they find us?"

Don't panic, West, you aren't in trouble, whoever was typing on the other end put into the box. *Well, not yet anyway.*

"Okay," West said after they'd spent a solid sixty seconds just staring at the blinking cursor. "What the hell is this?"

Jude pointed at the keyboard. "Ask who they are."

Who are you? Clover typed. Her heart beat like a trapped bird.

Ned Waverly.

Waverly-Stead Ned Waverly? "Ned Waverly?" she asked the screen, which of course couldn't hear her.

Bridget leaned in closer. "Isn't he dead?"

West shook his head. "Dead or alive, that isn't *Ned Waverly.* Come on."

Prove it, Clover typed.

Your brother is considering giving up his suppressant shots because you gave him an article that said they were the Company's way of keeping you under control, and he's afraid of being arrested if he goes to a bar. Little Geena wrote it.

West stood up. His chair teetered on its back legs and then crashed back into place as he grabbed Jude's arm and ripped him out of his seat next to Clover. "Is this some kind of joke?"

"That's what I'd like to know." Jude didn't break eye contact or struggle against West's hold on him.

"Stop it!" Clover pulled on West's other arm. "What's wrong with you, West? Let him go!"

West looked at her, and then Bridget, and finally released Jude.

Clover sat back down and typed: *How do you know that?*

You told me all about it in another time line. Is Jude okay? Your brother doesn't know his own strength.

Clover looked over at Jude, who glared at West but was otherwise unhurt. Then she typed: *What do you want from us?*

I need to talk to you.

So talk.

Not now. Bridget is about to faint. I'll contact you six p.m. the day after tomorrow.

West, Jude, and Clover all turned to Bridget just in time for West to catch her as she slumped into the predicted swoon.

chapter 12

There is a Destiny which has the control of our actions, not to be resisted by the strongest efforts of Human Nature.

—GEORGE WASHINGTON,
LETTER TO MRS. GEORGE WILLIAM FAIRFAX,
SEPTEMBER 12, 1758

Waverly's showing up on Jude's computer put an end to the night. West, Clover, and Bridget crowded into the bedroom adjoining Jude's on the fifteenth floor of the Dinosaur. West made a pallet on the floor, even though Jude offered to bring another bed into his room.

The next morning, West rolled over and opened his eyes to find Bridget looking down at him.

"Morning," he said.

"If you don't go, I don't go." She'd been awake awhile, he thought, thinking about this.

"You have to."

She sat up, cross-legged on the mattress. "They're at least as likely to be looking for me as they are for you. In fact, if they're looking for you, they're probably looking for Clover, too."

"Clover has to be dosed. She's a Messenger. The minute she doesn't show up somewhere she's supposed to be, the entire guard starts looking for her." They would search for her even harder than they'd search for a guy who hadn't killed anyone yet.

Bridget's hair was a mess, she had dark circles under her blue eyes, and her hands shook in her lap, but she stiffened her spine and said, "So you and I skip it."

West rolled over to his back and stared at the ceiling. "How can I send Clover to do something I'm too scared to do myself?"

"This isn't about fear."

He sat up. She was right. It would be harder to convince Clover. West could already hear her stubborn response, but in the end, he'd have to win this one, whether he wanted to or not. She'd have to take her chances that night at a suppressant bar. And he had to let her go.

"I'm worried about you," Clover said while they waited for Jude and the others to return. It wasn't like her to waste much time on worry she didn't think was necessary, so he believed her.

"Try not to be," he said. "It won't do any good."

"What am I going to do if the article is wrong and you die?"

"We have to trust something," he said.

He'd never questioned the execution of future criminals until he faced the same fate. In fact he was glad that capital crimes were firmly a thing of the past.

His whole life, he'd been taught that the current system was right. His father was an executioner, for God's sake. The tight hold on crime kept them safe, didn't it? It was brutal, but necessary. And never wrong.

Because of the portal in Lake Tahoe, it was never wrong.

Either the justice system was fatally flawed, or he was going to kill Bridget.

"We're going to figure this out, Clover." He sat at the table with her and picked at a small bowl of strawberries Emmy had brought to them before everyone left. They grew them in big tin cans on the balconies. Ingenious, really.

"Aren't you scared?"

Terrified. He'd lived through the virus when he was a little boy; he wasn't looking forward to it reconstituting in his body. He didn't have to catch it, because he already had it lying dormant in his cells. If the zine was wrong, he'd get sick. His skin would decompose off his living body. And if he couldn't figure out a way to save himself, he'd die a miserable, excruciatingly painful death instead of a quicker one in front of a firing squad.

Bridget had never contracted the virus during the Bad Times. Maybe she'd have a chance of staying healthy. But only, of course, if he stayed away from her so that she didn't catch it from him. If he got sick, she'd have to go home so she could be dosed and live.

Trying to figure this mess out was making his head hurt.

"What do you think about Waverly?" he asked, needing to change the subject.

"It's unreal. Like the president popping up to say hello."

Waverly and Stead were on a level with the president. Revered, distant even here in the Company's capital city, and working for the good of the people. Waverly wasn't associated with the Company that bore his name anymore, but West, like everyone he knew, was in awe of the man.

Waverly had saved his life, after all.

Clover bit into a strawberry and closed her eyes. "How are they eating like this?"

They were too young to pick up rations. The guards at the Bazaar checked ID at the elevators. It might be possible for them to get through the front door, but those elevators were guarded like they were the entrance to the kingdom's gold.

West guessed they were.

Maybe they somehow got in through one of the locked stairwells.

More likely, they were stealing what they had to, without taking enough to get caught.

"I don't know, but we should figure out how to get what we need out of the house this afternoon, before it's too late."

"West?" Clover rocked back against her chair, but only slightly. That was her maintenance rock. The one that kept her stable when things were under control, but only just. "Be careful okay."

"I will."

"And if it's your daddy that ratted you out?" Christopher asked as West walked with him toward the house. West liked Christopher. He was seventeen, nearly old enough to collect on his own rations. He was quiet, but when he spoke he didn't mince words.

"It's possible," West conceded. He didn't want to think it. But it was possible. Something broke in James Donovan when he went to work as an executioner. Maybe something broke in him a long time before. "But I don't think so."

"Yeah? But maybe you're just a daddy's boy and can't see straight."

"Not hardly."

His father was a Company man, through and through. He was on the first crews that cleaned the city after the virus and had worked his way up the ranks. He might not do anything to stop West's execution, but West didn't think he would go out of his way to expedite it either.

"Yeah, so you say. You sure walking around the neighborhoods is a good idea?" Christopher asked. "How you know we won't get snatched?"

"I don't know, but I'm pretty sure we won't."

"Pretty sure? I'm not about to tell your sister the guard caught you up."

"Sure enough to risk it. The guard isn't exactly sly. If they're waiting for me, we'll see them long before we reach my house. If they put out my dispatch flyer, the Bazaar will be papered with it."

The guard was notoriously visible. The ranks wore uniforms that resembled pictures West had seen of old-school army soldiers. But more important, they showed up in vehicles with sirens blasting and lights rotating on top.

Any sign of a guard vehicle on the watch for him, and they could turn back. It might not be parked right in front of the house, but if they circled around, they'd find it. A block or two away, no more.

Isaiah had told him about the process of picking up a criminal. Bragging, West thought at the time. Rubbing in his entrance to the guard program while West had to work at a cantaloupe farm.

"Your skin," Christopher said.

They walked the two miles to West and Clover's neighborhood, trying to stay out of view of as many people as possible. There were some who made a career out of the dispatch flyers, determined to have a Whole New Life, and West didn't want to run into one of them.

So they aimed for casual, but West was painfully aware that his neighbors would peg Christopher as an outsider as quickly as the Foster City kids had seen him and Clover as hoodies.

"I think it's safe," West finally said.

He led the way to the house he'd lived in his whole life. They came up the far side of the street, to avoid Mrs. Finch seeing them if she was at work in her garden. She must be so worried about them, but West couldn't think about that right now. He opened the garage door. No one jumped out of a dark corner or came roaring up in a government truck.

West uncovered the trailer his father had used years ago to pull Clover behind his bicycle. He and Christopher worked quickly and quietly, filling the trailer with garden tools, seeds, extra flashlights, the rest of Clover's meager candle stash, the three live chickens, whatever food they could carry, clothes, their laptop and a couple of books that West knew would make his sister happy. Almost as an afterthought, he took the box of their mother's letters from Clover's trunk, and the picture their father had looked at from the living room.

West attached the trailer to his bicycle and tipped his head toward his father's old bike for Christopher. They were at the end of the driveway when a voice called his name.

He spun, placing the voice immediately, which didn't stop a hard lump of fear from forming in his throat. "Mrs. Finch."

She looked at Christopher as one hand went to worry the top button of her housedress. She had a light blue sweater over it and a pair of sensible brown leather shoes on her feet. She looked entirely out of place outside her garden. "Isaiah said—"

She stopped and looked confused. Her eyes, the left still noticeably drooping since her stroke, darted again to the boy she didn't know.

"This is Christopher," West finally said. "Christopher, this is Mrs. Finch."

Christopher nodded but didn't smile.

"Isaiah was here this morning," Mrs. Finch said. "He said— well, I didn't believe him of course. How could I believe something like that?"

The guard was looking for him, and he was standing in front of the place they would look first. They had probably sent Isaiah, thinking he wouldn't run from or fight a friend. Either that, or Isaiah had come on his own, to prepare his grandmother. And maybe to warn West. "It's okay, Mrs. Finch. Try not to worry."

"We going or what?" Christopher asked, low, almost under his breath.

Their street was so quiet. Exactly as it had been for most of West's life. The same neighbors, the same trees and gardens. West looked past Mrs. Finch, and it was almost like seeing a photograph. Why wasn't the guard there already?

Didn't take much to get to the answer. He wasn't supposed to have advance warning. Now he'd had three pieces of it. He'd already seen the dispatch flyer. His father had shown up in his living room to warn him. And Isaiah had come as well. They weren't here yet, because as far as they were concerned, there was no rush.

That meant that neither Kingston nor Bennett had reported Bridget missing. Looking for West for a future crime was a whole other animal than looking for the headmaster's missing daughter. The idea that she could go missing at all was dangerous. It meant the system had failed to protect her.

West felt a little sick. "Yeah, we have to go."

He pulled his ration tickets from his pocket and pressed them into Mrs. Finch's hand. She grabbed his wrist with her other hand, her grip surprisingly strong, and held it long enough that Christopher started fidgeting beside him. Then she let him go and West rode away.

chapter 13

You cannot stop the spread of an idea by passing
a law against it.

—HARRY S. TRUMAN,
ADDRESS BEFORE THE SWEDISH PIONEER CENTENNIAL
ASSOCIATION, JUNE 4, 1948

"Clover's a weird name."

"Said the sister of a boy named Phire," Clover said.

One of the twins had braided Emmy's pumpkin-orange hair
into a thick rope that hung halfway down her back. She had a rash
of freckles all over her face, neck, and shoulders and down her bare
arms. At seven, she was nearly as big as her twelve-year-old runt
of a brother. "Our mama said we was bright like jewels when we
popped out. Got a big brother named Diamond. We call him
Mondo. Phire's real name is Sapphire, and I'm Emerald."

"Where's Mondo now?" Clover asked.

"A ghost. Same with our daddy and mama."

"You mean dead?"

"Dead or just gone." Emmy didn't look particularly sad. Maybe
she wasn't. Everyone had lost someone. Seven was pretty young to
be jaded, but Clover thought maybe that was what let the little girl
get through.

"What happened to your parents?"

Emmy sat at the table in the boiler room, drawing on some

recycled paper with the broken and well-used nubs of crayons. "The squads got my daddy before he got my mama, then she got herself."

She was so matter-of-fact. Didn't even look up from drawing oblong fish swimming in a green sea.

"You still have Phire," Clover said. "Same as I have West."

Emmy added a long strand of yellow seaweed to her drawing. "Phire takes care of me."

Phire still needed someone to take care of him. "How long has he taken care of you?"

"Since we went to Foster City, when I was almost six."

A year or so then. "Why did you leave Foster City?"

Emmy frowned and pressed harder on the tiny piece of golden crayon in her left hand. If it had been longer, it would have broken. "Daddy Martin liked Phire too much."

"He made you call him Daddy?"

"He said he loved Phire, but he made my brother cry. A lot. Jude snatched us up from there and now we live here."

Clover's stomach knotted, and she breathed through a wave of nausea. "Do you like it here?"

She smiled up at Clover, showing a gap where one front tooth had fallen out and the other had grown in crooked. "Yes, a lot."

"See why we can't go back?" Jude asked from the doorway.

She did. She didn't want to, but it was obvious. "I wasn't trying to pry. I'm just curious."

"I know. Don't ask Emmy questions around Phire, though. He's very protective."

Clover had a brother like that. "Is Bridget still sleeping?"

"I think she's in shock or something. Sleeping to keep from thinking about it. Can I talk to you for a minute?"

Clover studied Jude's face. He had smudges like bruises under his eyes, and he looked like he hadn't slept well the night before. Or any night. Ever. "Is everything okay?"

"Come with me? I have to get back to watch."

Clover followed Jude to his room with Mango at her heels. "But aren't you worried that someone will come in another way? Someone else, I mean."

"If someone came in, they wouldn't come all the way up here. We have a protocol if someone shows up."

Clover didn't say that their protocol had failed both times she and West came into the Dinosaur. Instead, she sat in one of the chairs. Jude stayed standing, inspecting the bean plants growing in cans in front of the window. He plucked off some ripe pods and handed a couple to her. Mango lay between them. Without his vest on, he was off duty and could laze around like a regular dog.

"I found something," Jude said. "On the nets."

"What is it?"

"Something about Waverly."

Clover took a bite of one the beans. "What did you find?"

Jude looked back out the window. "Waverly left the Company two years after the suppressant was developed."

"Everyone knows that." She'd learned it in primary school. Waverly was a recluse when he found the Lake Tahoe portal and pulled away from the Company when the publicity became too much for him.

"But did you know that Waverly spoke out against the Company privatizing everything?"

The Company took over most aspects of society after the virus. Clover had been taught that this privatization was necessary to keep peace and safety in the cities. It had never crossed her mind to question the Company's dominance over her country, her city, even her family.

The number of things she'd never thought to question was becoming alarming.

"How come I've never heard that?"

"You ever been on the open nets?"

She hadn't. Her access was limited to what the Company and the government wanted her to know. If what Jude said was true, that meant the Company had sanitized the story. Sanitizing helped keep order. It hurt Clover's brain to think otherwise.

"What happened?" she asked, pushing aside the disturbing idea that she'd been brainwashed. For now, anyway.

"I found an article someone wrote and posted just before the nets were closed. Listen to this. 'Even Waverly knew the truth, that the cities gave up too much freedom, and now who knows what they've done with him.' And then, '*Nip the shoots of arbitrary power in the bud* is the only maxim that can ever preserve the liberties of any people.' I haven't had time to find out what they meant about him knowing the truth. But it's here, somewhere."

Nip the shoots of arbitrary power in the bud? "Can I use your computer?"

She barely heard him answer before she was sitting in front of it, the wide open entirety of the nets at her fingertips.

"Nip the shoots of arbitrary power in the bud," she murmured as she typed the words.

"What is it?" Jude asked, behind her.

She looked over her shoulder at him. "John Quincy Adams."

"You guys need some security at these back doors," West said to Christopher when they rolled up to the back of the Dinosaur. Christopher held the door open wide so that West could park the trailer inside.

"No one comes here," Christopher told him.

"We did."

"Yeah, well," Christopher said. "You ain't exactly code red."

When they reached the fifteenth floor, West made it half a dozen steps before a door flew open and Bridget barreled into the hallway, then stopped with one hand on the wall and took a breath before walking toward him with Clover and Mango at her heels.

"You made it back," she said.

He nodded, thinking, *This time.* The Dinosaur was not a long-term solution. Not for any of them. Not even the Foster City kids. He didn't know how to even start talking about that.

"You have to go to the bar," West said.

Clover almost laughed. Not because any of this was funny, but because the miserably uncomfortable mass of fear and anxiety building in her chest had to come out somehow. "And if I do? You think my name isn't flagged?"

"Your name flagged won't mean the same thing as mine. I get executed. You go to Foster City. And don't forget that you're a Messenger. You miss your dose and the Company notices."

"I don't want to be the reason you're arrested," Clover said.

"I don't want to be the reason you're dead."

"At least you're acknowledging how stupid and dangerous it is to stop dosing!"

"I'll take her," Jude said. They were sitting in his room, Clover, West, Bridget, and him. Clover's dose was due in an hour.

"If I go, I might lead them back here. We did this so you wouldn't end up in front of a firing squad, remember?"

"So your big plan is for both of you to catch the virus and die here?" Jude turned to Bridget. "You agree with them?"

Bridget shook her head, her blond hair brushing her shoulders. "It's no use, Clover. You have to go."

"You don't get a vote," Clover said.

"The guard is probably already looking for West and me. You don't go, and you'll have the whole Company looking for you as a deserter. It'll be worse than telling them you don't know where West is if someone asks you."

"Damn it." She hated that Bridget was right. That West had been right that morning. But they were, both of them. If she was going to be arrested for questioning during her dosing, they wouldn't be sitting here. It would have shown up in the database, and she and West would have been taken a long time ago. Somehow, they'd managed to screw up the information the Company still believed to be true.

After much discussion, Clover left Mango at the Dinosaur. She wanted him safe if the guard showed up at the bar while she was dosing. Jude walked with her toward the bar where he and the others were dosed. She didn't get to a place of comfort with people easily. She liked Jude, though.

She'd gone to the same suppressant bar since she was a baby, except for yesterday. And now today. It was weird not to recognize her neighbors sitting on the stools along the two long bars. Or the Caramel-Camel Man or the dosers behind the bars.

Just like at her regular bar, the dosers here didn't make eye contact. She signed in with the woman at the door, then sat at the bar. When the doser came, she felt the pressure at her port. The sting was the same as always, like lava flowing against the curve of her skull. And then it was done. No guard, even though she was sure at each step in the process they would come.

"You're worried about West," Jude said as they walked back to the Dinosaur.

"Of course I am. He's my brother."

"I've been thinking. What if—"

Clover slowed to a stop. "What if what?"

"What if I give you some suppressant? In the future."

"How would you do that?"

"I don't know."

"If you can get suppressant in two years, why can't you get it now?"

"I'm not saying I can get it then. I'm saying—what if we agree that I will, if I can."

"It's not like you can pick it up in the Bazaar."

"But if I have two years; if *we* have two years, we can come up with a way. And if I bring it to you—in the future, like the zine— we can give it to West without him going to a bar."

Clover started to pedal slowly toward the Dinosaur. "I'm supposed to go on another mission tomorrow."

"We could decide on somewhere I can leave it for you."

"West won't like it."

"I suggest we don't tell him."

"I don't lie very well." Not that she wouldn't want to lie. West would hate this idea. A lot. But when she tried to lie, especially to her brother, it never worked. Transparent, he called her. Just to piss her off.

"Not telling isn't the same as lying. And it's for his own good."

Clover ran through her memory of the routes to the launch site, off the *Veronica* to the van, to the pickup box. "There's a building. A small, brick building near the launch site. It almost butts up against the mountain. If you leave it there, between the building and the mountain, I think I could get it without being seen."

Jude held up his right hand, lightly fisted with his pinky finger crooked toward her. "If I can, I will."

Clover hooked her finger into his and made her first pinky promise.

chapter 14

There is nothing wrong with America that the faith,
love of freedom, intelligence and energy of her
citizens cannot cure.

—DWIGHT D. EISENHOWER,
COMMENCEMENT ADDRESS, COLUMBIA UNIVERSITY, JUNE 8, 1950

Neither West nor Bridget got sick while Clover was
gone to the suppressant bar. Bridget stayed with him in their room
that night, and Clover slept on the second bed they'd finally moved
into Jude's room. Clover was relieved to find her brother and Bridget
still well in the morning.

"Don't look so shocked," West said. "I'm going to write an
article for that zine in two years. I'm not going anywhere."

Clover looked him over, just to be sure. He looked a little
flushed, but there were no sores. Bridget had her arm through his
and her cheek on his shoulder. She looked okay, too. "If the zine
is right, which it might not be."

"Geena wrote that the suppressant doesn't work the way we
think it does. I might not even get sick."

Clover looked at Jude, who lifted his chin a little but didn't say
anything about the plan they'd hatched the day before. She wasn't
risking her brother's life on something Geena had written. Between
the two of them, she and Jude would figure out a way to hide the
suppressant on the other end of the portal.

"I have a mission this morning," she said to West. "Try not to die while I'm gone. Also, you might want to stop hanging all over him, Bridget. If he does get sick, he'll be contagious."

"She'll be fine. And I'll try," West said. They'd already exhausted all conversation about whether she should go on her mission the night before. If she went AWOL, it would only make things worse. Much worse. The fact that she didn't have an article in the zine lived in the back of her mind, where it poked at her and reminded her that as far as she knew she'd be dead sometime in the next two years.

Clover half turned and said to Jude, standing behind her, "I have to go."

Jude stood up and handed the zine, which he'd been reading through again, to West, who said, "Clover—"

"I'm going." Clover stopped her brother before he could do or say something that would tip over her carefully balanced emotions. "I'll be fine."

West closed his hand around her upper arm. She kissed his cheek, then pulled away from him and knelt to hug Mango. She wasn't taking him for the same reasons she'd left him behind when she went to the bar. If this went badly, she didn't want him caught up in it. It was hard enough trying to figure out how she was going to manage without Mango, without having to worry about him being taken from her permanently.

Jude followed her out of the room.

"Don't let him die," Clover said as she hefted her pack. She hadn't spent more than a workday away from her brother in her whole life. "Don't you dare let him die."

"I won't."

"You have to remember the hiding spot for two years."

"I'm sure you won't let me forget."

Clover stopped, a few steps down from Jude, between the thirteenth and fourteenth floors. "This could be a mistake. We might be setting ourselves up for a . . . I don't know, a major time loop. Or something even worse."

"Like what?"

"*I don't know.* That's the point."

"What do you want to do?"

"This has never been about what *I* want." Before she started down again, she added, "Take care of my dog."

When Clover arrived at the Mariner offices, she spent a few minutes pacing in front of the main entrance before she finally made herself go through into the cool, sterile lobby. The same receptionist who had been there on her first day smiled at her.

"Hello, Miss Donovan," she said.

"I'm . . . it's a workday for me."

"Yes, of course. I have you on my list. Have a good mission."

Clover ran her sandpaper tongue over her bottom lip and hurried toward the elevators. Through the nerve-racking wait for the doors to open and close and the ride seven stories up, she could not stop thinking about Bennett in Bridget's house. It made a strange kind of sense that maybe Bennett had placed the arrest warrant for West when he was surprised in his efforts to do something bad to Bridget, although it made Clover's head hurt to think about how it could have happened. Or why West was allowed to take Bridget away from her house at all. Or why no one seemed to be looking very hard for Bridget.

Her theory was that Bennett had come to do something bad to Bridget and was surprised by finding West in the house. Because Jude had warned them about West's arrest early through the zine, whatever information the guard had about West and Bridget had changed.

Clover shook her head to clear away the complicated thoughts that cluttered it. She opened her closet and reached in for the jumpsuit. West couldn't die, she decided as she took it off its hanger. That was all she had to think about right now.

She went into the bathroom and took a hot shower, dressed in her new uniform and her boots, and went back downstairs to meet the trainer who would take Leanne's place until her leg healed. Clover half expected Bennett instead, there to demand she produce her brother the moment the elevator door opened, so she shouldn't have been surprised to see him leaning against the receptionist's desk. But she was. Her heart stuttered, then restarted painfully.

He straightened when he saw her walking toward him and met her halfway. "Ready for your mission today?"

"What are you doing here?" She should have answered that she was ready for her mission and asked about his weekend, but she thought of it too late.

"We weren't able to free up a trainer for you today. You did an excellent job on your own. Are you up for another solo run?" Bennett looked around. "*Really* solo this time, it looks like. Where's our Mango?"

"I decided to leave him at home. How was your weekend?"

"Just fine, dear. Just fine."

Bennett opened and closed his hands at his sides, and his mouth was set in a stern line, even though his tone was friendly.

"Are you sure?" Clover asked him.

"Quite. Let's go, shall we?"

Clover walked behind Bennett outside and to the parking lot. He went to the driver's side and she followed him. And then he got in. "I thought I was going alone."

"You are, from the dock." He closed the door and stared at her through the window until she went around and got in the passenger seat.

"I hear your brother is in some trouble," Bennett said as he pulled the van onto Virginia Street.

"He—" Clover didn't know what to say. "Yes, I guess he is."

"Have you seen him?"

The motion sickness hit all at once. "No, sir."

"You aren't staying at your house alone?"

Oh, God. She wasn't good at trying to come up with clever answers without time to think. "I'm fine."

It was the wrong thing to say. She knew it immediately, but it was too late to do anything about it. She was prepared for him to push her about West. Why hadn't he done that? What difference did it make to him where she lived?

"We can't have that," Bennett said. "I'll make sure someone from the emergency center at Foster City comes by to see you after your mission. You're going to be just fine, Clover. You belong to the Company now. We'll take good care of you."

Clover rolled down her window in hopes that she wouldn't add to Mango's pee stain by puking all over the carpet.

Sitting in the Messenger cabin inside the *Veronica*, Clover couldn't stop thinking about the two years passing as the big steam-powered machine slipped through the portal and up on the other side. West might be dead now. Long dead. She might get off the submarine in a time when her hardest mourning for him was done.

If there were no suppressant syringes in the hiding spot, did that mean that she and Jude had decided they weren't necessary?

If there were some, did that mean that everything would be okay?

If there were none, it could mean that she didn't make it back to the Dinosaur. She might get caught trying to steal the suppressant. Or Bennett might have the emergency center employee at the barracks take her into guardianship, stolen syringes and all, before she was released from her quarantine.

What if Jude had kissed her out of sadness because she was executed for trying to save her brother? She tried to imagine standing in the concrete Kill Room she'd only seen pictures of, while faceless executioners trained their rifles to the red X over her heart. She hadn't written any of the articles in the zine. Not one. That had to mean something, right?

She didn't realize she was rocking until her head hit the curved wall behind her.

"I'm okay," she whispered. She would have done anything to feel Mango pressing his body against her legs. "I'm okay."

She was alive now and not in any kind of trouble at the moment. And the syringes wouldn't be there if her having them meant she'd die. She needed to hold on to that. The ship docked and Clover climbed out of the dark hold and into the sun on rubbery legs with her stomach turning itself inside out.

At least she really did feel sick. In fact, it didn't take much to fake a choking gag for the benefit of the Mariners still milling around the dock as she climbed out of the submarine. She lurched off toward the brick building, felt her way along the side wall, and slipped behind it.

She didn't actually throw up, but it was close. She was so busy thinking about her stomach and what the odds were that she was having a heart attack that she almost missed what she'd come back there for. All she saw were rocks and short little shrubs, stunted by lack of sun between the building and the cliff side behind it.

Panic made her stomach turn over again. It had to be here. It had to be. She got on her hands and knees and dug through the brush and the sharp little stones.

And there it was. Sitting in the dirt behind a larger rock. A leather belt with a pouch exactly like the one she wore around her waist. Clover picked it up and sat hard on her butt with her back against the rock, the pouch in her lap.

Her hands shook as she opened it. Inside, she found a cloth-wrapped bundle that she didn't dare unwrap. She stood up and took off her belt, retched one more time for good measure, and tossed it over the cliff to the lake below. She threaded the new belt around her waist, the pouch settled over her hip, and came back out to the dock.

The illegal syringes felt like a beacon in neon light that might draw the attention of every Mariner on the dock. There were only a few people left at the launch site, though, and none of them even looked at her. Clover fumbled for the van keys in her pocket and forced herself to walk slowly to the vehicle. She tried to look as normal as she could, but her limbs were stiff and weird and she knew she was failing.

A man and a woman, both in black Time Mariner jumpsuits, stood talking. A small group of Static Mariners stood together at the end of the dock like they were waiting for something. It occurred to her that they were waiting for her to bring back the disc before they arrested her. So far, this whole thing was so easy, except for her own panic, that Clover was paranoid she was being set up. She actually looked back over the van seats to make sure Bennett or a guard wasn't hiding there. She drove, her hands sweaty on the steering wheel, wondering if she would be arrested at the pickup box. Or meet Jude there again.

But she didn't see anyone. With time to spare, she returned to the dock, parked the van, and went back to the Messenger cabin and buckled herself in. She wished the cabin door locked, but it didn't. The Static Mariners were gone when she came back to the ship. She wasn't sure whether the Time Mariners were inside already.

She was sure she would never do this again as she settled back in her seat and the submarine came to life under her. Never travel, never drive. She'd never see Leanne again.

Before the *Veronica* began its descent, Clover cracked open her fortune cookie. She read the little slip of paper out loud with just seconds to spare.

"Do not fear what you don't know." Clover shoved the paper into her pocket. "Yeah."

The van waited for her in the dock parking lot. Bennett must have had someone drive it over, rather than come for her himself. The relief at not seeing him was almost overwhelming, and she had to get herself together before she started the engine. She drove to the last turn in the road before she'd be visible to the guards at the gate and pulled to the side of the road.

For a few minutes, she sat there with everything in her screaming at her to go back to the Dinosaur now, skip the quarantine and the possibility that Bennett would somehow force her to give up her brother.

The guard would turn over every rock in Reno looking for her if she disappeared with a disc. Even if she left the disc in the van, he would not let her just go. The Dinosaur would go from being relatively safe to the place where she waited to be arrested and maybe executed. Bennett had called her involvement with the Company a draft. He'd drawn a comparison to war. Clover was smart enough to know she didn't understand everything that was going on here. She was missing something. Something big. And that something might get her or her brother, or the other kids at the Dinosaur, killed.

Why hadn't she thought this part out more thoroughly before now? She opened the leather pouch Jude had left for her. Or maybe she'd left it for herself. There was no way to know for sure, but it comforted her to believe that Jude had done what he'd promised.

Inside the pouch was a soft cloth cushioning a dozen syringes filled with the thick suppressant. Would that be enough? Was there some significance to the number that she didn't know, or was this just all they could get?

The syringes were warm to the touch, and Clover wondered if they'd stay fresh this way. She had no way to refrigerate them in her room at the barracks, except maybe to fill her sink basin with cold water and submerge them. And then pray that no one came in and saw them.

Each syringe was topped with a nasty-looking needle. West and Bridget would have to get dosed the old-fashioned way. She wrapped them up again and slid them into the top of her jumper. The belt around her waist kept them from slipping too far down. She was able to separate them and lay them flat, so they didn't add a noticeable amount of bulk. She felt them there, though, and they kept her hyperfocused.

She would not survive being taken in for questioning about West with these syringes on her person.

She drove through the gate, lifting a surprised hand in response to Isaiah, who waved at her from his position just outside it. She slowed the van to a stop and rolled down the window when he took a step closer.

"What are you doing out here, Clover?" he asked. He looked over to the other guard, who seemed curious but not concerned. "They got you out here all by your lonesome?"

"Leanne broke her leg." Clover forced herself to keep her hands on the wheel and not let them fuss with the front of her jumper. "Her good one."

"I heard. I didn't know you could drive. Where'd you learn to do that?" Isaiah stepped a little closer to the van and leaned in enough that Clover felt compelled to lean back. She forced her hands to stay down and not flutter to the syringes against her belly.

"Leanne taught me."

"You always were a quick learner." He looked back at the other guard again before he added, "They're doing some roadwork near your house, I hear. My grandma's been housebound for days."

Clover ran her tongue over her upper lip. "Roadwork?"

"Yep. Be careful over there."

Clover nodded and said, "Yeah, I will," then put the van in gear and drove away. Maybe a little bit too fast. Gravel kicked up under her tires. Isaiah was trying to tell her something, and even though her brain wanted to take him literally and brought up whatever pictures and film she'd ever seen of roadwork, she repeated what he'd said to her over and over so she could tell Jude and West later.

When she reached her room on the seventh floor of the barracks, she saw Leanne leaning against the wall across from her door. In this time line, Leanne didn't have a broken leg. She was sidelined by something that would happen to her two years from now. It made Clover's head swim to try to figure out why she didn't just not do what would break her leg, since she knew it was coming. She also couldn't come up with a good reason for her to be in the hallway.

"Hey, doll," Leanne said. "Miss me?"

"I've been doing okay on my own." Clover pulled the key from her pocket and opened her room. She looked at Leanne, whose face had fallen a little, and said, "What are you doing here, anyway?"

"Bennett asked me to debrief you."

They sat together at the round table. The curtain over the window was open, letting in the sun. It took a few minutes for Leanne to debrief her, during which time Clover was barely able to focus on anything but the syringes pressed between her jumper and her T-shirt.

What if one of the needles poked her?

What if a syringe broke and the suppressant leaked out?

What if Leanne tried to hug her and felt them there?

When Leanne was done with the debriefing, Clover asked, "Aren't you still recuperating? You know, on the other side."

"I was going stir-crazy just sitting in my room waiting for a leg I hadn't even broken yet to heal."

"What have you been doing to keep busy?" It would make her insane to sit in these barracks with nothing to do.

"Ah, you know." Leanne hesitated, her forehead wrinkled like she was trying to figure something out in her head, and then she said slowly, "Happiness lies in the joy of achievement and the thrill of creative effort."

Leanne looked at her for a long moment, but Clover didn't say anything else. She knew that one. It was FDR.

"Why won't they let you do your job on this side?" Clover asked, with the same kind of uncertainty that she'd heard in Leanne's voice.

"I'm not sure. I just know I was benched for a while."

"But—"

Leanne shook her head. "I really don't know."

It didn't make sense. It was like Bennett wanted Clover to be alone on her missions. Why wasn't he here, debriefing her himself? Clover was certain that he had questions about West, but he'd sent Leanne to talk to her instead.

"Don't look at me like that," Leanne said. "I'm your friend."

"Really?" Everything in Clover wanted to believe that.

"Really."

"You're supposed to ask about my brother, aren't you?"

Leanne shrugged one shoulder, just a little. "Is there anything you want to tell Mr. Bennett about him?"

"No. Why did you quote Roosevelt earlier?" Clover asked. She knew she should be careful. Cautious. But the words tumbled out. " 'Happiness lies in the joy of achievement and the thrill of creative effort.' Why did you say that?"

"It's true, don't you think?"

"That's not why."

Leanne sat still and looked at Clover for a long moment before she pushed her chair back and stood up. "I'll see you soon, Clover. Take care of yourself."

Clover was a wreck by the time she made it back to the Dinosaur the next day. Every time she fell asleep, she dreamed about a representative from Foster City coming to collect her. She got up twice, sure there had actually been a knock, but was wrong both times. Was he bluffing? Maybe Bennett had threatened her with Foster City to throw her off. If that was it, he'd done a good job.

Add Leanne's strange behavior and Isaiah's warning about road-work the day before to her lack of sleep and worry about Foster City, and by the time she left the barracks with the syringes hidden under the cardboard bottom of her pack, she was so wound up she was afraid she might not be able to make it home. Why hadn't she asked Jude to come back today and walk with her to the Dinosaur? She stopped for a minute and looked around, hoping maybe that somehow just wishing it was true would make it so.

It didn't.

She would have loved to run, and for Mango to be there running with her. The rhythm would make everything better. But Mango wasn't there, and she couldn't risk jostling the syringes, so she walked downtown, following the Truckee River as it cut through the imposing buildings. It seemed to her that every single person she passed stared at her. Like they had X-ray vision and could see through her pack to the stolen suppressant syringes.

Everything in Clover screamed at her to get rid of them. Dump them in the river. Everything in her, that is, except the part that was certain her brother was lying in that huge, empty casino dying.

If someone was following her, they were looking for her to lead them to West. Or maybe Bridget. Clover was certain the rest of the kids probably hadn't even occurred to Bennett or Kingston or the guard. In fact, she doubted that anyone outside the Dinosaur thought about those kids at all, except for their house parents, who most likely hoped they were never found.

She couldn't lead the guard to them. She couldn't stand here by the river for the rest of her life, either. She climbed up out of the river walk and onto First Street, where a few people were milling around. She looked over them, trying to decide if any were paying particular attention to her.

No one stood out. She turned toward the service road that would take her to the Dinosaur. No one back here at all. She let her guard down when she had less than a mile left to walk. And then she saw him. A young man, maybe two or three years older than West, wearing brown pants and a white shirt. *Brown for the dirt slingers.* He was too clean to be a farmer and his hair was cropped short, like the guards wore theirs, not longer to keep the sun off his neck like West's. Plus, no farmers would be walking around downtown this early in the day.

Clover veered between two buildings and over a couple of blocks to Virginia Street. A few minutes later, she passed a plate glass window and saw the fake farmer's reflection, doing a really bad job of secretly trailing her. She did the only thing she could think of. She turned fully to face him, planted her feet wide, and screamed.

The fake farmer stopped, looked back over his shoulder like there might be someone else she was screeching about, then backed up when dozens of people turned their attention to her, moving in closer.

"Please, help me!"

Someone took her by the arm. "What? What's wrong?"

Clover pulled away. If the fake farmer wasn't really chasing her, she was about to get him into serious trouble. A middle-aged man who probably had daughters her age tried to put his arm around her and she puddled to the ground, taking care not to land on her pack as she slithered out of his grasp. "No, don't touch me."

There weren't too many people out, not at this time of day. Most were working. A woman knelt next to her and said, "Are you sick?"

The fake farmer stood in the shadows of the alley, watching. She lifted one arm and pointed at him. "That man was chasing me."

The man who'd tried to comfort her spun around, and the fake farmer looked alarmed. He backed up more deeply into the alley.

"Hey, get back here!" The graying man chased after her stalker, and several others followed.

"You okay?" a woman asked her. "You don't look so well."

She didn't feel so well either. She needed to get out of here, right now, so she could get to the Dinosaur while her stalker was otherwise occupied.

"Stay with her, Donna," another woman said. "I'll call for an ambulance."

Oh, boy. She stood up again. "Wait, no, I'm okay, really."

"Maybe some water? Get her some water."

The second woman went into the building behind them. The people who'd chased after her stalker were gone, leaving her alone with Donna. She didn't see the fake farmer in his too-clean dirt slinger uniform anywhere, and she didn't see anyone else standing around waiting for her to lead them to West and Bridget. It was just her and Donna.

She kept a death grip on the straps of her pack with her other hand, in case someone thought to take it from her. "I think I'm okay now. Really."

"Where are you going? I'll walk you home at least." Donna didn't look happy about that, even though she offered readily.

Clover did her best to look recovered. "Just a block or so up. I'm fine now, really."

She needed to go before someone else picked up the fake farmer's slack. She wasn't sure what to do about Donna and the other woman, who came toward them with a glass of water, so she just walked away without looking back. They asked each other what they should do, but neither of them tried to stop her.

By the time she reached the Dinosaur she was half convinced that she'd just managed to scare some poor farmer friend of West's half to death. Or get him arrested for something he didn't do.

She was sure she'd upset all the people on the street, who were used to men who stalked young girls being dealt with before they got to the point of chasing them in the street.

"You look terrible," Jude said when he met her in the hallway on the fifteenth floor.

"Thanks a lot. Where's West?"

Jude rubbed the bridge of his nose. "In his room."

"Oh, God." Clover finally realized that it was Jude who really didn't look well. "Oh, God, he's sick, isn't he?"

"No."

Clover barely heard him. She took off running toward the room she shared with West, fumbling with her pack as she did, trying to get to the syringes.

Jude wasn't lying. West looked fine. Well, he looked a little pale and exhausted, but he didn't have any sores or anything. He didn't look sick.

It was Bridget who lay on one of the beds, moaning as she folded in on herself as if she could contain whatever pain she felt. Sweaty sheets tangled around her legs and torso, and her hair was plastered to her flushed face.

The pressure cooker of fear in Clover's chest released as the fear for her brother eased, even as it was replaced by fear for Bridget. The whole mess of emotions came out as anger she knew was misplaced but couldn't hold in. "Does she have a fever? Why aren't you guys taking care of her?"

"We're doing the best we can," West said.

Clover knelt by Bridget and looked her over. No sores. A hard spasm wracked through the other girl, and she moaned when it passed and said, "Oh, God, that hurts," without really gaining consciousness.

"West?" She put a hand on his shoulder. Bridget was sick. Really sick. And West, who'd had his last shot nearly half a day after Bridget had hers, wasn't far behind. For a second, she almost saw the virus crawling through him, worming its way through his veins. Stealing him from her.

A hard shiver passed over West, and he said, "I've been better, we both have, but we'll be okay. She doesn't have any sores. Maybe this isn't the virus."

A crush of emotions hit Clover with no warning. Her face crumbled, even though she tried to keep from showing West how upset she was. Tears streamed down her face, and despite her best efforts, she rocked from foot to foot with enough sudden vigor that Mango let loose a short, startled bark.

"Try to breathe," West said. "Please, don't do this now. Everything will be okay. I promise."

For the first time in her life, West couldn't make everything okay. But she could. This time she could. She had, already. West wouldn't get sick. Bridget would get better. As quickly as she'd become overwhelmed, she drew a breath and was in control again.

She pulled the package of syringes from her pack.

West looked at her like she'd pulled out a live rattlesnake, instead of the stuff that would save him and Bridget. "Where did you get that?"

Clover backed up when West came closer to her. She had averted a full-on meltdown, but she still felt like she might fall apart if West touched her. Jude caught her from behind but let her go when she struggled.

"What did you do, Clover?" West asked again.

"We left it for me to find on the other side of the portal."

"You could have been killed."

"They're syringes with needles," she said. She showed West and Jude the syringe with its thick, sharp needle, not designed for insertion in his port. That thing would have gone all the way into their brains.

"You helped her do this?" West asked Jude, who looked about as equally close to being sick as West did.

"She needs you," Jude said, quietly. "We had to do something."

"You could have been arrested," West said, his voice raw and painful. "Do you know what they'd do to you for stealing suppressant?"

"Yes," Clover said. Of course she knew. She had the same executioner father that he did.

"I don't want it."

"Don't you want Bridget to have it?"

West clamped his mouth closed and looked at the sick girl on the bed. Finally, he inhaled deeply and said, slowly, "Only if she gets sores. The article said there would be withdrawal. That's all this is."

"You don't know that," Clover said.

"You shouldn't have done this. Stealing suppressant is . . . it's . . ."

West collapsed, sliding almost gracefully to the floor. Jude moved quickly, positioning himself over West's limp body, holding up an arm. "Come on, Clover. Do this before he wakes up."

Somehow, Clover managed to pull the plastic tip off one of the needles. She didn't really know what she was doing, but she'd learned at a first-aid class in the library to push up the plunger until a thick drop of suppressant oozed from the hole in the needle.

She plunged the needle into her brother's bicep before she lost her nerve. His skin was tougher than she expected it to be, and she had to push hard to get it in. He came to then, and Jude had to practically sit on his chest to keep him still. It took what seemed like an eternity to depress the plunger all the way. After she pulled the needle out, she rubbed the spot with her fingers to make the medicine work through faster.

"Jesus, Clover," West moaned. His face was damp with sweat, and he couldn't get out from under Jude, even though he should have been able to easily push the smaller boy away.

"I'm sorry," she whispered, then wondered if West could see through her glass face to the truth behind that lie. She couldn't lose him.

While Jude helped West into the other bed, Clover dosed Bridget as well. The girl didn't move, and only a soft, low moan escaped when Clover pulled back her sheet and pushed the thick needle into her upper thigh.

"Make sure you get it all in," West said quietly behind her. "If you're going to do it, might as well make sure you do it right."

Clover turned her head, still depressing the plunger, and looked at her brother. "Do you have any sores?"

"No. But I don't feel very well."

West fell asleep, and Bridget never really woke up. Clover covered them both, resting the back of her hand on their damp, hot foreheads, even though there was nothing she could do about their fevers.

She finally left them and went into the adjoining room, where Jude sat on one of the beds waiting for her. She sat on the other bed and told him about Leanne giving her a presidential quote and about her maybe-stalker. She hesitated before telling him about Isaiah talking to her about roadwork in front of their house, because it felt like she should talk to West about that first. In the end she let it all come out.

When she finally stopped to catch her breath, Jude stood up without saying a word. He went to the parcel of syringes and came back with one.

"What are you doing?" she asked.

"I don't think you want to dose yourself." He tilted the big needle and peered at it. "This thing is a monster."

"Those are for West and Bridget."

"Here's the thing. I'm not doing this without you."

Clover sat on the other bed, without looking away from the needle.

"I'm serious, Clover," Jude said. "You can't go back to the bar. And I'm not going to let you get sick."

He *looked* serious. His dark eyes didn't move from her face, and his scarred jaw was set in a hard line. For the first time, Clover saw a hint of the older Jude who had started all of this.

chapter 15

Change will not come if we wait for some other
person or some other time. We are the ones we've
been waiting for. We are the change that we seek.

—BARACK OBAMA,
CAMPAIGN SPEECH, FEBRUARY 6, 2008

Clover's nerves were a frayed mess. West had regained some color after she dosed him and made him eat a few bites of eggs and beans. Bridget was resting more comfortably, although she still didn't look like herself.

Clover's arm stung from where Jude had injected her with one of the stolen syringes of suppressant. That was what made her stomach turn now. For the first time since she was just a few weeks old, Clover had not shown up for her dose when she was supposed to. Because of her job, because Bennett had West on his radar, her subversiveness would be noticed. Until tonight, Clover had felt like she would be able to just slip back into her normal life when all this was over. Not anymore.

Waverly had better have a plan for them. And a good one.

"Where is he?" Clover's legs shook with impatience, and Mango pressed against her shins. She waited with Jude, Christopher, and Marta in front of the computer for Waverly to show up. Geena stood watch, and Clover had no idea were Phire and Emmy were.

"It isn't six yet," Jude told her.

"Are you sure?"

That was some risk you took, Clover. Especially considering you didn't really need to do it.

Clover stared at the screen until she'd absorbed the words that popped up in a communication box in the center of it. It took two or three readings. Whether or not they were actually talking to Waverly, the person on the other side of the nets knew things he shouldn't. That she and Jude had stolen the suppressant. That she'd gone on one last mission to get it.

So, how is our girl?

Bridget's sleeping, Clover typed.

Good. She'll need her rest for the trip. And your brother, he's managing?

"This guy is freaking me out," Jude whispered.

Marta inched in a little closer. "What's it say?"

What trip? she asked Waverly, ignoring Marta. Jude read out loud what had been said so far.

To visit me, of course.

"He's in the city?" Clover said.

"What if it's not Waverly? What if whoever it is, he's some kind of creeper?" Marta asked. "Some of us have been through enough already."

"All of us—"

I'm not a creeper. What an odd word. And I do not live in the city.

So, what are you then? Jude reached over Clover to type.

A scientist. A revolutionary.

"A walking ego," Jude muttered.

Clover shushed him and typed: *Where are you?*

At my ranch, outside the walls.

Jude peered over her shoulder. "He may or may not be a creeper, but he's definitely plain crazy."

Be nice, Jude. I'm not crazy.

"Oh, my God! Stop that!" He backed away from the screen. This time Clover read out loud.

"I've been careful to make sure that what I've told myself about the future is enough to convince, but isn't enough to put us all into a loop. Well, not a devastating one anyway. I don't know how you'll get here. But I know you make it safely."

"The only way he can know this stuff is that at some point, we tell him," Clover pointed out. "He must be traveling through the portal somehow."

"Still?" Christopher asked from the doorway.

If it makes you feel better, I don't know much more than the parlor tricks I've already shown you.

How are we supposed to get out of the city? Clover typed, before Jude could say again that Waverly was freaking him out. As far as she could tell, freaking them out was Waverly's whole point.

By the power of your own ingenuity.

Jude made a sound behind Clover that sounded like a half laugh, half sob. He fell back into the slang the other Foster City kids used. "I got the Academy in two weeks. Two weeks! I ain't slipping on that. Not for anything or anybody."

"Maybe West and Bridget and I will be safer out of the city."

"Yeah, well, they're never going to go for it," Jude said, jerking his thumb over his shoulder toward the adjoining room where they both slept.

They'll follow you, if you lead them, Jude, Waverly typed. *And you want to lead them, don't you?*

Jude nudged Clover out of her chair in front of the computer and sat there himself. *What is that supposed to mean?*

I know what Foster City was like for you. What it's like for the kids who are still there. It's what you were born for, isn't it? To change things.

Christopher and Marta peered at the screen, and Clover whispered the words.

How can I change anything?

You can't by yourself. But all of you. All of you are going to change more than Foster City.

"I'm the only one who has to go," West said when everyone but Bridget, who still slept in the other room, had gathered in the boiler room and been brought up to date. "But Bridget should come with me, at least until she's safe back in the city. Everyone else can decide for themselves."

Jude stood up. "I say we stick together. That's what Waverly said, and he was right."

"Well, I ain't going, and Emmy, too." Phire hovered over his sister as if they might try to force her outside the walls. "I don't care what the rest of you do."

"I'll go," Christopher said. When Phire glared at him, he added, "What I'm gonna stay for? A cantaloupe farm?"

West sat in the chair, a little heavily, and Jude passed a glass of water down the table to him. He drained the glass, then looked at Clover. "It might be hard to bring Mango. If you go."

"If? You don't think you're leaving me here? And Mango's coming, too."

"Any ideas for actually getting over the wall?" Jude asked.

The wall was twenty feet high, the surface smooth, slick concrete that curved steeply, so that on the inside it was shaped like a letter *C* and on the outside it bulged like a pregnant woman's belly. "No one is going over that wall," Clover said.

"How will we get outside, then?" Christopher asked. "We gonna just walk out past the guard, like nobody's business?"

Clover took a bite from a carrot, turning the idea of leaving the city in her mind so she could see the problem from every angle. Christopher had a point, even if it wasn't the one he thought he had. "We actually could just walk through the gate."

The idea didn't excite her, but she knew instantly that it would work. Outside the wall was the Bad Times. Inside the city, order and safety ruled. The city's citizens had the rebellion scared out of them sixteen years ago. Their suppressant was in the city. The guard was in the city.

If anyone ever thought about leaving, she'd never heard talk of it. Never daydreamed about it herself, either. Sometimes she wondered what other cities might be like, but never the space between. That was no-man's-land, and no one wanted to be in it. The whole city was indoctrinated to stay. Their lives depended on obeying the rules and being near a suppressant bar.

In other words, no one ever tried to leave and there was no one left outside to try to break in.

Clover had been through the gate three times. Every time, it was wide open and watched by only two young guards. Isaiah was one of them. They sat in chairs with rifles nearby but not at the ready. The rifles were more for bears than people.

"We can't just walk right through," Christopher said. "Can we?"

"Well, not as easy as that." It was possible the gates were opened during the time the Messengers and Mariners went through, and kept closed and locked the rest of the time. But she didn't think so. The Company was cocky. Men like Bennett believed that no one would want to leave the city. "All we need is a distraction. Just five minutes to get through and hide. The gate opens right into a stand of trees. If we can get through, we can hide there."

"And how do we make that kind of distraction without getting arrested?" Jude asked.

The answer came in a flash of inspiration. Fully formed. "We don't. Waverly does. He'll drive up to the gate and cause a scene."

The inexperienced guards weren't about to arrest him. Sane or otherwise, he was *Ned Waverly*. It was foolproof. Waverly had saved the lives of everyone left living. The two guards would try to calm him and turn their attention away from the gate, which no one in fifteen years had tried to slip through.

"And if you're wrong?" Phire was paying attention now, even if he still had a scowl on his face.

"I'm not."

"Everyone is sometimes."

"But I'm not this time. They won't let him in. He's from outside. As far as they know he hasn't been dosed in years, and it's only dumb luck that he's still alive. The virus doesn't get into Reno. That's their only job. They'll fall back on it when they don't know what to do."

"So he distracts them, and we sneak out," Jude said.

"Pretty much."

West shook his head. "We won't be able to use this plan twice. Any ideas for getting back in?"

"Not yet," Clover said. "But we'll think of something."

"To get back in, I just need to tell the guards who I am. While they find my father, you all can slip back in."

The room went quiet as everyone turned to where Bridget stood in the boiler room doorway. She looked a little better, but Clover still thought a strong breeze might blow her over. She was obviously well enough to come up with an idea. A good one, too.

"It might work," Clover said. "But it's dangerous."

"Not if we wait until after my . . . my death date."

"It's dangerous, because we've already changed the future," West said. "Too dangerous."

Clover sat back in her chair. "You can't keep trying to save everyone from taking risks, West."

"Maybe Bennett—" West stopped talking. "Damn it."

Bridget blanched, but to her credit, she didn't give in. "I can do this."

"Okay, so let's vote," Jude said. "Who's in?"

Christopher, West, Clover, and Bridget put their hands in the air. The twins hesitated a little longer, but then did as well. Everyone looked at Phire, who was holding Emmy's hands down on the table.

"This is so stupid," Phire said.

But his hand went up and he let go of Emmy so she could put one up, too.

"What about our doses?" Geena asked.

Clover looked at Jude, not sure whether this was the time to reveal that they had nine more stolen syringes.

"We have a plan," Jude said. "Let's have some faith that the details will work themselves out, okay?"

Phire banged his fist on the table, making his plate jump. "Don't act like we can't question them, Jude. Three days ago, we didn't even know them. Now we're putting our lives at risk on their say-so?"

"Three days before we came here, I didn't know you or Emmy. We're *supposed* to be together. That's what the zine's about. *Freaks for Freedom.*" Jude thumped his open hand on his chest, then opened it wide at them. "*We* are the freaks."

Geena shook her head when Phire started to argue again. "I want to write that article."

"When do you talk to Waverly again?" West asked.

"Tomorrow night at six o'clock," Jude told him.

West rubbed a hand over his face, then through his hair. "Okay. So we're going to be here at least tonight and tomorrow. We aren't going anywhere right now. Not until we let Waverly know about our plan."

Clover closed her eyes and pictured herself typing their plan to

Waverly the next night. He would tell himself. Somehow. It hurt her head to think too hard about it, but he knew. Just like he knew all the other things about them. "Actually, Waverly has known for the past two years."

"He said he didn't know how we get out," Jude said. "And we haven't told him yet."

"Not in this time line. He's caught in so many loops, we probably don't need to talk to him at all now. We needed to think of it on our own for it to work. It's our plan; he wouldn't know all the intricacies. But he knows his part. I guarantee it."

chapter 16

All my children have spoken for themselves since
they first learned to speak, and not always with my
advance approval, and I expect that to continue in
the future.

-GERALD FORD,
NEW YORK POST, AUGUST 13, 1974

Clover stood next to Jude near the lookout window
and picked at the edge of one of her nails. "Are you excited for the
Academy semester to start?"

"I don't know anymore. It's so mixed up. If anyone belongs at the
Academy, you do. Who knows if either of us will be able to go now."

Clover shrugged one shoulder and petted Mango so she'd have
something to do with her hands. "You'll be back in time. I know
it. Kingston didn't think I belonged. And I don't think I want to
go anymore, anyway. They don't want autistic students."

"There have been plenty of Academy graduates with autism."

"Mine is worse, I guess."

"You know better than that."

Clover let her other hand flap at her side. It was her most reliable release valve.

"Kingston really should have let you stay. What was that about,
anyway?" Jude asked.

"It wasn't about anything. I can't be around people, I can't handle too much noise or too much—of anything. Kingston didn't want me at his school, that's it."

"If that's true, then Kingston is an idiot."

"Kingston is the headmaster."

"Then even headmasters can be idiots."

Before she could stop them, tears slipped down her cheeks. She brushed at them angrily with the backs of her hands, but more fell. "This is so stupid."

Jude opened his arms without moving any closer to Clover. He let her come to him and didn't hug her until she hugged him. Even then, he didn't pet her or move his hands behind her where she couldn't see them. He just held her like that until she could breathe again, and then let her go.

Somehow, he knew how to touch her without triggering her natural tendency to pull away. Just like he would two years from now. He reached up, slowly, and brushed a strand of her hair from her forehead.

"Who do you know who has autism?" she asked.

"My brother."

"Where is he?"

"He's a ghost." Dead or missing. "If we save his daughter, Kingston will have a place for you at the Academy. I know he will."

Clover wiped her face on her sleeve and desperately needed to change the subject. "What do you think about the classifieds?"

"You mean the quotes?" Jude asked, backing up to just outside Clover's personal space. "Tell me one."

The quotes were too frequent to be random, and her gut told her they were important. She flipped through her memory of several she and Jude had found on his stolen laptop. They came from several states and, other than quoting an old president, didn't have anything in common.

"*Victory has a thousand fathers, but defeat is an orphan.* John F. Kennedy said it."

"Some kind of replacement alphabet?" Jude asked. "Or maybe an anagram."

"Not one I've been able to figure out."

Clover looked at her feet, at the red Chucks that someday would wear through. At least West had saved their mother's letters for her. He would never get to work for the Company. She'd worked her last day for them, too. If they survived this, they would both be blacklisted. At least. Clover really had no idea what would happen to her. She knew all too well what they'd do to her brother, and that there was a real possibility she'd share his fate.

"I keep thinking," she said. "Maybe it's wrong for me to go with you guys to meet Waverly."

"How can that be wrong?" Jude held up a hand to stop her from talking. "We stick together. That's the plan."

"The Company will look for me, if I leave. Harder than the rest of you, except maybe West and Bridget. If I stay, maybe it will take some of the pressure off you."

"Don't say that again. I'm serious. I don't want to hear it."

"Just think about it."

"Just think about this. You said your trainer gave you a quote. Maybe she was trying to warn you against doing something stupid like staying behind in the city by yourself."

Clover tracked West down outside, standing with his back against the wall next to the door, where he could get inside again quickly if he needed to. He looked stronger. Healthier. His color was back, anyway.

"How're you feeling?" Clover asked.

"Much better."

"That's good."

West turned to face her directly. "Is everything okay with you?"

"I feel like there's something we're missing," she said. "About the quotes. Remember, I told you about the Roosevelt one. What do you think they mean, West?"

"I don't know. Maybe they don't mean anything. Maybe someone just thinks they sound cool."

"But people from all over the country are leaving them. They must mean *something*."

"What are you thinking?"

"I think they're some kind of communication. They're in the classifieds; that means whoever is placing them wants them to be read. Everyone reads them. Everyone but you, anyway."

"So what, like a secret handshake in the newspaper?"

"Maybe. Or a message. A code or something."

"You'll figure it out, Clover."

She looked up at him. He'd changed in the last few days. Something about him was different. "I'm scared."

"Of what?"

"All of it. Talking to Ned Waverly on the nets, him knowing stuff about us, never going home again. What if you're arrested because of my idea? You'll be executed. What if everything falls apart because I go AWOL from the Company?"

"I won't be arrested, and everything won't fall apart."

"You can't know that."

"No, but I believe it. Or I want to, anyway. Waverly says we all get out safe. And I had an article in the zine."

He did. "I didn't."

"Don't overthink this. You'll only drive yourself crazy. We have to move forward. We have no choice."

"Do you think Waverly will agree to our plan?"

"Yes, I do."

She was already driving herself crazy. Everything depended on Waverly agreeing to a plan that she would never have any memory of telling him about.

It took an hour to organize and prepare the Dinosaur for their absence. They arranged the rooms they'd slept in like no one had been there and moved their storage into a room at the end of a hallway where it would be less likely to be found.

Phire and Christopher let the chickens go in the yard of a house they'd taken food from before. Clover hoped they'd be taken care of.

"I still think this is a crazy plan," Phire said before they left.

Jude pushed the last bird into its cage. "We should eat these birds, at least."

Maybe, but they didn't have time to butcher them. What Clover wished was that they were just leaving the chickens at the Dinosaur. Giving their birds away was a silent acceptance that they might not be back.

Jude set the cage with the others, against the wall. "Just be careful, okay. You see the guard, get out of the way."

"Fine," Phire said. "But if after all this, 'Waverly' turns out not to be *the* Waverly, I'm going to shove a big piece of I-told-you-so in your face."

"Agreed."

"What did you say?" Clover asked. She had a strong mental image of a groom shoving cake in a bride's face during a wedding reception. She'd never been to one, but she'd seen it happen in old movies. There was a picture in her trunk at home, one she'd probably never see again, of her father with white frosting all over his face and her mother laughing with a chunk of cake in her hand.

"It just means he's going to rub it in my face."

Laughter bubbled up and out, and it felt good. Like a teakettle releasing steam. Both boys looked at her like she'd lost her mind, but she didn't care. "Maybe Waverly will know what Bennett wanted with Bridget in the first place."

"She's a pretty girl. Could be he's just a perv," Jude said.

Clover sobered as she remembered feeling uncomfortable when he touched her. "He put a dispatch out on West. He's more than a perv."

"The headmaster and the man in charge of student recruitment at the Company," Jude said. "They're an odd couple, for sure."

"Kingston sent me to Bennett directly. He gave me a letter—" Clover inhaled, and blinked several times as she tried to remember something that flirted around the edges of her memory.

"What?" Jude asked. "What is it?"

She closed her eyes and saw Kingston's office. The picture of Bridget on the bookshelf, the window that opened out into the campus courtyard. The electric lights that were such a waste. The huge desk with a thousand drawers.

"When I came to Kingston's office, the letter was already written. Already addressed to Bennett."

"Maybe it was just a standard letter of introduction or something."

"No. It had my test scores inside. And information about my brother and our dad."

"He knew he was going to send you to the Company before your interview?"

"Where's West?"

Clover flung open the door to West's bedroom and nearly gave him a heart attack. She barreled in with Mango at her heels. *How can someone so small be so much like a hurricane?*

Their father used to say that, and it was true. She slid to a stop with Jude right behind her.

"I think your dad has something to do with this," she said to Bridget.

"What's going on?" West put a hand out to stop Bridget from getting defensive too quickly.

Clover pointed a finger at Bridget, then flapped both of her hands a few times and started to bounce on her toes. Mango huffed and pressed against her legs. "Her dad had a letter of introduction all ready for me when I got to my interview. It was in his desk, addressed to Bennett with my test scores inside. Before he ever met me, he planned to send me to work at the Company. I want to know why."

"Calm down, Clover. Whatever happened at the Academy, it isn't Bridget's fault."

"Stop protecting her!"

"Stop attacking her."

"What did your father get out of sending students to Bennett?" Jude asked Bridget.

"What do you think he got? A promotion he had no business getting. A big house, enough food. Horses, for God's sake. My father traded kids like Clover for advancement and security and comfort for himself and me."

"Kids like me?" Clover said. "Like with autism?"

The room went silent. Could that be it? It seemed so obvious once Clover said it out loud.

"Why does Bennett want kids with autism?" Clover asked Bridget.

"She doesn't know," West said.

Bridget cut him off before he could defend her further. "You don't understand."

"What is there to understand?" Clover's voice rose almost to the point of yelling. "That he needed an *estate*."

"That's enough," West said.

"No. She's right. He's greedy. Do you think I don't know my own father?"

Clover split a glare between West and Bridget. "You should have told us."

"You're right," Bridget said. And then directly to West, "I should have. I'm sorry I didn't."

Jude went to the door between their rooms. "We're going to have to talk about this eventually. But there's no time right now."

Clover stood and stared at West until he said, "Please, Clover."

"This is my room."

She was right. But he wasn't about to leave Bridget alone with his blunt, pissed-off sister right now. "Go talk to Jude. I'll be in soon."

She glared at him another minute, like she might argue, and then stalked off and slammed the door behind her.

chapter 17

If you are not too large for the place you occupy,
you are too small for it.

—JAMES A. GARFIELD,
SPEECH AT SPENCERIAN BUSINESS COLLEGE, JULY 29, 1869

"The plan is simple," Jude said. "We get as close to the gate as we can without being seen. Waverly drives up, causes a scene, and we sneak out into his van."

Clover had a sudden attack of second thoughts. Maybe they *should* wait until tomorrow, to be certain that Waverly was aware of his part of this simple plan. Maybe her time-loop theory was wrong. They might be better off really making sure he knew the plan, rather than assuming they'd told him in some other time line. What was a day, really? She tried to calm down before she let those thoughts come out of her mouth. She wouldn't be able to take them back, and they would make everyone else doubt her.

They had a date with Waverly at nine. She'd picked the time, because whatever after-dark procedures happened at the gate would be settled by then. The guards would assume they were in for a long, quiet night and might be easier to take by surprise. All she could do was hope that in some other version of tonight, she'd told Waverly the same time. And he'd be there. He had to be.

Because West was right. This wouldn't work twice. They might not even make it back to the Dinosaur after curfew.

If his hair standing on end all over his head was any indication, her brother had been giving this a lot of thought, too. "Wear dark clothes, and hats if you have them. Maybe we can even figure out some way to darken our skin. Maybe the ash from the rocket stove."

"Ashes all over your pale faces ain't going to make you *less* noticeable," Christopher said.

"It's a mission. And we have to get it right."

"Christopher's right. A bunch of white kids in blackface will draw attention," Jude pointed out. "It's not even dark out yet."

"Okay, fine. Whatever. Has anyone been to the gate at night?" No one spoke up.

"There are floodlights," Clover said, closing her eyes to picture the gate. "I've only been there during the day, but there are lights."

"Maybe someone should go scout out the area. See where we can hide," Jude said.

"We don't have time for that. Clover's seen the gate, up close, inside and out," West said. "It'll have to be enough. There's something else to think about. Isaiah might be there."

Clover shook her head. "I saw him on the day shift."

"Just be prepared, in case."

"Who's Isaiah?" Phire asked.

"My friend in the guard."

"Well, that's okay then, right? He's your friend."

"I don't know."

It took them almost ninety minutes to get to the gates. The timing was perfect. Church bells all over the city rang to announce curfew fifteen minutes before they approached the gate.

Clover was relieved to see that her memory hadn't failed her. There were floodlights attached to the guard stations right inside and outside the gate. Even though it was still just dusk, the lights were turned on. They seemed to be mostly for the comfort of the guards. They were angled downward, rather than casting a wide circle of light.

The guard on the city side sat in a chair with his back against the guard booth, examining his fingernails with his hat pulled down low over his forehead.

Clover and the others crouched and moved through the trees. One by one, with West in the lead and Christopher in the rear, they slipped along the wall to the place where the guards had parked their Company van and knelt behind the vehicle.

Jude looked at his watch and whispered, "Two minutes."

The watch belonged to his brother. He wore it like Clover wore her mother's shoes. Clover petted Mango's head, to keep him calm. She felt a little sick. If this went badly, it would be on her. Her idea might get her brother killed. It might get Jude and his friends sent back to Foster City. Or worse.

They might all end up in front of the squad. Her father might shoot—

"Clover," West hissed. "Stop."

She forced herself to stop rocking, one hand on the van, the other tight around Mango's lead and resting on his head. She stood up just enough to see the closest guard through the van's windows. He looked up just then, and she ducked. "I was wrong."

"What?" West asked.

"It's Isaiah."

West lifted his head and then sank back against the van. "It'll be okay. Nothing changes."

They squatted there for what seemed to Clover like a hundred years. *He's not coming. He's not coming.* But then she heard an engine approaching and the night was split by a long, loud bleep of a horn. "It worked. I can't believe it worked."

Clover stood up and saw Isaiah drop the book he'd been reading when Waverly started his racket. He stood up too fast and knocked his chair over. She barely heard him say, "What the hell?"

"Here we go," Jude whispered.

"Someone in a Company van," the other guard said. That wasn't Isaiah.

"Well, Jesus. He doesn't need the horn."

The other guard joined Isaiah on the outside as the van came to a stop in front of them.

"Wait," West said.

Finally, he started toward the wall at a fast, silent pace. They all followed. One of Clover's hands was caught up in Mango's leash and the other flapped like it had a mind of its own and wanted to detach itself from her body.

She was the weak link. She was going to get them all killed, because she couldn't do this.

Jude slipped his hand around her flapping one and squeezed it. "Breathe," he said. "We got this."

West held an arm up, then lowered it quickly and went through the gate with Bridget in tow, slipping around it to the left. The twins went next. Jude pulled Clover, who brought Mango with her, one hand being led and the other leading.

Phire and Christopher were right behind her with Emmy.

They would have made it. The plan worked flawlessly. Except a rabbit darted out of the woods and across the road in front of the van just before Emmy made it into hiding. Mango barked just once. He was a good dog and well trained. He didn't try to run after the rabbit. He just couldn't help announcing it.

Phire had gotten up the incline into the trees and turned back to help his sister, but it was too late. Isaiah turned toward Mango's bark. Maybe even recognized it, even though he couldn't see them in the trees. He did see Emmy, though. Isaiah grabbed her around the waist, up against him, just as Christopher yanked her brother deeper into the trees.

The little girl squirmed and reached toward where Clover watched in horror. "Let go of me! Phire! Phire!"

"Stop kicking me!"

"I don't want to be a ghost! Phire!"

Christopher put a hand over Phire's mouth and managed to quiet him before they were all caught. West whispered in the smaller boy's ear, "Wait a minute."

"Phire!" Emmy screeched again when her brother didn't come for her.

"Where? Where's the fire?" Isaiah indicated with his head for the other guard to check inside the gate.

"I don't see nothing," he called.

"I swear to God, little girl, if you don't stop—ouch!" Emmy had her teeth in Isaiah's forearm, and even then he didn't let her go. He shook her instead, until she loosened her jaws.

"What's wrong with you? You want to get eaten by a bear out here?"

The second guard came back and picked up the gun he was issued to keep himself from being eaten by the same bears Isaiah had warned Emmy about.

"Who're you with?" Isaiah asked. "What's your name?"

"What the hell are you doing outside the gate?" The other guard looked at Emmy. Clover was willing to bet this was the first time he'd ever seen anyone other than Mariners and their crew on the other side of the gates.

"Phire, help me!" Emmy bit Isaiah again, on the wrist this time, and he let her go, but when she tried to run to the woods, he yanked her back.

"I told you, you don't want to go there. And you bite me again, you're going to get a visit from the tooth fairy."

Christopher grunted, and Clover thought maybe Phire had bit him, too. West waved and whispered for the twins, Bridget, Clover, and Jude to circle through the woods to the rear of Waverly's van.

"Let Phire go," he said. "It's okay. He'll be quiet, won't you?"

Christopher waited until Phire nodded his ability to stay calm, and then they all took off. As Clover took her turn running to the back of the van, she saw her brother step into the light and skidded to a stop. "Oh, no."

"It's okay," Jude whispered, pushing her along. "He knows what he's doing."

Waverly kept up on the horn, but he didn't look back at them as they piled into his vehicle.

"Isaiah," West said.

Clover maneuvered herself so she could see West and Isaiah through the van's windshield while she hid behind the driver's seat. She was acutely aware of the man sitting in it. Could smell him and hear his breathing, even over the sound of the horn he never let up on. But she watched Isaiah put his hand on the baton at his hip. It didn't shake and there was no hesitation. For a split second, Clover was sure her brother was going to be executed right here.

"Let her go, Isaiah," West said. "Please."

"Jesus Christ, West, what are you doing here?" Isaiah looked over his shoulder, and then toward the woods where they had all been hiding. "What the hell is going on? Who is this kid?"

Emmy threw her arms up and kicked back, hard, catching Isaiah in the knee. Isaiah, whose attention was divided, stumbled backward; his center of gravity shifted and his leg buckled under him. She wiggled away and threw herself at West, wrapping herself around him when he lifted her. Clover covered her mouth with her hands and leaned into Mango, the pressure of his heavy body keeping her from screaming. "No, no, no," she whimpered.

"Wait, Clover. Watch." Jude was behind her. Close, but not touching.

Somehow Phire had come around behind the second guard. Clover didn't see him, but she saw the guard go down to his knees when a rock hit the back of his head. The kid was a dead-on shot. Isaiah went down with the next stone. Phire dove into the van and was followed seconds later by West and Emmy. Christopher pulled the back door closed.

"You know," Waverly leaned out the open driver's-side window and called to the fallen guards, "I don't think I need to get in the gate after all."

"What? Wait a minute," Isaiah called, rubbing the back of his head and coming to his knees.

Waverly put the van into reverse and waved through the windshield at Isaiah, who looked unsure as to whether to help the other guard, who was still lying on the ground, or chase the van on foot.

"Well, you kids sure know how to make an entrance," Waverly said after he had the van turned around and they were speeding away from the gate. "Or was that an exit? Yes. It was an exit. A spectacular one, too."

"We're going to be caught," Phire said. "That guard knew West. He saw Emmy."

"He thinks we're in the woods," West said.

"He'll figure it out!"

"I don't think so. Not right away, anyway."

Christopher knelt near the back of the van's cargo area and looked out the small rear window. All the seats had been removed, but Waverly had put blankets down over the bare metal floor for them. "No one is chasing us."

After a while, the adrenaline ran itself out and the chatter in the van quieted as Waverly drove. "I can't believe you showed up," Clover whispered, mostly to herself.

"Did you really doubt me?"

"Yes," Clover said. "We have to get off the highway."

"Don't worry, we will."

chapter 18

The only thing new in the world is the history you
don't know.

—HARRY S. TRUMAN,
AS QUOTED IN *PLAIN SPEAKING: AN ORAL BIOGRAPHY OF HARRY
S. TRUMAN* BY MERLE MILLER

"Where we going, anyway?" Phire asked. "We could ankle
it faster than this."

"We're driving forty miles per hour. And you walk at about one
tenth that rate. Not much faster than that." Waverly didn't move
his hands from the steering wheel or look back as he spoke. "Of
course you could jog, or you could run, but even then you might
go five, maybe seven miles an hour, and not for very long. We'll be
there when we get there, as my mother used to say. And not a
moment before."

Clover watched the shadowy trees, caught in the van's headlights, as they drove until her stomach turned over and she had to
look away. The lake would come up on their left soon, but she
wasn't sure they'd see it in the dark.

"Are you okay?" West asked her. He sat between her and
Bridget, leaning against the side of the van.

"You could have been killed."

"But I wasn't." He tried to put a hand on her arm, but she
yanked away from him. "Isaiah wouldn't hurt me."

"That other guard would have. In a heartbeat. And you don't know what Isaiah would do. He's a guard, West. It's his job to stop people from coming in and out of the city."

"I'm fine."

Clover pulled her knees up under her chin. It was crowded, cold, and uncomfortable in the van. "I'm not."

"Try not to worry so much, Clover," Waverly called back. He didn't even pretend not to eavesdrop. "You're going to love the ranch."

"Don't you think Isaiah probably connected you to the van, West?" Clover asked.

"Isaiah couldn't wrap his brain around any of this if I told him flat-out."

Emmy had fallen asleep with her head in her brother's lap and stretched just then, her small foot connecting with Mango's hip. The dog lifted his head, startled, but didn't make a sound.

"Almost there," Waverly said, turning the van off the highway.

Five minutes later, the van stopped. They were there. Not that Clover could see where *there* was. "Where?"

"Our ranch, of course. You'll have to wait until morning to really see it." Waverly turned down a long drive and then stopped and cut the engine. He turned around in his seat to look at them. "I can hardly wait until you do."

Ned Waverly was sixty-three years old. He had curly graying hair growing in shoulder-length tufts around the edges of a bald scalp. He wore a purple t-shirt and a pair of blue jeans cut off at the knee. When he got out of the van and came to let them out, Clover glimpsed open-back leather sandals with two straps over the tops of his feet.

He was lean with a potbelly and stood several inches taller than West. Taller even than Christopher. He looked like the pictures she'd seen of him, only less well groomed and far more casually dressed. And with considerably less hair on top. More on the sides. They all climbed out of the van and stretched. The rush of adrenaline, followed by a long car ride, had taken a toll. Clover guessed that, except for her, none of them had ever been in a car that they could remember.

The air smelled strongly of pine and had a chill bite to it that surprised her. When she looked up, Clover was stunned by the blanket of stars above the ridge of treetops just barely illuminated by the night sky. She'd had a dusk curfew her whole life. Clover had never been outside this far past sunset, except in her own backyard.

She squinted her eyes, trying to see more of the ranch, but it was no good. "There's a house, isn't there?"

Waverly swung his flashlight ahead of them. "That way. *Vamanos, mis amigos.*"

"*Hablan Español?*" Jude asked.

"Not much. Or well." Waverly started down the path and they followed, fumbling their own flashlights out of their packs as they went.

"This guy is weird," Jude whispered to Clover as he cranked the handle on his, then clicked it to life.

"Takes one to know one," Waverly called over his shoulder.

The dirt path led to a large, wooden house. Clover caught glimpses of other buildings and strange structures as the flashlights flitted over them, and then Waverly opened the door and held it while they filed in.

He flipped a switch and electric light flooded the room. "Just for tonight, girls on the left and boys on the right. We'll get you set up in your places tomorrow."

"We got our own rooms?" Emmy asked. "Are they upstairs?"

"No, no, those stairs don't lead anywhere."

Emmy rubbed at her eyes with the palm of one hand and seemed ready to question that, but just followed the twins to the girls' side of the room.

"You have electricity?" Clover asked. They were in some sort of big living room, with a fireplace in one wall and heavy wood furniture pushed out of the way to make room for thick cushions on the floor.

"Electricity, of course, but no wasting. Fuel is precious, you know. Contentment consists not in adding more fuel, but in taking away some fire. That's Thomas Fuller."

"Thomas Fuller wasn't a president," Clover said, mostly to herself.

"No. But Jimmy Carter was. He said, 'Put on a sweater.' Damn shame we didn't listen to him, isn't it? Damn shame." Waverly waved her away to the girls' side. "I'm afraid you'll have to use the bushes just outside the door if you can't wait until morning. Can't go roaming around here at night, when you don't know where you're going. Lions and tigers and bears, oh my! Okay, just bears, but they're bad enough. Good night, children. And welcome home."

He turned out the light and used his flashlight to pick his way around them to a door to Clover's left.

As soon as he was gone, Phire and Marta and Geena all turned their flashlights on.

"What did he mean, 'Welcome home'?" Geena asked.

"We're all tired." West lay back on his cushion and moaned softly. "Let's just try to get some sleep."

Emmy squeezed between the twins. One by one the lights went out. Clover was asleep within minutes.

"Christopher went up the stairs, just to see. They really don't go anywhere. Who builds stairs that don't go anywhere?" Jude asked the next morning. Clover sat with him, cross-legged on his cushion, the computer open in front of them.

"That whole side of the house slides open, too," Waverly said as he came out of the other room. He'd changed into a red and white striped shirt and worn blue jeans that went to his ankles this time. He was barefooted. "Remind me to show you that sometime."

"What? Why?" Phire sounded more fascinated than scared, which Clover considered a good thing. He could be a little unpredictable. "Why would the side of a house open?"

"So they could take a long shot, of course. Don't you know where you are?"

"No."

"You don't recognize the old homestead? Now that's a true shame. Well, come with me, then."

Waverly slid his feet into the same sandals he'd worn the night before, which he'd left near the front door, and waited while they all scrambled to get their own shoes on. The sun was up, but the day was still cool. Clover inhaled deeply, and the sharp scent of pine made her nostrils flare.

Waverly's ranch was a whole little town. Brightly colored buildings lined both sides of a dirt path. Wooden sidewalks ran along the front of them. A pair of fake horses stood near a church down the road.

"I want to see them!" Emmy struggled against Phire, who had a firm grip on her hand. "Let go!"

"Not now," Phire said.

Clover peered at a grassy area next to what looked like a church. "Is that a cemetery? What is this place?"

"It's the Ponderosa Ranch. Don't you just expect Hoss to come out of the saloon any minute now?"

"What?" She turned and looked at the little buildings.

"No, I guess you wouldn't know. You're too young. Maybe getting rid of television was a good thing, but now some things are just lost forever, aren't they?" Waverly shook his head. "They used to film a television show here. Or part of it, anyway. A western called *Bonanza*. This place is a piece of American history. Now it's mine. Well, ours. Okay, it's ours."

"Ours?" West came up next to Clover, and Mango pressed his head into her brother's hand.

"Sure. I've spent two years getting it ready for you to show up."

"You've been here alone for two years?" Bridget asked.

"I've been here alone for most of fourteen years. I only found out you all were coming two years ago."

No wonder the man was a little off his rocker. Clover didn't like to be around too many people, but that was too much solitude, even for her.

"Come on, let me show you around."

Waverly walked ahead, toward the tiny town.

"They meant this to be Virginia City, you know." He looked back at them. "Of course, it isn't. The real Virginia City is a ghost town now." Waverly stopped at a building marked *Taxidermy*. "Here we are."

"Here we are where?" Clover asked.

"Why, your house, of course." The old man opened the door and swept his arm toward the inside of the building. "Enter the Donovan abode."

The whole bottom floor was a single room with a wood floor covered by a worn rug. A squat black wood-burning stove sat in one back corner with a staircase near it. The room was furnished with two overstuffed chairs, a small couch, and a table with four chairs. Smaller tables sat on either side of the couch, with a lamp on each one. Waverly went to one and clicked it on and then off again.

"Electricity via generator. Be frugal with it or you won't have it for long. Two bedrooms upstairs. Now that you're all here, we can work on getting plumbing into these buildings, but for now, there's a bathroom with a shower in it near the restaurant. That's the only kitchen, too."

West sat on the little couch and bounced a little, like maybe he was testing to make sure it was real. "This is unbelievable."

"What about us?" Geena asked.

"You and your sister are in the ice cream shop. Phire and Emmy in the justice of the peace, and I paired up Christopher and Jude in the gift store. I hope you boys don't mind."

"Can I see my room?" Emmy asked. When Phire elbowed her, she added, "Please?"

"'Course you can."

Everyone left but Clover, West, and Bridget.

"He didn't make a place for me," Bridget said. "I guess that means I'm going home."

"Of course you're going home." West pulled her into the seat next to him. "We all are. Until then, you'll stay here with us."

Clover ignored them both and snapped the lamp on again. "How do you think he's running electricity in here?"

West reached over and turned the lamp back off. "I don't know. But we don't need lamps in broad daylight, regardless. Let's check out the upstairs."

The first bedroom was clearly Clover's. The walls were painted yellow, fluffy white curtains fluttered over the open windows, and one whole wall was covered in shelves lined with hundreds of books.

"Oh," Clover said, staring at the books. "This is—West, look, he got me *Gone with the Wind* and *To Kill a Mockingbird*. And look at all these books about beekeeping!"

Two beds sat on either side of the window. Each was made with a comforter covered in white lace. A huge dog bed took up a lot of the space between them. "See," West said. "He did mean for you to stay at least for a little while, Bridget."

Clover did her best not to let her instant dislike of the idea of sharing her room show. "Let's look at your room. Maybe it has two beds, too."

Waverly obviously had some fairly traditional ideas about gender. The walls in West's room were painted navy blue and the window was covered with red cotton curtains. West had just one bed. A double with a comforter covered with baseballs and bats.

"Baseball?" Bridget asked.

West tried to shrug it off. Clover would have bet that not many people knew about the baseball card collection in the top of West's closet at their house. It used to be their father's. She knew that he still took them out sometimes. Somehow, Waverly must have found out, too.

Once everyone had seen their new rooms, they gathered in the living room of the little house Waverly had called the Donovan abode. West sat on the couch and watched them all get comfortable. They were, too. Far more than they had the first time they all sat together like this.

"We need to get dosed soon," Christopher said.

Clover dug the leather pouch out of her pack. It was too early for her, but after the initial shock that she had them, and Jude taking time to explain how she did, everyone else got a dose in their upper arm. That raised up a round of gasps and moans as the thick needles went in and the fiery medicine flowed through their veins.

Phire sat on the floor with Emmy softly crying in his lap when the dosing was done. "Why would the old guy give us houses? How do we know he won't just let us catch the virus and die now that we're out of doses?"

"Not everyone is out to get you," West said. Clover thought the real question was how they were going to get back to their lives, now that they'd all officially missed a dose.

Phire let Emmy go when she wanted to sit up. "Maybe that's how *your* life has gone. Not mine. Not any of ours, except maybe yours and your sister's, and the rich—"

"No, West's right," Jude said. "We need to stay calm. We weren't dragged here; we agreed to come. Waverly is a weird dude, but he hasn't done anything to make anyone uncomfortable, has he?"

Clover looked around the room, and one by one everyone shook their head, even Emmy.

"There's only one of him and nine of us," West said.

Geena looked around the room. "The Freaks."

Marta pointed at Bridget. "Except her. She ain't a freak."

Clover expected West to defend Bridget and was surprised when the girl sat up straighter and said, "Like hell I'm not. If you don't think being the headmaster's daughter makes me a freak, you're crazy."

"Freaks," West said. "All of us. Until we know more about Waverly and what's going on here, we stay in pairs at least. Agreed? No one is alone, ever."

Everyone nodded again.

There was a knock on the front door. Mango sat up at the sound and Clover scratched his ears as West went to let in Waverly, who carried a large silver tray in both hands. Nine syringes were lined up in a neat row on it. They were fitted with an attachment that would allow the suppressant to go into their ports.

"I've brought your suppressant," he said.

"I can't have mine until tonight," Clover said. She lifted her chin toward the pile of empty syringes sitting on the table. "Everyone else is okay for today."

Waverly froze for a second, like a deer caught in the headlights, staring at the syringes on his tray. Then he shook himself and made a loud honking noise that made Emmy giggle. "Wrong. The time restraint was designed to make it easier for people to remember to be dosed, and to keep order and control at the bars."

"She'll be overdosed if you give it to her now," West said.

That honk again, and this time the twins laughed out loud. "Wrong again. Any of you could have a dose every twelve hours without being overdosed."

"I don't understand."

"You have to miss three doses before the withdrawal kicks in. I would be willing to place even odds that our own Miss Kingston here didn't get sick until thirty-six hours after she missed her dosing time. I'm right, aren't I?"

Bridget said, "Just about."

"Aha! See? You missed three doses, not just one. One twelve hours after your last shot, one at the next regular dosing time, and one twelve hours later. Thirty-six hours is when your body starts craving it." Waverly placed the tray on the table.

Clover stood up from where she sat on the arm of the couch. "You're saying the suppressant is addictive?"

"West and Bridget really just had the shakes?" Christopher said. "Like my dad did, from booze. He got sick, had to start drinking again. Killed himself with the stuff he made."

"Withdrawal. We'll talk all about that, soon." Waverly brought a chair around in front of him and bent over to pat the seat. "Let's get you all on the same schedule, shall we?"

Clover and West looked at each other, and then Clover sat in the chair.

"Wait a minute," Bridget said before Waverly could dose Clover. "It doesn't look the same."

"It's not. But it'll work, trust me."

Clover leaned away from Waverly. "Why isn't it the same?"

"Look, it doesn't matter to me if you take the dose. You won't die if you're never dosed again, although I'd be willing to bet you'll wish you would."

At some point they were going to have to trust someone, and they'd already decided to trust Waverly. She settled back in her seat again.

"What do you think?" he asked Clover.

"Everyone is going to have to take it eventually."

"Very good." He moved Clover's hair away from her port. "These are a real travesty, you know. A real travesty."

"The needle is too big to inject into our skin every day," West said as Waverly pushed the syringe into Clover's port.

"The drug wasn't intended to be used this way, you know. It just wasn't."

"What are you talking about?" Phire asked. "The suppressant was a miracle. You're the one who gave it to us."

Waverly crossed his legs and his arms, the spent syringe dangling from his long fingers. He looked more somber than West had seen him so far. "Xanverimax was a miracle. A cure and an inoculation all in one."

"Xanverimax." West let the odd word roll around his mouth.

"That's right. You probably received it as a baby. I can see that it saved you."

West ran a hand over his scarred cheeks. "What are you saying, Dr. Waverly?"

"I'm saying that Xanverimax only needs one dosing. Once is enough for anyone. Forever."

"I don't understand," Jude said.

"It started honestly enough. We weren't sure how it worked. There was no time for the kind of testing drugs used to be subjected to before we started administering Xanverimax, which, by the way, is the biggest time loop of them all. We really did suspect it was a suppressant at first."

"I told you he was cracked," Geena whispered.

"My wife was dead, and my work became an obsession. I'm an anthropologist, you know. Not a virologist or chemist or even a medical doctor. I studied prehistoric things, like Lake Tahoe."

They listened as he told them about going through the portal, finding it after fifteen years of looking. He nearly drowned, because his scuba gear stopped working. "I thought my car was stolen, when it wasn't where I parked it. I had to walk ten miles toward Carson City before someone stopped to pick me up. It didn't take long to realize that I wasn't in my own time. The place was ravaged, but the people weren't ill."

"What did you do?" Bridget asked.

"I met a woman who told me about the suppressant. She must have thought I was out of my mind, not already knowing about it. She took me to a clinic. They were still injecting it the old-fashioned way, of course. I stole a syringe and brought a sample of Xanverimax back with me, contacted a chemist named Jon Stead, and the rest, as they say, is history. I spent years trying to figure out how to manipulate the portal, so that I could go back to my Veronica. It was no use. The portal is like a doorway. On one side is today and on the other is exactly two years from today."

"But Jon Stead was the one who discovered the suppressant in the future," Clover said. "That's what I was taught in primary school. Jon Stead was already working on the suppressant when you brought him the sample of his own work."

"I had to find someone who knew what to do with what I'd brought back with me. And fast. People were dying all around me. You have to understand." Waverly's voice took on a defensive tone. "We expected someone to come forward and say that they'd been working on the same formula, but they never did."

"You stole the suppressant?" Clover looked a little off-balance to West. Like she couldn't find her place. She kept shifting her position.

"Oh that, sweet girl, that was all ours, I'm sorry to say."

"You aren't making any sense," Clover said.

"The world was in chaos. None of you are old enough to really remember. Most of you weren't even born yet. There were so many dead. Almost everyone, just gone. So many that the continuation of the species was called into question. Can you imagine that?" Waverly shook his head and looked as off balance as Clover did. "Did you know that there were only two hundred people left in Kansas, and two-thirds of them were younger than twelve. We had to bring people in, just to fill Wichita enough to keep it viable."

"We know the world was busted," Christopher said. "It still ain't so great for some of us."

Waverly started nodding and then didn't stop for a good minute. Like he was stuck. Long enough for Emmy to start fidgeting and Marta and Geena to make some noise about how they knew he was crazy, and now look at him. West leaned forward on the couch and watched him a little more closely.

"At first we really did think Xanverimax was a suppressant that had to be given daily. And as soon as we had the dosing organized, everything slid into place so quickly. It was like the country was starved for some way out of the chaos and dove at it when it showed itself. After we knew better, we thought—Jon convinced me—that we could help by giving people something to hold on to. That was the suppressant. Only we needed something to make the dosing itself less distressing, so we developed the port."

"The shots really aren't necessary?" West asked.

"Don't you see? It worked so well. The suppressant kept people from turning into animals in the aftermath. It happens like that. Tragedy brings out the worst in people. And we managed to help keep order. Peace. They gave us the Nobel Prize, you know. The last one. I'm still not sure how that happened, because the system for honors like that had disintegrated. No nominees or votes or anything. No reward, either. We got called to the White House, and after traveling for four days by train, the president gave it to us. He was the thirteenth in line for the office, you know. The secretary of housing and urban development. There were some who thought maybe that was a blessing in disguise."

Jude rubbed at the back of his neck, just under his port. "So, what is the suppressant, then?"

"It's a clone designed to look like and feel like Xanverimax. Only newborn babies get the real stuff, at birth, to protect against a new outbreak."

"Why did Bridget and I get sick, then?" West asked.

"I've already told you. You're addicted to the clone. All of you are. Everyone in the country is. Your body needs the clone and rebels after thirty-six hours without it."

"The shakes," Christopher said.

"That's right."

"You addicted the whole country?" Clover asked. "Why would you do that?"

"Why do you think?" Marta ran her palm over the stubble on top of her head. "He's got this big old place and you can take it to the bank he ain't living on rations."

"No, it wasn't that," West said. "Was it, Dr. Waverly? It was power. The Company runs everything. Not just here, either. Everything, everywhere. Even in the places that pretend to be independent, because the Company supplies the suppressant. Waverly-Stead has more power than the government. More than any government has ever had. More than all of them combined now."

Waverly looked at the ground while West spoke, his shoulders sagging. "In my defense, in our defense, ending the virus was its own reward at first. We started out on the right path."

"We don't need the shots?" Emmy asked. "I don't like them."

"You won't like being sick, either," Phire told her.

"I have enough of the clone here to keep you all dosed up for a while. A good long while. No one needs to go cold turkey. We ease you off the stuff. It'll take a while, but you won't get sick the way West and Bridget did."

Geena stood up and looked around. "You're all sitting at this guy's feet taking every word he says like he can't be lying."

"Why would I lie to you, Geena?"

"Because you want to get a bunch of kids up here to keep you company? You like kids, don't you, Waverly?"

"I love children. Veronica died before—"

"Oh, he *loves* children."

"Geena," Jude said. "Sit down."

"This is Foster City all over again."

"Foster City was necessary," Waverly said. "There were too many orphans. So many. You can't imagine. People managed to keep their children from being infected long enough for Xanveri-max to save them, but the parents died. The crews found houses with starved children crying over their rotting parents. What else could we do?"

Geena's hands fisted at her sides. "What else could you do? Do you *know* what happens in Foster City?"

Waverly looked around the room, and when no one else spoke, he said, "The intentions were good."

"Your good intentions don't mean shit," Marta said. "The guard swoops up anyone who even thinks about murdering or raping a hoodie before the bastard even knows he was going to do anything wrong. But our house mother can kill our little sister and just bury her in the backyard? Where were the squads then? Screw your good intentions."

That was the most West had ever heard Marta say at once.

Waverly stood and took a hard breath. "All I can do now is try to make it up to you. Lunch will be ready in the restaurant in an hour."

He left the house, taking the suppressant with him. For a long time, the Freaks sat silently, trying to understand what Waverly had told them.

chapter 19

A preemptive action today, however well-justified, may come back with unwelcome consequences in the future.

—BILL CLINTON,
LABOUR PARTY CONFERENCE, OCTOBER 3, 2002

Clover sat with Jude in his house, which was very much like the little house Waverly had given her and West. They sat on the couch in the main room downstairs. Waverly fed them a sort of vegetable pizza on a crust he made out of ground corn and pine nuts topped with cheese made from the milk of goats he kept on the ranch.

"I like it here," Clover said. "Maybe I shouldn't so soon. But I do."

"Some of the others are having a hard time trusting Waverly. I had to convince Geena and Marta to eat this morning. They're worried he's going to poison us."

"What do you think?"

Jude stretched his legs out, propping them on the table in front of the sofa. "I don't know what to think. Geena's article was right. The suppressant is a goddamned fraud. That's like finding out the earth really is flat."

"You think he's lying?"

"I don't know. I don't even know *how* to know."

Clover picked up the laptop computer from the couch cushion

between them and balanced it on her knees as she pulled up the classifieds. "He knows about us. Weird stuff that he could have only found out by talking to us. He has about a thousand pounds of dog food. Not old stuff either. Fresh dog food, for Mango. Where did he get it? How did he know we'd need it?"

"We told him. Think about it. We must have."

"I *have* thought about it, until I feel like my brains are going to leak out of my ears."

It made sense. Sort of. They'd say things to Waverly sometime in the future. He'd write notes about what they said. Sometime in the last two years, he read those notes. That much was clear. There was no other way for him to have information about them. He was close to the lake, and he'd discovered the portal. He was obviously still using it.

He gave himself the information about them in advance. Once he knew about them, he couldn't unknow, so they didn't have to tell him again. In their timeline, they would never tell him.

"I found another quote," she said, needing to change the subject to ward off a headache that was gathering at the base of her skull. "'Farming looks mighty easy when your plow is a pencil and you're a thousand miles from the cornfield.' Eisenhower."

"He was right," Jude said. "People can talk about how great it is that everyone has work, but they don't know anything until they're out there."

Clover searched Jude's face. "That's why the Academy is so important to you, isn't it? You don't want to work at the farms."

He studied the floor between his feet as he talked, as if imagining the soil that would be there if things were different. "My parents were migrant workers. It was only dumb luck we were in Reno when the virus hit. Farming is in my blood. But after the virus killed my father, my mother couldn't work and take care of a five-year-old and six-month-old baby, too. She and my grandmother managed between them, until my grandmother died when I was ten. There was no one else to take care of me while my mother worked. The social worker came and got me one day. I never saw my mother again. I don't even know why she never came to see me. She was just gone."

"I'm sorry, Jude." Clover forgot, sometimes, how lucky she was. What would have happened to her if West had gone off to the Academy three years ago? Or if Mrs. Finch hadn't helped raise them?

"It's like Waverly knowing stuff about us. In some other time-line, I would be a farmer by now. And that would be okay. But the Bad Times came and changed everything. The Company acts like they've put a stop to crime, like nothing bad happens anymore. Meanwhile, they have a whole *city* of kids left completely unpro-tected. I have to do something to help them."

"Are all the house parents bad?"

"Some are there for the right reasons. But the job draws people like my house father like flies. No one monitors them. There's a theory that the Company doesn't execute all of the future criminals. Some of them, they put in Foster City as house parents. We don't matter."

"You matter to me." Clover chewed at her bottom lip before going on. "I should have been in Foster City three years ago. Maybe if I had been, I could have helped you. You wouldn't have—"

"No," Jude said, cutting her off. "Don't say it. Don't think it."

Clover let it drop but couldn't brush off the crumbs of guilt. "We need to ask Waverly about the quotes. Maybe he knows something."

Jude and Clover met West and Bridget coming out of the restaurant.

"Maybe they're some sort of secret society," Bridget said after

Jude explained where they were headed. "I've heard of those, from before. They named themselves after animals. Like Elks and Lions and Buffalo."

"What do they do?" Clover asked.

"I don't know."

They found Waverly in a small but lushly green garden near the front of his house. As far as Clover knew, none of them had spoken to him since he dosed her and West.

"Can we talk to you?" Jude asked when they came close enough.

Waverly froze for a second but then brushed off his hands and stood up. He put on a bright smile for them. "Of course. Let's go inside. I picked some blackberries this morning that will be just the thing, I think."

Waverly had put away the mats they'd slept on the night before, and his furniture was back in place. He set a bowl of plump berries in the center of his table, and they all sat around it.

"What can I do for you?" he asked.

Clover set the paper she'd written the messages on in front of him. "We want to know what these are."

Waverly looked at the page without touching it. "You found them already?"

"They're right there in the classifieds," Clover said. "We aren't blind."

"What are they, Dr. Waverly?" West asked.

"Meetings, of course."

"It *is* a secret society, I knew it!" Bridget leaned in to see the paper. "Are you part of it, Dr. Waverly?"

"A secret society. Yes, I suppose that is exactly what they are. They call themselves the Freaks."

Jude and Clover looked at each other.

"Like you, right?" Dr. Waverly said. "It's okay. You tell me later, anyway."

"How do you know so much about us?" West asked. "It's pretty . . ."

"Weird?"

"Yes."

"I take notes and leave them for myself. I have two years' worth regarding you all, although I've been pretty careful not to tell myself too much of importance."

So Clover was right about how Waverly knew things he shouldn't know. Somehow knowing that she'd figured it out didn't ease her mind much. "You still travel through the portal?"

"I have to know," Waverly said. "I have to know. Even though it puts little holes in my memory, like Swiss cheese."

"You must be stuck in dozens of loops," Clover said.

Waverly gave half a nod. "At least. Hundreds is probably more like it. But I have to know."

Clover put up her hand to stop him from talking. "Wait a minute. What do you mean, your memory is Swiss cheese?"

"We never really figured out how or why it happens. The brain is such a fragile, mysterious thing."

"How what happens?"

"You stay on the other side of the portal more than thirty minutes, your old memories are replaced with new ones. Maybe you lose your tenth birthday party and have a memory of sitting on a stone near the lake in the future where it used to be."

"You mean you forget things, while you're over there?" Clover's stomach twisted, like a fist had reached in and grabbed her insides. "Why didn't they tell me that?"

"The human mind wasn't designed for time travel, Clover. Some things are only in my notebooks now."

"If you know that's a problem, why would you stay more than thirty minutes?" Jude asked.

"I try not to. Sometimes I lose track of time."

The air went out of Clover's lungs, and taking another breath was painful. "So if a Messenger missed a return trip?"

"The memory loss isn't minute-for-minute. The replacement is exponential. Twenty-four hours would be devastating."

"How did you figure that out?" Clover asked.

Waverly rocked in the chair. "We had to know. You have to understand. We had to."

"What did you have to know?" West asked when Waverly petered off, like he'd lost track of what he meant to say.

"They were volunteers, all of them. We tested their memories and sent them through. The first half hour doesn't affect much for those with the strongest memories."

West looked at Clover, and she shook her head. "I don't think I've forgotten anything."

"Not in the first half hour. But after twenty-four hours, a person would return with no memories except for what they'd done on the other side. They'd remember to breathe. How to walk. Whatever they did during those twenty-four hours, they'd keep, but when they came back through the portal everything else would be gone."

"The fortune cookie," Clover said. The idea of forgetting how to read made her feel sick. "That's it isn't it? I had to read a fortune cookie so I wouldn't forget how to read."

"Yes," Waverly said. He looked like he might want to go on, but he didn't say any more.

"But they can relearn things they forget, right?" Jude asked.

"Sure, but it's the difference between knowing something happened and remembering it happening to you." Waverly looked at each of them, as if trying to judge their understanding. "Some things take years to learn. Like speaking or reading. Some people have strong memories that can handle traveling."

"What do you mean by *strong memories*?" West asked.

"Some people are special." Waverly smiled at Clover. "They can afford to lose more, because they remember more."

"Like me." Clover clenched her hands together on the table in front of her.

"Like you."

"You still go," Jude said. "Even though it's stealing your memories?"

Waverly pulled at a lock of his hair and didn't comment on that.

"So, what about the quotes?" Bridget didn't even bother to disguise the gigantic subject change. "What do they have to do with us?"

"They can't have anything to do with us," West said.

"They know about you. Oh, yes they do." Waverly drummed his fingers against his thighs. "And they know that a revolution is coming."

"How do they know?" Clover asked. "*We* don't even know. I've been through the portal three times. Things are just the same in two years."

"Are you sure?" Waverly said. "Jon would work hard to keep the present time line from finding out about problems in the future."

Clover tried to think. All she really saw was the lake and the road to and from the pickup box. The last time she went, even though she was acting strangely, all the Mariners were preoccupied enough not to notice. And somehow, Jude was able to approach her with the zine. And leave the suppressant syringes. And then there was Leanne.

"My trainer broke her leg. That's why I was alone when I met Jude at the box."

"Leanne Wood didn't break her leg," Waverly said. "In two years, she'll be dead."

Clover covered her face with her hands and forced herself to breathe until she could speak. "Dead how?"

"I don't know for sure, but the rumor is she was killed to stop her efforts in the rebellion."

"Leanne is a rebel?"

"Most definitely."

"If that's true, why would Bennett let me travel at all? He must know what's happening in the future."

"Having information from the future is like a drug. It's . . ." Waverly looked around the table at each of them, his face contorted with discomfort. "It's addictive. He used you to bring him what he needed."

"Why me? He could have used anyone."

"That may be."

"You must know what's going on two years from now," Jude said when Waverly didn't answer right away. "You leave yourself notes about everything else."

Waverly shook his head. "I have almost no notes about the revolution. Just enough for me to know that it picks up speed when you get here. I'm not sure why I haven't told myself more, but there must be a reason."

"Why would people revolt at all?" Bridget asked. "Things are good inside the walls."

Jude snorted, and Bridget's face flushed. Things were good for her. And they were okay for people like Clover and West. They were scary bad for Jude and the other kids from Foster City.

"It's been brewing a long time, Bridget. It started with a baby who was allergic to the suppressant. I heard about it, and helped him."

"You can be allergic to it?" Bridget said. "How is that possible?"

"It's not really a miracle, despite what you were raised to believe. That baby survived because I told his parents that he didn't need daily dosing."

"Why haven't I heard about people having trouble with the doses before?" Clover asked.

"We knew there could be allergies, but one person, for any reason, not on the suppressant and not contracting the virus . . . you can see what that would have done, can't you?"

"Kept us from having to take your fake dope for our whole lives," Jude said, his voice devoid of emotion. "What made you take a stand finally?"

"So many were already dead. Hundreds of millions of people just in the U.S. So many that we can never name them all. I couldn't stand to let that baby be another one lost. Not from the virus, and certainly not from the cure."

"You saved him," Clover said.

"His parents were the first. It's taken nearly fifteen years, but they built a network that communicates with each other, across the country, through the classifieds."

"The messages," Clover said. "I can't figure them out."

Waverly touched his finger to his nose. "That's the whole point."

"She figured out they were messages," Jude said. "And she figured out that they were probably only markers, leading people to the real messages."

"Impressive," Waverly said. "Much more than I expected."

"Are you going to tell us what they mean?" Clover asked.

"Tell me one."

"'Genius is sorrow's child.'"

"Ah. John Adams. It's easy, really. The first three words give you the time of a meeting. In this case, six twenty-seven."

It took a minute, but then the solution popped out as clear as a picture to Clover. "You count the letters!"

"That's right, and the words. And because Adams was a president pre-twentieth century, that's six twenty-seven A.M. A more recent president would mean P.M. Since there are four words in the quote, the meeting will be held the next time the fourth day of a month comes around."

"That early in the morning—before curfew ends some times of the year. How do they do it? Where do they meet?"

Waverly smiled as he listened to Clover's questions. "They have places. Like you have the Dinosaur. And they're careful not to get caught, if they have to meet during curfew. They're sneaky."

"What do they talk about?"

"They share ideas," Waverly said. "And they plan for now."

"Now?" Clover asked

"Now that you're here."

"Me?"

"All of you. We've been waiting."

"Waiting for what?" Jude asked. "We're just kids."

"You are the Freaks. You've left the walls. I told you, I'm not sure what you're going to do. But I know it will change everything."

West pushed his chair back and stood up. "What are we supposed to do?"

"I can't tell you."

"You told yourself I like baseball, but you didn't keep a record of what exactly is expected of us?"

"I've already told you, I don't know much about what happens after you get out of the city. There are some written records, but I didn't read them. We can't risk changing the future by knowing it too soon."

"Where are these records?" Clover asked.

"They're hidden safely away at the other end of the portal. No. No, don't even think about trying to find where. This has to happen in its own time; a loop won't do."

"Unbelievable."

Waverly looked rather proud of himself.

"Look," West said. "None of this matters if we don't figure out what Bennett wanted with Bridget. It's great that we're part of some new wave revolution, but if we're dead, what does it matter?"

Waverly thought about that for a minute, then seemed to come to some conclusion and nodded resolutely before saying, "You're still alive in two years, West. You and Bridget both."

The room exploded into chaos. Everyone wanted to know, all at the same time and at the top of their lungs, what would happen to them in the next two years. Waverly tried to wave them off, but they wouldn't stop.

Clover clapped her hands over her ears. West wouldn't be executed. They did it. They'd saved him and Bridget, too. She left the table and went to the fireplace.

West was at her side a few seconds later, and she turned into him, hugging him tight. She stayed there until the noise dulled. Everyone, Clover supposed, was figuring out that Waverly had said all he was going to. She'd just about come back to herself when West stiffened. She turned to look at what he was staring at. "What is it?"

West reached over her head and took a framed photograph from the mantel.

"That's Bennett." He turned the picture and showed it to her. "It is, isn't it?"

Langston Bennett. Much younger, standing next to Jon Stead. Their arms were thrown around each other, and off to the side, farther away than is usual when posing for a picture, was Waverly, tall and lanky, with already thinning dark hair and a haunted look on his face.

The three men stood in front of a crew of workers just installing the gates to the wall around Reno.

West turned the picture to face Waverly. "What is this?"

"That's Jon and I, on our way to meet the train to take us to receive our Nobel Prize."

"But why is Langston Bennett in it?" Clover asked.

"Of course. You don't know."

"What don't we know?" West demanded.

Waverly hesitated for a minute, looking around the room. *He's scared*, Clover thought. His shoulders were tight and his jaw twitched. "Langston Bennett and Jon Stead are brothers."

"That can't be right," Jude said. "Jon Stead lost his only brother in the Bad Times, to the virus. Everyone knows that."

Waverly took the photograph from Clover. "Langston was very close to death when he was dosed. This picture was taken a year later, and he was still recovering. His face was eaten by the sores to the bone. You could see his teeth through his cheeks. That's how bad it was."

"Why would you and Stead tell the world that he'd died?" West asked.

"I don't understand why this has you all so upset."

"This isn't something that you put in your notes?"

"Obviously not."

Maybe it was the tone in his voice that set Bridget off, Clover wasn't sure, but she took the picture from West and thrust it at Waverly. "This man takes kids and sometimes they don't survive whatever it is he does to them."

"Wait a minute," West said. "What do you mean they don't survive?"

Bridget pulled away from him, wrapping her arms around her body. "I don't know."

"You don't know? You said it!"

"There was a kid, okay. A kid named Max. I heard my dad trying to make Bennett tell him what happened to Max. He didn't get a straight answer, except that something went wrong and that Max was gone."

West looked from Bridget to Clover and back again. Even Clover caught the anger in his eyes. "You should have told me sooner."

"I'm not used to being surprised." Waverly's voice took on an edge of irritation and cut off whatever Bridget might have said to West. "I want to know what you're talking about."

"Langston Bennett is the head of the Messenger program," Clover said. "He drafted me into the Mariner track."

Waverly looked up and exhaled slowly. "I didn't know he was still . . . that he still . . ."

"Why did he want me so badly?"

"Because you're autistic."

"So what if I am?"

"Another thing we've never really figured out. Brain chemistry is our best guess. Something in our makeup makes it possible for us to go through the portal and come out on the other end of a two-year-long tunnel."

"Us?"

Waverly exhaled slowly. "Only people with autism can travel through the portal."

chapter 20

I believe there are more instances of the
abridgment of the freedom of the people by gradual
and silent encroachments of those in power,
than by violent and sudden usurpations.

—JAMES MADISON,
SPEECH TO RATIFY THE FEDERAL CONSTITUTION, JUNE 6, 1788

"You're autistic." Not particularly clever, but West was having a hard time keeping up with the revelations.

"I'm on the spectrum." Waverly sat in a chair near the fireplace. The old man suddenly looked every one of his sixty-three years.

"Why all the secrecy?" West asked.

Waverly leaned back in the chair and looked at the ceiling. "I wish I'd prepared myself for this."

"Dr. Waverly," West said when Waverly didn't speak again. "Dr. Waverly! Please, we need to know why Bennett would want to hurt Bridget. What was he doing at her house, looking for her?"

"I haven't seen the man in more than a decade. I don't know what he's doing. His brother either. Jon hides himself, doesn't he? Makes sure that if his secrets ever become public, no one will know where to find him in the aftermath."

"The Company ran low on adult volunteers," Clover said softly. "I mean, how many autistic adults could have survived the Bad Times? That's it, isn't it? So you took off, and Jon Stead started taking kids. The tests had been done. They figured they could keep us safe by choosing those of us with the strongest memories and giving us a time limit."

"Jon needs autistic people to travel for him. He can't do it himself. It was the one thing that eluded him. He dove, over and over, and the portal never opened for him."

"Couldn't he go in the *Veronica*?" Clover asked.

Waverly shook his head. "They tried to send someone off the spectrum, early on. He drowned when he didn't go through the portal with the ship."

"Jesus," West said. "You're sure you didn't write yourself anything about this, Dr. Waverly? Some clue or something?"

"I'm positive. And I'm glad I didn't. I wouldn't have liked to sit with this information about my old friend for the last two years."

"If you knew Stead was doing something bad to autistic kids, you could have stopped him," Clover said. She focused over his shoulder, and for once West wished she'd rock or tap or flap or even scream. Something other than hold herself so tight that he was afraid she might break.

"I didn't know that. And I am old and selfish." Waverly stood suddenly, nearly tipping back the chair. He set the framed picture carefully back in its spot. "When *you* are old and selfish, you can have opinions about right and wrong. I must get ready for my dive now."

"My brother might be executed because you didn't—"

"I already told you, I knew he wouldn't be." Waverly walked away, to the other room, and closed the door firmly.

"Geena and Marta were right. He's crazy," Clover said.

West tried to gather his thoughts. He didn't know what to believe or whom to trust.

No. That wasn't true. "Find the others. Tell them to meet us in our house. Fifteen minutes."

He grabbed Bridget by the hand and went out the door.

"Waverly's diving tonight," West said, after everyone had gathered. "He'll be gone to the lake for at least ninety minutes. I think we need to search."

"Search for what?" Jude asked.

"Waverly can't get out of the future. He's like an addict. Somewhere, he must have stuff written down about Bennett and Stead and what the hell is going on in the Company. Why we're here. What we're supposed to do."

"So we toss his house?" Christopher asked. "What if he finds out? What if he already knows, because he wrote about it somewhere and telling us he's going diving is some kind of setup?"

"It's a risk we have to take," West said. "We need to know what's going on, and I don't think he's going to give us the whole story."

"I been thinking. Any of you ever know a kid at Foster City that just poofed? You know, a kid like—" Phire tilted his head toward Clover.

Clover shot Phire a dirty look. "You mean autistic? It's not a dirty word. You can say it."

"Fine, any of you know an autistic kid that went ghost from Foster City?"

"Oh, my God." Clover covered her mouth with one hand, and breathed into it for a few seconds like you might into a bag if you were light-headed. Then she pulled her hand away and said, "Your brother, Jude. That's what happened, isn't it?"

The whole room turned toward Jude, who looked a little green around the gills. Jude opened his mouth, but nothing came out. Then he stood up and left the room. Clover started to get up, to go after him, but West put a hand on her shoulder. "I'll go."

It was warm outside, but the sky was overcast and everything had a sort of grayness to it. Jude leaned against the side of the little taxidermy house. He looked up when West came out.

"I don't want to talk about Oscar," Jude said. "I really don't."

West didn't blame Jude. When Clover was missing for just a single day, he'd been frantic enough to knock on the headmaster's door. He tilted his head toward the watch Jude twisted around his wrist. "Was that his?"

"He always wore it. He left it behind for me, on my bed."

"How long has he been missing?"

"Three years." Jude tipped his head back and looked at the sky. "Looks like rain, doesn't it?"

"Yeah, little bit."

"Oscar loved the rain. He knew everything about every major storm for the last hundred years."

"Was he younger than you?"

"Almost four years older."

West had about a dozen questions jostling for position in his head, but he didn't know how to ask any of them. The best he could do was say, "I'm sorry I didn't get to meet him."

"Maybe they just have him in the Mariner program somewhere. They don't see us as real people, you know. Foster City kids, I mean. It wouldn't occur to them that taking Oscar and leaving me behind would be a problem to anyone. He could still be alive."

"We'll find him," West said. "I don't know how. But if he's alive, we'll find him."

"He wasn't always all that easy to live with. Sometimes he would get so angry over something that no one else could see. But we took care of each other."

"I know."

Jude stood up from the wall. "I'm glad they let Clover come home."

West was, too. He was almost sick with relief. "We better get back inside."

"I want to go with him," Clover was saying when they came back to the table.

"I don't think so," West said at the same time that Jude said, "No."

"I'm the only one of us who can travel through the portal. I need to see how he does it. What if I have to sometime?"

Jude took his seat next to her again. "Why would you ever need to?"

"How could I know that?"

"You don't even know how to swim," West pointed out.

"I don't want to dive tonight, for God's sake. I just want to watch. I want to see what happens."

Arguing with Clover was like beating yourself against a brick wall. West felt the headache coming on to prove it. "The portal is deep. You won't see anything."

"Come with me if you want. I'm going."

"I'll go, too," Jude said. "The more we know the better, including about what he does when he goes out to the lake."

Everyone wanted to go then, and there was a little chaos as they jockeyed for a spot on the team that would head with Waverly to Lake Tahoe.

"Wait a minute," West said. "We don't even know if he'll allow it."

"Nine on one? He won't have a choice," Geena said.

Jude put his arms up to stop the noise. "Raise your hand if you want to go."

All hands went up.

More noise that made Clover cover her ears with her hands and start to rock in her chair.

"Someone has to search the house. That was the whole point," West said.

"I'll stay," Bridget said. "Me and Emmy. We'll be the search party, won't we, Emmy?"

The little girl took a long time to think about that and then finally nodded very seriously.

It took less to persuade Waverly to let them come to the lake with him than Clover anticipated. He agreed almost immediately, which made her think maybe he already knew they'd ask. They all piled into the van. Clover left Mango with Bridget and Emmy. He would warn them when the van returned.

"Sit up here with me, Clover," Waverly said when she was about to climb into the back, which had its seats replaced now. She hesitated, but then climbed into the passenger seat.

After they were on the highway, Waverly reached down between their seats and pulled up something that looked like a rubber bag with a long strap and a mouthpiece. "This is how I do it."

Clover took the bag and Waverly put his hands back at ten and two on the steering wheel. "What is it?"

"An air bladder. I know, I know. Terrible name. But it stuck. Air tanks won't make it through the portal with the electronics intact. I'll fill the bag with oxygen, and it'll give me just enough to get me through and back."

"The water must be cold down there. Do you dive in the winter?"

"Not as much. Sometimes I have to risk it." He didn't say more, and she didn't ask what might make him dive into nearly frozen water. "My suit keeps me warm enough."

"What do you do on the other side?"

"I write in my notebook. I read what's been said earlier. I keep the current one there, so I'm not tempted to spend too much time with it here. A built-in restraint."

"Where do you keep the notebooks?"

Waverly was silent for a minute, and then he said, "In good time, okay?"

"Does Jon Stead know you still dive? Do you ever see him?"

"We didn't part well, me and Jon."

"What happened?" As soon as the question was out, she wondered if she shouldn't have asked. But Waverly didn't seem upset by it.

"I couldn't be part of what he was doing anymore. And he didn't want me to leave the Company. I know too much. Even Langston doesn't know everything that I do."

"Does Dr. Stead know where you are?"

Waverly shook his head. "I don't think so. I was on guard for years, waiting for him to find me. I stayed in houses around the lake at first. Then I found the ranch. It was perfect. Jon never came. I guess as long as I kept my head down, finding me wasn't a priority. He'd have to do it himself, wouldn't he? Everyone else left alive thinks I'm their savior."

"Aren't you?"

Waverly drummed his palms on the steering wheel to the time of some music only he heard. "I suppose so."

"Do you know where Jon Stead is?" West asked from behind Waverly, who looked through the rearview mirror at him.

"Yes."

"Where?"

Waverly adjusted the mirror. "Everything you need to know is where all the information is."

"What's that supposed to mean?"

"When you need to know, you will. We're meeting the train first."

"What train?" Clover asked. She'd never actually seen one. When she was still a baby, work was done to extend tracks around the city, so that train deliveries could be made without breaching the walls. The trains stopped just outside the city. Guards with trucks brought the goods in from them and out to them.

"This is why I was so glad you wanted to come. You'll meet Frank tonight and his daughter Melissa. She's about your age, Clover."

"We get to see a train?" Christopher asked.

"We do indeed."

The energy in the van changed, from wary distrust to excitement.

Waverly drove quietly for a few more minutes, then pulled onto an unpaved service road and finally turned down a nearly invisible path that was hidden by the trees. They all sat there, their eyes and ears trained toward the tracks in front of them.

"When will it be here?" Phire asked.

"Soon. Listen."

Clover did, straining, then cranked the window down halfway. After about fifteen minutes, she heard the rumble of an approaching train. It came around a curve with its lights glowing and steam billowing from its stack. The whistle blew once, then twice, and the noise seemed to fill Clover up.

Then the train screeched to a stop in front of them. A few minutes later a middle-aged man with red hair going white and a girl with long hair the same shade without the white walked toward them.

Waverly opened the van door. "Okay, everyone out."

"They'll see us," Clover said.

"Frank and Melissa are the whole crew, and they're anxious to meet you."

Clover walked toward the man and the girl but couldn't make eye contact. Instead, she walked on by, toward the train. It was magnificent. The engine made the ground under her feet rumble, and the lights were dazzling. The engine, with its big steam stack, pulled three freight cars.

"Frank," Waverly said. Clover turned and saw the two men

shake hands. "Frank and Melissa, meet West and Clover, Jude, Christopher, Sapphire, Geena, and Marta."

"Oh, wow." Melissa grabbed Clover's hand and started to pump it. "I can't believe you're finally here, Clover."

Clover yanked her arm back.

"Clover," West said, almost under his breath.

Clover tried again. "I can't believe I'm here, either."

"I'm Melissa," the girl said. "Wait! I have something for you."

She dug into her pack and came out with a packet of letters held together with a rubber band. "There's one from all the way in Pennsylvania," she said. "Can you believe it?"

Clover took the letters and turned them around in her hands before looking up at Waverly, who was talking to Frank. When she turned back around, Melissa had her arms around Jude's neck, and he stumbled back a step before hugging her back.

Even covered in soot and wearing filthy work clothes, Melissa was pretty. She was tall and lanky, and her auburn hair was pulled back into a braid that hung halfway down her back. Clover thrust the letters at Jude, holding them there until he untangled himself and took them.

"What are these?" he asked.

Clover shrugged and looked at Melissa.

"Well, they're letters," she said.

Neither Jude nor Clover responded to that.

"I mean, they're the information. The information that we gather. Don't you know this?"

"I haven't had a chance to tell them," Waverly said.

"Dr. Waverly gathers the information." Melissa looked at Waverly and then her father, looking for assurance. "We bring it to him and he puts it in the book."

"There's a book?" Clover looked to Waverly. "What is she talk-ing about?"

"I keep a book full of the letters," he said. "It's really quite incredible. They come from all over."

"Why haven't we seen this book?"

Waverly took the letters. "You will."

"Where is it?"

"On the other side of the portal."

"In the future? You keep this information in the future?"

"I'll bring it back tonight."

"Denver sent information about a new calorie crop that grows like grass," Frank said. "Sent some seed, too. Lots of the cities just send updates about how they're surviving. Recipes for things they can't get from the Bazaars. That kind of thing."

"That doesn't sound like it needs to be hidden."

"They send information about their resistance efforts, too, Clover," Waverly said.

chapter 21

The tree of liberty must be refreshed from time to
time, with the blood of patriots and tyrants. It is
its natural manure.

—THOMAS JEFFERSON,
LETTER, MARCH 24, 1818

The train left after Frank told Waverly he'd have oil
to deliver in two weeks. Every first and third week, the train delivered convicts from around the country to the Justice Center in
Reno, and Frank couldn't stop when he had live passengers. Melissa
hugged everyone again, including Clover, who wanted to hate the
girl, or maybe just resent her, but didn't.

"You liked her," she said to Jude while the others were getting
back in the van.

"She's a likeable girl."

"Yeah."

Jude had the nerve to chuckle.

"What?" she asked.

"Not a thing. Ready?"

She climbed into the backseat of the van, as far from Jude as
she could get.

"I dive right in front of the *Veronica*," Waverly said as he backed
out of the path and turned onto the road to the highway. "You'll
be able to watch from the dock."

"What if someone sees us?" West asked.

"Not at this time of night."

"Still, might be better if we stay hidden, don't you think?"

"Suit yourself. You can watch from the trees nearby."

"But I want to see him dive," Clover said.

Waverly tilted the rearview mirror so he could see her through it. "You won't miss a thing."

During the day, the lake was spectacular, mirroring the blue and white sky and the mountains around it. When they approached it a few minutes later, the stars reflected in it, and with an almost full moon, the lake glittered like a giant bed of jewels.

"I can't believe Bridget's missing this," West said.

"She'll have a chance to see it later." Waverly pulled into a spot in the trees, facing the van so that it pointed toward the lake, where they saw the *Veronica* in front of them. "You'll have a good view from here."

He got out before anyone could say anything else and went behind the van to undress and get into his wetsuit. When he came back, he looked to Clover like a giant seal. He reached into the front seat for his air bladder and a small tank of oxygen, which he used to fill it. He slipped that over his shoulders like a backpack and picked up a pair of something that looked like duck's feet.

"Time me," he said as he adjusted a mask over his eyes and nose. "Less than thirty."

They watched him in complete silence until he was at the dock and walking down it.

Christopher leaned forward between the seats. "I didn't even know people could dive through the portal."

"It's how he found it," Clover said.

"Yeah, I guess so." Christopher gave up trying to see from inside the van and opened the door.

"Hey!" West said. "We're hiding."

"I can't see from here. Can't we get out of the van and stay in the trees?"

Before West could answer, everyone came out of the van and crowded around the edge of the stand of trees, hushing each other and generally raising a stage-whispered racket.

"Just be quiet," West said.

"Look, he's going!" Clover pointed toward Waverly, poised at the end of the dock, positioned about ten feet from the nose of the *Veronica*.

A sharp, painfully loud noise took Clover so by surprise that she froze, like the bear she'd nearly hit with the van. It came from a tunnel over the highway leading back to the city, about a hundred yards from where they stood and collectively stopped breathing.

"Oh, God," Geena said.

Waverly collapsed like a puppet with cut strings. Just folded in on himself. Clover started toward him, but her brother held her back forcibly enough to hurt her.

"We have to get out of here," West said, his voice barely a whisper.

"We can't just leave him," Clover said.

"He was shot. We have to take the van and go before we are, too."

Apparently, Clover was the only one concerned about Waverly. Everyone else started toward the van.

"Wait a minute." Clover turned back to the dock. Her heart stopped when she recognized Langston Bennett walking down it toward Waverly's body. Before she could say anything, there was another shot. One of the twins cried out in surprise somewhere behind her.

West took her hand and yanked her toward the trees. "Run," he said as softly as he could.

Clover wasn't sure that any of them knew where they were going. If they started out wrong, they might get lost and never find their way back to the van. Especially not in the dark. They were breaking branches and kicking pine cones all over the place, besides breathing like a bunch of freight trains.

"We need to stop," she said.

West pulled her a few more steps.

"No, wait. We're making too much noise. He's going to find us."

He might stop chasing if he couldn't hear them stampeding through the woods like a pack of elephants. Everyone stopped, except for Geena. Christopher reached for her, but she broke through the brush and for a moment was on her own. West made a hushing noise and a downward motion with both hands.

Clover heard Bennett coming just before the third shot rang out.

Geena yelped, just once. And then there was no other sound except Bennett moving in to see what he'd done. Clover stood, frozen in the trees. Her brain screamed at her to do something, anything, help Geena, run, scream. Her body couldn't sort those signals out as she watched Bennett walk to Geena and turn her onto her back. He put a hand to the side of her neck, then sat back on his heels and scanned the woods.

West took Marta and Christopher each by one arm and man-handled them behind a boulder five feet to their left. Jude and Clover followed. She leaned against the cool stone and shook. Jude gathered her into his arms and sat them both on the ground.

Bennett searched some, cursing under his breath, then walked back toward the lake, where he must have had a car. If he'd looked even a little harder he would have found them. They were in no condition to be stealthy. Not with Marta burying her sobs in Christopher's chest and Christopher barely keeping himself from leaving their hiding spot to go to Geena.

Clover stayed where she was and rocked against Jude. She wished that Mango were there, to help her get her thinking straight, and then was grateful he wasn't. He would have barked or made some other noise and they'd all be dead.

Finally, West let Christopher and Marta go out of hiding.

Christopher knelt beside Geena's body. There was a small hole in her forehead, above her left eye. Clover wondered if Bennett was that good a shot or poor Geena was just very unlucky, and then hated herself for thinking about that.

A low, painful wail escaped Marta, and Christopher pulled her against him. It hurt Clover to watch them. West lifted Geena. The hole in the back of her head was much larger than the one in her forehead.

"Jesus," Phire said under his breath. "Oh, my God."

"We should bring Waverly back to the ranch," Jude said.

"We can't," West said. Geena's blood seeped into his shirt and Clover looked away. "Bennett will be back for the body. If it's gone . . ."

"We can't just leave him here," Phire said.

Jude shook his head. "No. West is right."

"We need the air bladder." Clover took a few steps toward the dock. "We have to have it."

"Clover, get back here." West shifted Geena's body in his arms. "Let's just go back to the van."

"Don't you think Bennett will notice the van is gone?"

"It doesn't matter. We can't carry Geena back."

"Well—"

"We aren't leaving her." Marta's voice was toneless. As dead as her sister.

"I need that air bladder if I'm ever going to dive through the portal," Clover said. "We have to have it."

West transferred Geena's body to Christopher, who held her to him as if she were a sleeping baby. "Get everyone into the van. I'll get the bladder and be right back."

Clover wasn't sure taking the van was the best idea. It would tell Bennett that Geena wasn't alone if her body and Waverly's vehicle were both gone. But no one seemed to care what she thought, and she was too heartsick to force the issue, so after West came back, white-faced and holding the full air bladder, she drove them all home.

"Are you positive it was Bennett?" Bridget asked much later.

"It was him." Clover was curled in a corner of the couch in their living room. Jude was next to her, but far enough that he didn't touch her. She might have shattered if he touched her.

"You're sure Waverly's dead?" Bridget ran a hand through her hair. "I can't believe it. I can't believe Bennett did it himself."

Clover was not far from the edge of her ability to cope. "Do you think we're lying to you?"

"Clover," West said. "She's shocked, that's all. We all are."

"He must have left half Waverly's skull in the lake," Jude said. Clover closed her eyes against the image. "He did it all right."

The others were somewhere else, sitting with Geena, consoling Marta. They all did that, for a while, but Christopher finally took West aside and told him they should go to bed. Not exactly a dismissal, but close. Jude went with Clover after a whispered conversation with Christopher.

"I can't believe he shot Geena," Bridget said. "I can't believe any of this."

"Too bad that doesn't mean it didn't happen." Clover stood up from the couch and made it outside just in time for the little bit of food she had in her system to come back up in the bushes near the door. She knelt on the stoop, because her legs weren't strong enough to hold her up anymore.

The front door opened and Mango was at her side, pressing his body against her for support. She wrapped her arms around his neck, grateful again that she had left him home when they went out with Waverly.

Jude sat next to her. And when she was sick again, he whispered something soothing in Spanish but still didn't touch her. When her stomach was empty and settled at least enough for the dry heaves to stop, she said, "She wrote that article. How can she be dead?"

"Knowing she'd write it changed things," Jude said. "Just knowing something is supposed to happen changes everything."

Clover felt another wave of nausea but had nothing left in her. "We shouldn't have come."

"Don't blame yourself, Clover. You weren't the one running around the woods in the middle of the night with a gun."

She petted Mango's head. The repetitive motion helped. "What if Bennett finds us here tonight?"

"I don't think it would occur to Langston Bennett that there is an *us*, much less to come looking for us."

"But Geena? He'll know she came from somewhere."

"I don't know, Clover. We'll figure out our next step tomorrow. Christopher, Marta, Phire, and Emmy are spending the night in the main house, with Geena. Do you want me to stay with you?"

Clover nodded. Jude opened one arm. She curled into him and let her tears come.

The next morning, Christopher, Phire and Jude took turns digging an actual grave in front of a fake gravestone in the cemetery. They dug it deep. As deep as Christopher was tall, so that animals wouldn't dig it back up again.

Marta washed her sister and wrapped her in a white sheet. *This is where ghost stories come from*, Clover thought. She felt so out of place, and so tense from working so hard to keep from saying something that would hurt someone, that all she really wanted to do was go home and hide in a corner somewhere. Knowing that she'd never go home again didn't help.

Christopher stood in the grave and West handed Geena down to him. Her body was so small. Like she'd shrunk when her spirit left it. Christopher laid her carefully on the freshly turned earth, then climbed back out of the hole. Everyone stood around the open grave.

"Geena wanted to write that story," Marta finally said. "She talked about it a lot. She wanted to be smart enough to have something important to say. I'm going to do it for her."

"She liked to braid my hair," Emmy said. "And she told the best stories."

Phire wrapped an arm around Emmy when she started to cry. "I trusted her."

Marta looked up at Phire and nodded. He didn't give his trust easily.

"I wish I had time to know her better," Bridget said.

Marta wrapped her arms around Christopher's waist and buried her face against his chest, and silent sobs shook her whole body.

"Geena was one of the bravest people I've ever known," Jude said. "It was her idea to leave Foster City in the first place. She saved my life."

"Mine, too." Christopher had one big hand against Marta's nearly bald head, smoothing his fingers over it in an effort to soothe her.

"She was my friend," Clover finally said. It was the most important thing she could think of between her and Geena.

Once everyone had said something, Christopher led Marta away and Phire brought Emmy and followed him. Clover slipped her hand into Jude's while West sprinkled lime he'd found in a shed over the body at the bottom of the grave and then started to shovel the dirt back in. It took a long time, but the four of them finished burying Geena.

"What did you find while we were gone?" West asked Bridget when they were all sitting around the main house later. He was exhausted. Every muscle either burned or ached. Some of them did both. He wasn't sure he cared what she found, but he guessed it needed to be discussed tonight.

Bridget stood up from the couch and went to a corner of the room where she'd stashed a box. She lugged it to them and pulled out several black and white spiral-bound notebooks. "Two per year," she said. "For almost fourteen years. The most recent ends about five months ago."

"The notebooks with future information and the book with the letters in it are on the other side of the portal," Clover said.

"What do they say?" Marta asked. Her face was swollen and splotchy, but for the moment, she seemed to be able to be part of the conversation. West wasn't sure what he'd do if it had been Clover shot in the woods, but whatever it was, he'd probably regret it later. And Marta might have something like that in her, too. Christopher was staying close to her, though. Keeping a good eye.

"They're pretty random. Notes to himself about things like how he's organizing a search of nearby houses. Lists of supplies. Information about the crops and animals here. I've seen a couple notes about things that don't make a lot of sense to me. Lists of cities, names, dates."

"We'll have to read them all," Clover said.

"The most recent books say a lot about us. The stuff he used to get us here. Stuff we never even told him. This is so messed up."

"He can't ungive himself the books or unknow the things he's written in them, just because we don't tell him in this time line."

"That's so weird," Phire said. Emmy was asleep with her head in his lap.

"Waverly keeps the most important junk on the other side, right? About where Stead is, and where he hid the notebooks," Marta said. "We need to find that."

"Maybe it's not in the future. Or at least not all of it. He said he keeps his notes about the Company and Stead where all the information is," Clover said. "That's what he said. Maybe he means it's somewhere on the nets."

"Tomorrow," West said. "We all need sleep now."

Clover sat on her bed with Mango lying across her feet and tried to wrap her head around everything that had happened that night. Geena and Waverly were both gone. Thinking about them felt like a fist closing around her heart, and she forced herself to think about the notebooks instead.

The time lines were like a giant case of déjà vu. Something almost remembered, but for the wrong reasons. Things she'd never do had changed her whole life. Changed everyone's life.

Nothing in Waverly's life happened organically. He lived in the present and also in about a thousand time loops that he used the notebooks to keep straight.

The only way for them to get their hands on the most recent notebooks was to figure out where Waverly kept them. Then wait two years to catch up with them. Or for her to dive for them. She had the air bladder, but the idea of learning how to swim and then diving into the lake deep enough to reach the portal terrified her.

There was something else. Something Waverly seemed to think they would need. The information about Stead was hidden. *Where all the information is.*

Where was all the information? She nudged Mango off her feet and they both went to go look for Jude and his computer.

"Do you have any idea where to start?" he asked when they were sitting at the table in the house he shared with Christopher.

"Maybe he's got it written down somewhere." Clover leaned over to the box on the floor and pulled out Waverly's very first notebook.

"Any idea where that is?" Jude asked. "There's nothing about it in the notebooks."

"There's this." She turned the notebook toward him. It was the first one, dated fourteen years ago. On the inside of the cover, in thick black ink, was a quote. *Oppressed accumulate a sense of humor that few can fully appreciate. Thomas Jefferson.* "Maybe that's a clue. He doesn't have any quotes written on any of the other covers. In fact, I didn't see any presidential quotes anywhere in any of the books. Did you?"

Jude typed the quote into the computer, then shook his head. "It's not Jefferson."

Clover looked at the quote until the words swam in front of her eyes. The other presidential quote codes were so easy, they'd gone right over her head while she was trying to make it complicated. "Type this in," she said. "Nine, one, zero, one, five, two, five, four, three, three, five, one, zero."

"Jesus, Clover. It's an ISBN number. *A Child's View of the American Revolution,* by William Matthews."

It took most of the afternoon for them to search every book they could find on the ranch. *A Child's View of the American Revolution* wasn't there. Anywhere. When they couldn't find another stash of books to check, they returned to Jude's house. "This isn't a library," Clover finally conceded. "Even if he has a lot of books."

"Do you think he hid it in a library around here? Maybe in Truckee?"

She picked up the notebook again. *Oppressed accumulate a sense of humor that few can fully appreciate. Thomas Jefferson.*

"Wait. Thomas Jefferson? That's it. It has to be." It was the name of the Reno city library.

"Mr. Donovan?"

James held the door to his barrack open a little wider. "Yes, sir?"

"James Donovan?"

"Yes."

The man came into the room. "Do you know who I am?"

James tilted his head, looking more closely at the other man. "Of course, I do, Mr. Bennett."

Langston Bennett nodded. "And you know what I do, then."

"You're the head of the Mariner program. How can I help you, sir?"

Bennett sat in the chair behind James's desk. "Can you imagine why I might be here?"

James exhaled and then couldn't draw another breath fast enough and the room started to spin. He fought hard to keep his moment of off-balance to himself. "Is it Clover? Has she been hurt?"

Bennett flipped through the file folders lying in a neat pile on the desk. "You mean to tell me you don't know your children have left the city?"

James did step back then, and put a hand on the side of his bookshelf to steady himself. "That can't be true."

"Your daughter missed a mission yesterday, and your son hasn't been at work for a week."

"Mr. Bennett, you have to find her. You have to . . ."

"Her. Not him? Do you think your son might have hurt his sister?"

James shook his head. He couldn't think that. Not if he wanted to keep his sanity. "No."

Bennett stood up and came around the desk to James. He brushed his hands over James's shoulders, then gave him a two-handed pat. He stood too close, but James didn't step back. "We will find your children, Mr. Donovan. Both of them. You can be certain of that."

"I hope so," James said.

Bennett slipped a card into James's shirt pocket. "If you hear from either of them, you'll call me."

And then he was gone, leaving James to hyperventilate all on his own. He sat hard on the edge of his bed. His hands shook as he leaned over and pulled a file folder from its hiding spot between his mattress and box spring. He opened it and read West's dispatch. He'd done it. West had left town, just as James had told him to.

And he'd taken Clover with him. They were both out there, somewhere, without their suppressant. Without anyone to help them. He took the folder into the bathroom, pulled out his lighter, and lit a corner of it on fire. He held it while it burned, then dropped it into the bathtub and watched it smolder until he could rinse the ashes down the drain.

Clover put a hand back and felt the port at the base of her neck. This whole thing suddenly seemed just too *big*. "What about the suppressant? Does anyone know where it is?"

"It's in the restaurant. I don't know where he got it, but there are hundreds of bottles. Enough to keep us going for a long time, but not forever," Jude said. "Do we trust that if we wean off, we won't get the virus?"

"What choice do we have?" Clover asked.

Jude waited until they'd all nodded or voiced their agreement, then said, "Then we'll start weaning off tomorrow. That will leave us with plenty to help others."

"Others?" Marta asked. "Where are others going to come from?"

"This is a revolution, Marta, not an isolation camp."

"A revolution?" Emmy asked. "What's that?"

"It means change, Emmy," Clover said.

"We tackle the Company?" Marta said. "No way it'll work."

West laughed a little. "That's what we're doing, though, isn't it? What's the choice? Go back to the Dinosaur and pretend we don't know the Company has everyone in the country strung out?"

"I like it," Christopher said. "A revolution."

Jude stood up. "First things first. We have to think about how to wean off the dope. Anyone have any ideas?"

There was some discussion about weaning, but they were all emotionally and physically exhausted, and it wasn't long before they went to bed on the pallets. Clover lay on her back on her mat with Mango asleep near her feet, listening to the sleeping sounds of her brother and her friends.

The only way to stop what was happening—to other kids like

her, to kids like them, to the whole country doped up on the Waverly-Stead suppressant—was from the inside.

It turned out that Phire was good with fire. In the morning, after everyone had slept as well as they could on the floor of the main house, he lit up the grill and Christopher and Marta made breakfast of roasted sweet potatoes, scrambled eggs, and green beans.

"We can eat some of the chickens," West said. "There are more than we need for eggs."

Clover pushed her plate away. "I have something to say."

"Me, too," Bridget said.

Clover felt a kick of irritation. She'd spent all night thinking about how she'd put her news, coming up with just the right words. She didn't want to wait. But she figured it would be better to have all the information she could, so she nodded for Bridget to go first.

"I need to go home," she said.

Everyone looked at West.

"Bennett will kill you, Bridget. Do you understand that? He will kill you," West said.

"Not if I wait until after my death date." Bridget took a breath and wet her bottom lip before going on. "Jude can come with me."

"What?" Clover looked at Jude and then back at Bridget. She was ruining everything. Everything.

"Someone has to be on the inside," Jude said. "It has to be me. Me and Bridget."

"You can't just walk back in," West said. "Even if you slip in, what about the dope? They'll know you've missed doses."

"They don't pay as close attention to Foster City kids as they do to the hoodies," Jude said.

"You seem pretty sure of that."

"We're listed by house number, not by our names. We don't even get ID like you do, until we get our own rations."

West shook his head, like he was trying to shake that idea into some kind of order. Clover couldn't wrap her own head around it.

"Never mind that right now. Bridget, are you sure you want to go back?"

"Yes."

"You don't even know what your death date is now. We've changed the future."

"It's not right for me to stay just because I'm scared."

"I know you miss your father," West said. "But he wouldn't want you dead."

"It's not that."

"Then what?"

"If I go back and tell them that you're dead, Bennett won't try whatever it was he was going to do to me again." Everyone else stayed silent, like they were holding their collective breath. "And if he's looking for you, he'll stop."

"I don't want you to go," West said, his voice barely above a whisper.

"It's the only way. This place is too important. The Freaks are too important. And Jude is right. We have to have some people on the inside."

"It doesn't have to be you," West said.

"Who else?"

West just grunted, turned to Clover, and lifted his eyebrows. "And what about you? What's your big announcement?"

Clover wished she'd gone first. "I want to go back, too."

West left the restaurant. Bridget reached for him, but he brushed past her.

The awkward silence West left behind was thick, and Clover

escaped it by following her brother, Mango padding alongside her. She had to run to catch up to him. "Wait. West, wait for me."

"This isn't fair," he said, turning to look at her. "You can't do this to me."

"Do what?"

"You really want to go back and work for the Company? After all this?"

"No."

"Then what? Move back to the Dinosaur? They won't let you live in our house alone, or with Mrs. Finch. She's still too frail."

"I know that. All of that. The safest place for me is the Academy."

"How do you plan to swing that?"

"I wasn't sure until now." Clover remembered what Jude had said to her earlier. "Kingston will let me in if I bring his daughter to him."

"Why? Why is this so important to you?"

"We need what he left us at the library in the city. And on the other side of the portal."

"You can't travel through the portal if you're in the city."

"I need to learn how to swim first. There's a pool at the Academy. And I have to find that book."

"Jude can get the book."

"I want to be part of the revolution, West."

"You *are* part of it."

"I have to go back. At least for a little while."

For a minute Clover was sure she would have to defy her brother to go. He was going to tell her she couldn't, and she'd leave anyway. They'd spend who knows how long apart and angry at each other. But then he said, "Revolution isn't easy, is it?"

Clover shook her head.

West hugged her, and she let him. He smelled a lot less like goat manure these days. "You know I'm going to ask Jude to watch out for you, right?"

"Yeah, I know."

West nodded slowly. "I'm going to be really angry if you get yourself killed."

Clover thought it best not to point out that if that happened, his anger wouldn't do either of them any good.

chapter 22

This country, with its institutions, belongs to the
people who inhabit it. Whenever they shall grow
weary of the existing government, they can exercise
their constitutional right of amending it, or
exercise their revolutionary right to dismember or
overthrow it.

—ABRAHAM LINCOLN,
FIRST INAUGURAL ADDRESS, MARCH 4, 1861

Time was sticky and slow, except when it moved like
it was greased. Work made the daylight hours fly by. They took an
inventory of the entire property. West did his best to outline a plan
not only for making the most of the current harvest, but also for
the next season. And he lay awake every night, tossing and turning,
thinking about his sister alone in the city, or Bennett going after
Bridget again.

Two nights before the date they'd decided that Clover, Jude,
and Bridget would go back to the city, West asked his sister to teach
him how to drive.

"Someone will have to drive you to the gate."

"You're right. But if the guards recognize you, the whole plan
is shot. I should teach Christopher."

"I'm driving you to the gate. Don't argue."

She shot him a quick salute. "Fine, you're the boss."

"And don't you forget it."

Clover stuck out her tongue, then went back to pulling carrots
out of the ground. Mango was asleep in the shade of the restaurant's

awning. He didn't have to work so much here, where Clover had far fewer triggers that he had to help her overcome. She was learning to just be a girl, without primary school bullies to whip her into a frenzy. And West thought Mango was learning how to be a regular dog.

He would miss her when she was gone, but it seemed even more of a tragedy that she'd lose the calm she'd taken on in the last couple of weeks.

"What, right now?" Clover asked when he didn't go away.

"No time like the present."

She stood up, wiped her hands on the back of her jeans, and walked with him to the main house, where she could wash up and grab the keys.

"Do you ever feel like you're in some kind of alternate universe?" Clover asked him when she came back. "Or on a different planet, maybe?"

"You've been reading too much science fiction," he said, but he knew what she meant.

Sometimes, when he couldn't sleep, it seemed like someone had stripped him of a protective layer. All the lies he thought were the truth had buffered him. He couldn't go back to what he was just a couple of weeks ago, even if the opportunity smacked him upside the head.

"Put the key in there," Clover said, pointing to a spot under the steering wheel once they were in the van. "Good, now put your right foot on the right-side pedal, just a little, and turn the key."

The engine roared to life, and West's foot came down harder on the pedal before he could stop it. The noise was like a living thing, and he took his foot off altogether, which caused the engine to stall.

"Well, don't do that," Clover said.

Driving was both more difficult and much easier than he had anticipated. His first lesson was on the wide, winding highway leading away from the ranch. The pedals were delicate; if he stepped too hard on either the gas or the brake, he sent both of them flying against the back of their seats or toward the windshield until the seat belts tightened and choked them. But the transmission was automatic and once he put the van in gear, he only had to focus on learning how to manage speed and the wheel.

He'd driven the tractors at work a few times, and it wasn't too different. The most difficult part was knowing he had to learn fast. Fuel was too precious for him to waste taking his time with this.

"Turn the wheel the way you want the tires to go," Clover said. "Don't drive too fast. Just turn gently, a little at a time . . . That's it. See how it works? If you turn the wheel to the right, the van will go to the right. Don't turn too hard."

Clover loved driving. West thought he liked his feet on the ground better. Still, he made it back to the ranch, parked, and pocketed the keys as he got out of the van.

Jude held up one of Waverly's journals. "Frank and Melissa bring corn oil into the biofuel plant just outside the Sacramento city walls. Apparently, he siphons off just enough to give Waverly to keep the van and the generators going."

"Did he put down how he turns it into fuel?" Christopher asked.

"Not that I've found, but there are books."

Christopher got up and went to the shelves, filled with books West knew he couldn't read. Or he couldn't very well. They'd have to take care of that. Soon.

"I can probably figure it out," Christopher said.

West looked around the room. When Jude, Clover, and Bridget left, he'd be here with Christopher, Phire and Emmy, and Marta. He was the only one of them who could read or write. If something happened to him, they'd be lost.

"We start reading lessons tomorrow," he said. Christopher

looked uncomfortable, but nodded. "Not just for you. Every Freak needs to know how to read and write."

Marta darted her blue gaze to Christopher. She didn't respond, but West was pretty sure if Christopher was into it, she wouldn't fight it either.

"Me, too?" Emmy asked.

Jude tugged on her braid. "You especially."

"We have a lot to do in the next few days," Phire said. "Maybe that should wait."

West shook his head. "After dinner tomorrow, just for an hour."

"I've been thinking," Jude said. Something about his posture caused West to pay attention. "I think I know how I can get back into the city."

"How?" Clover asked.

"There's another train tomorrow night. Remember, to bring more oil?"

Clover hesitated, then said, "Yes."

"I think Frank and Melissa can sneak me in. Melissa told me there's a truck at the stop for them to drive into the city when they arrive with a shipment."

West waited for Clover to tell Jude what a bad idea that was. When she didn't, he said, "Don't you think that someone will notice an extra person?"

"That's why I said *sneak*."

"What if you get caught?" Clover asked.

Jude ran a hand over his mouth and turned to look at her. "I'll talk to Frank and Melissa about it, at least. They'll know if there's a way."

"But what if you do get caught?" Clover's voice rose an octave, and West saw the signs of an impending meltdown. "Then what? Then what if I get into the city and you're not there?"

"Okay," West said. "Breathe, Clover. Let's wait until tomorrow, when we can talk to Frank and Melissa before you get yourself all worked up."

"I'm not worked up!" She stalked out of the big house.

West sighed. He was so tired. More tired than he could ever remember being. Finding a rhythm for the farm wasn't difficult. This was one of the busiest times, with the harvest starting to come in. It was all the rest that threatened to overwhelm him. What were they supposed to do out here, besides run the farm? Would others come? Were the people who wrote the letters expecting something of them?

"I'll go after her," Jude said.

West let him. It was a sign of his exhaustion that he was grateful not to have to deal with Clover's meltdown on his own.

Jude calmed Clover down, and the evening proceeded without any more drama. As tired as West had been all day, when he finally lay down to sleep, his brain wouldn't shut down. The idea of sending Clover and Bridget into the city alone made him sick.

There had to be something he could do. Staying on the ranch while Clover and Bridget went back to an uncertain future in the city felt so wrong.

It took a couple of hours of tossing and turning for the solution to hit him square in the gut. He put on his pants, with the keys to the van still in the pocket. He eased past the sleeping bodies of his friends, then went outside.

Jude sat on the porch, leaning back in his chair so that only the back two legs teetered on the ground. He looked up from the notebook he read by flashlight. "What's up?"

West was tempted to tell Jude he was going to the bathroom. That would be a useless lie, though, because Jude would hear the van start. And even if he didn't, he'd come looking for West when he didn't come back.

"I'm going for a drive," he finally said.

"Why?" West didn't answer right away, and Jude didn't back down. "Joyrides aren't a good use of our fuel."

West shifted his position, squaring his shoulders. "Don't try to stop me."

Jude didn't move and he didn't raise his voice when he said, "We're going to miss that van if you don't come back."

"I'll come back."

"What happened to staying in pairs?"

West took a deep breath. "You're on duty."

"Take Christopher."

West knew his resistance came from guilt. He shouldn't be anywhere near the gate. But he had to talk to Isaiah. He trusted Jude and Christopher, but he'd known Isaiah his whole life and he wasn't sending his sister, or Bridget, back into the city without talking to his friend first. Or at least trying to.

"Your friend's a guard," Jude said, reading his mind. "Are you sure his loyalty hasn't been trained out of him?"

"How did you know?"

Jude put his book down. "I've been waiting for it. Makes sense you'd try to talk to him, and there's not much else you'd need to sneak out in the middle of the night for."

West had to trust this kid with his sister and his girl. He guessed he'd better start now. "We need as many allies as we can get. Isaiah is one of the good guys."

"He's been a guard for three years. And you left the city. You might not know him now as well as you think you do."

"I know he tried to warn Clover."

Jude didn't say anything to that. West wished he weren't at least possibly right. Isaiah might believe that he was doing the right thing, even protecting Clover and Bridget, if he took West into custody. "I have to talk to him. I have to go now, so that he'll think I'm dead when Clover and Bridget say I am. I won't tell him anything he won't find out anyway—that Clover and Bridget have been outside the city walls all this time. That they're coming back and need protection."

"I'll take care of Clover," Jude said.

"And who will take care of you?"

"You think working a hoe and living in the neighborhoods without enough rations was hard?" Jude asked, his voice low and calm. "I said I'll take care of her and I will."

West was losing his baby sister. Right here, on this porch. He hoped Jude was as tough as he thought he was. "I'm still going. You're the one who keeps saying change starts on the inside."

"You really believe this guy is a Freak?"

"He tried to warn us. Twice," West said. "He deserves the chance."

He didn't tell Jude that he had a hunting knife in his back pocket. Or that the one question that haunted him was what would happen to Clover and Bridget if Isaiah wasn't part of the revolution after all. If he wasn't a Freak.

Jude nodded. Maybe deciding, like West had, that they had no choice but to learn to trust each other. "Take Christopher with you or I'll have the whole house up."

West went back in and shook Christopher by the shoulder. Five minutes later, he pulled the van out onto the highway.

Christopher's adventurous spirit was addictive. Fifteen minutes into their drive toward the gate, West had caught the excitement himself.

"Watch for bears," Christopher said. "Clover said she almost smashed one out here. Would be cool to see one, though, wouldn't it? I almost hope we do."

West was driving twenty miles an hour, which felt like flying, but he knew enough about driving to know it wasn't very fast at all. He was barely comfortable behind the wheel as it was; he wasn't about to speed around the dark curves.

Christopher drummed a chorus on his thighs with his hands. "I can read some, you know."

"I know."

"Be good to read better, though. And write. I'm not so good at writing."

"I'll teach you to write. You can teach me about fixing things," West said.

"Sure. I need to figure out how to make the biofuel. You can help me."

"Sounds good." West sneaked a sidelong glance at Christopher. "You've been real good with Marta. I don't even know what to say to her."

"We were in the same house in Foster City, you know. The three of us since we was just little. Their baby sister, too. You wouldn't know the twins were seventeen, would you? Same as me."

That did surprise him. He thought fifteen was pushing it, even though they sometimes acted like they were going on thirty. West should have left the city by himself, or maybe with Clover and Bridget. Then Geena would be alive. He tried to think of a way to articulate that and came up with nothing.

Christopher didn't seem to notice. He went on talking like he was alone in the van. "I almost didn't leave. Bad as it was, and it was real bad, at least I knew what to expect, yeah? Then our house father broke my leg. Swung at it with a golf club when I tried to stop him from—from doing what he did with the girls in our house. Wouldn't take me to the hospital. Guess he was afraid I'd talk."

"Would you have?"

"You think anyone would listen if I did? Soon as I could walk again, limp or whatever, we went with Jude."

They drove in silence most of the rest of the way to the gate. When they were a mile away, West turned the van around so that it faced back the way they'd come and pulled to the side of the road. He shifted in his seat so he could see Christopher. "Listen to me."

"Oh, no. I'm going with you."

"If things don't go well, you have to take this monster back to the ranch. Do you hear me?"

"West."

"I mean it. I know learning how to drive alone in the dark isn't ideal, but you can figure it out. You just turn the key, put your foot on the brake, and shift to drive. That's the *D* in the window there. Gas on the right, brake on the left. Turn the wheel the way you want the car to go. The right-hand pedal is the gas. You press it easy, you hear me? Pull this out to turn on the headlights. Don't you drive off a cliff."

West got out of the van and walked away before Christopher could argue. The mile walk, in the dark, to the gate felt like a hundred. The guard on the outside wasn't Isaiah. West had to crouch behind a tree and wait for them to change positions. Long enough to build up a nice head of concern that Isaiah might have the day off, or maybe he'd rotated to a different shift. Also long enough to worry that Christopher might decide to go back to the ranch without him.

But twenty minutes later, Isaiah came to the outside post and sat on the chair.

West hadn't thought this out well enough. Whether he called for Isaiah or just emerged from the woods, he was likely to get shot. He picked up one of the big pine cones scattered on the ground and took a deep breath before rolling it hard toward Isaiah.

Isaiah kicked his foot out in surprise and looked in West's direction.

Here goes nothing. West stepped out.

"What the hell?" Isaiah brought up his gun, and his call brought the other guard.

"What? What is it?"

West retreated, as silently as he could. He tensed, expecting shots to ring out, but they didn't.

"I don't know," Isaiah said to the guard, as he still looked in West's direction. "Thought I heard something."

He didn't mention the pine cone. Maybe that was good. Maybe not. West's heart beat so hard, he was afraid they'd hear it. Every instinct he had insisted he turn tail and get back to the van.

"Must have been a deer or something," Isaiah said. "I need to take a leak."

There was some kind of answer from the other guard, but West couldn't make it out. Then Isaiah picked up his gun and walked straight at him.

"Isaiah," West said, once his friend was close enough. Isaiah raised the gun and pointed it at his chest. "God, don't shoot me."

"What are you doing here? It's way past curfew." West nodded slowly, not sure how to answer that. Curfew was the last thing he had on his mind, and Isaiah knew he hadn't been in the city for weeks. Isaiah looked around and seemed to finally realize that West was on the wrong side of the gate. "They're looking for you."

"I know."

"You took Bridget Kingston. They're saying she's dead."

"She is not dead. And I didn't take her, she came with me."

Isaiah narrowed his eyes. "Then where is she?"

"She's safe. She's coming home soon, now that her death date has passed. You can be the one to give her back to her father." That would mean recognition, a big reward. Not a Whole New Life, but something. Enough to make a difference. Maybe a pass out of gate duty, at least.

"My grandma is out of her mind worried about you and Clover. Where is Clover, anyway? She with you?"

"Clover and Bridget are both coming back. I need you to look out for them, Isaiah. Both of them."

"What about you?"

"Promise me. If Clover or Bridget needs you, you'll be there. If they come to you and ask for help, you'll give it to them. And you'll believe what they say, even if it seems crazy."

"Isaiah!" the other guard called. "What the hell are you doing out there?"

"Promise me."

"Fine. Fine! I promise."

Isaiah ran back to the gate. "Way to give a guy some privacy," he called to the other guard. West was already picking his way through the trees back to the van.

"Are you out of your mind?" Clover had found out about his middle-of-the-night adventure, and she was not happy. She stood with her hands in fists, looking like she'd like to knock him out. West did his best not to laugh. Or do anything to make her feel like he wasn't taking her seriously. It wasn't easy. Her cheeks were red and the ends of her hair trembled as she shook with rage.

"I brought Christopher with me."

"Christopher? You brought Christopher? Neither of you know how to drive well enough to be out on these roads in the dark. And what was Christopher going to do to keep you from being shot?"

"Isaiah wouldn't shoot me."

She blew a breath out through her nose. "You didn't know that! Not for sure, anyway."

"I'm sorry I scared you."

"You should apologize to Jude. I had to beat him up to make him tell me where you were."

West looked at Jude, who stood not far away. The other boy lifted his shoulders.

"Hopefully no one got hurt," West said. "I needed to know Isaiah would be on our side."

"How much did you tell him?"

"Just enough to make him think. And to convince him to look out for you and Bridget."

"If he tells someone that you're not dead, it'll mess up everything."

"He won't know I'm not dead," West said. "You'll tell him I am, just like you'll tell everyone else."

"So you don't trust him."

"I trust us. I'm not sure he's one of us yet. When he is, *if* he is, then he'll know what he needs to know."

chapter 23

I am surprised at the suddenness as well as the
greatness of this revolution . . .

—JOHN ADAMS,
LETTER TO ABIGAIL ADAMS, JULY 3, 1776

Clover watched Melissa climb out of the train, then run to them and throw herself at Jude. His hand disappeared into Melissa's thick auburn hair, covering her back as he caught her. "Whoa," he said.

She hugged him, then stepped back. "I'm so happy to see you. All of you. I wasn't sure you'd be here."

"Of course we're here," Clover said. "We said we would be."

"We don't have much time," Frank said as he climbed out of the engine car as well. "We're running late already. Maybe some of you kids can help me get your oil barrel down."

The train had only two cars this time. Clover guessed it would pick up at least one in Reno, and maybe another in Sacramento before the whole thing turned around to head east again.

"Waverly is dead," Clover said.

If she'd meant to stop everything in its tracks, she couldn't have done a better job. Melissa turned toward her father and made a strangled little noise.

"What did you say?" Frank asked.

"Clover," West said from somewhere behind her.

Melissa was crying and Frank's face lost all its color. Clover felt so uncomfortable in her own skin, she wished she could crawl out of it.

"How did he die?" Frank asked.

"Langston Bennett shot him," Clover said.

"My God. Are you kids okay?"

"Bennett killed Geena, too," Marta said.

Frank shook his head, and for a few heartbeats, no one said anything.

"Some of us are going back," Jude finally said.

"To the city?" Frank handed West a packet of letters, a lot like the packet that Melissa had given Clover the first time they met. "Is that a good idea?"

"There isn't any way to know," West said. "Waverly thought that we were meant to do something big. If we're going to try, some of us need to be on the inside."

It took a few minutes for West and Jude to explain their plans to Frank and Melissa. Clover waited, feeling like she might be sick, for one of them to bring up the real reason they'd come to meet the train.

"Can you get me into the city?" Jude finally asked.

"Well, probably," Frank said. "But maybe it would be better for you to come farther east with us. We could take you—"

"No," Clover said. "He needs to be in the city."

Jude slipped her hand into his and squeezed it gently. "I appreciate it. But Clover and Bridget have a plan for getting back through the gates. I need another way in."

"Well, okay," Frank said. "If you're sure. Let's get your oil off the train. We need to get moving."

It took a few minutes to maneuver a barrel of corn oil from the train to the van. They had to take out the very back seat and leave it hidden in the trees to pick up later.

Frank climbed into the engine car. Melissa stood outside, waiting for Jude.

"I'll be at the Dinosaur," Jude said. "Be safe, Clover."

She started to say she would be, but Jude hugged her until she put her arms around him and hugged back.

Three afternoons later, the rest of the Freaks piled into the van for a somber drive to the gate. Clover glanced away from the road for a second, through the rearview mirror, at West and Bridget sitting in the seat behind her, their heads close as they whispered to each other.

Phire, Emmy, and Marta sat on the long bench seat behind them that Clover and West had gone back for the night before. West had wanted them to stay behind today but lost that battle.

"You okay?" Christopher asked from the passenger seat.

She shrugged without looking away from the road. "I guess so."

"You'll see him again, you know."

"Of course I will. He'll be at the Dinosaur." Christopher didn't say anything until Clover looked at him. "What? He promised me."

"I was talking about your brother."

Clover put her eyes back on the road and tried to ignore the hot flush that crept up her neck and over her cheeks.

"You don't have to do this, you know," West said from behind her. "You could stay."

She'd thought of little else since announcing she was going to try to get back into the Academy. If Kingston's answer was no, she wasn't sure what she'd do. She'd be trapped in the city, at least for a while. Bennett would probably take her back to the Company. He'd gone to a lot of trouble to get her in there in the first place.

Having someone inside the Company would be good for the Freaks. It had crossed her mind to get in the gate, away from where West could make decisions for her, and then get herself back to work. But the risk was so high. Bennett could just leave her on the other side. After a while no one would care what had happened to her except Jude and her brother and the other Freaks.

No. Kingston would take her back. She'd make it happen somehow. It would mean telling the whole city that her brother forced her to leave. When she and Bridget were done with him, West would never be able to return to the city. His bridges would be so burned, there would be no rebuilding them.

And no backing out of their course of action. No slipping back into the comfortable patterns of the life she'd lived until three weeks ago.

"I have to do this," she said. "I want to."

Clover slowed as she neared the gate and parked the van around a curve so the guards wouldn't see them coming, far enough back that their engine didn't give them away. They'd have to walk in and hope that Isaiah was already on duty. If he wasn't, they'd wait. He had to be there for their plan to work.

Everyone got out of the van and moved into the woods. West wrapped Clover in a tight hug, and even though she stiffened at first, the sudden closeness taking her breath, she didn't fight it. After a while she hugged him back, and her cheeks were wet with tears when he let her go.

"I love you," he said. "Please, be careful."

"I will."

"Say it."

"I'll be careful. I promise."

"Two o'clock," he said. "Every Saturday. If I log into that computer and you don't show up—"

"I love you, too."

Everyone else hugged her and Bridget. Emmy cried a little and wrapped her arms around Mango's neck, but Phire hushed her.

Clover's heart beat in her throat. What if Jude had been caught sneaking in on the train? What if he'd already been arrested? He'd be executed for possibly introducing the virus back into the city.

Her father would probably be on the firing squad.

And if he'd been caught, and forced to talk, she and Bridget could be walking into an ambush.

"Breathe, Clover," West said.

Clover hugged him again, hard and quick, then went to stand with Bridget on the road. Bridget took her hand, and they walked together down the middle of the road, with Mango on his lead.

Clover forced herself not to look back. It took only a few minutes for them to come around the corner and see Isaiah sitting in a chair outside the gate.

"Clover?" Isaiah stood. "Christ, Clover. Are you okay? Where's West?"

Clover didn't give herself time to chicken out before she said what she had to say. "West is dead."

Isaiah froze. And then he drew in a hard breath and let it out slow. "Oh, God. Oh, Clover, I'm sorry."

He seemed to want to hug her, but he didn't. He'd known her all her life, after all. He looked to Clover like someone had stuck a pin in him and deflated him.

"Where did you come from?" the other guard asked. He was older than Isaiah. Maybe thirty. They'd sent in someone with more experience, then, after the whole Waverly incident. His black hair was cut short and bristly, and his mouth was set in a hard line. "What the hell is this?"

Isaiah turned to him and said, "Don't you recognize the headmaster's daughter? The whole city is looking for these girls."

Then the guard evidently did recognize Bridget. His eyes widened and his mouth softened. "We thought you were dead."

"I'd like to see my father, please. Will you call him?"

The older guard turned to Isaiah like he expected his partner to fulfill Bridget's request. Isaiah said, "Call this in, Greg."

Greg looked annoyed at the younger man telling him what to do, but he turned and went to the guard station anyway, probably wanting the fame of being the one to report that, against all odds, the headmaster's daughter had been found alive.

Isaiah looked at Clover again when they were alone. "West is really dead?"

Clover cleared her throat. "A bear wandered into our camp and West distracted it so we could get away. It attacked him."

Isaiah's mouth hung open. For a second, Clover was sure he'd call her on her lie. But then he said, "I'm so sorry, Clover."

The other guard came back, walking as fast as he could without breaking into a run. He was afraid he'd miss something. "Adam Kingston is on his way."

"Have them find James—"

Clover clutched Isaiah's arm and cut him off. Panic burst in her chest and it was all she could do to keep from screaming. In all their preparation, neither West nor Clover had thought of their own father.

She suddenly wanted him, more than she could have imagined she ever would again. More than she had in years. But if he came, she'd never get away. And she needed to find Jude.

"No," she said.

"You can't stay alone, you know."

"I'll find him," she said. Isaiah knew too much about her family. He was part of her family. "Please. I'll find him on my own. Tomorrow. I'll stay with your grandma tonight. I'm just not ready to see him yet."

"Kingston's on his way," Greg said again. "Who else you want?"

"No one," Isaiah said. "Never mind."

"Thank you," Clover whispered.

"Okay, we'll talk about this later. You go to my grandmother's in the meantime, you hear me?" After Clover nodded, Isaiah said to Bridget, "Your dad will be here soon."

It took less than five minutes for a small white car to come careening toward the gate so fast that for a second, Clover was afraid it wouldn't be able to stop. She backed up and almost tripped over Mango.

Adam Kingston threw open the driver's-side door with its gold Academy logo, and pulled himself out. "Bridget?"

Bridget stayed near Clover. "I'm here, Dad."

Kingston seemed younger than he had at the Academy, in that way that old people can revert to looking like children when they are confused. His face was blotched, like he'd been crying. He had lost weight, so his clothes, usually perfectly tailored, hung on him.

He didn't have any of the air of authority Clover associated with him.

"Bridget." He wrapped his arms around her and pulled her against him. "Are you hurt? Did that boy hurt you?"

Bridget hugged him back. "I'm fine. No one hurt me."

The car's other door opened, and Langston Bennett stepped out of the passenger side.

"Your daughter is safe, Adam. What a relief." Bennett turned his attention to Clover. "And our wayward little Messenger is as well."

Bridget didn't look at Bennett. "I just want to go home."

"I bet you'd like to get home as well, Clover," Bennett said. "Has your father been contacted?"

"How did you get away from him?" Kingston asked his daughter.

"Not now, Daddy, please. I'll tell you everything later. Can't we just go home?"

"Yes, of course."

"Clover needs debriefing," Bennett said. "You can drop us both at the barracks."

"Surely that can wait until tomorrow. The girl looks ready to collapse. Let her go home."

Something passed between the two men that Clover didn't quite understand. Finally, Bennett said, "Is that what you want, Clover?"

"Yes, sir." The plan was to let everyone think that West had forced her out of the city with him. She was terrified that she would reveal too much, say something wrong. The longer she could put off the questions, the better, as far as she was concerned.

All she wanted right now was to get away from these people, so she could find Jude and know that he made it back into the city safely.

"The city will rejoice that you girls are both home and safe," Bennett said. "Tell us where West Donovan is. The guard will pick him up, justice will be served, and this whole incident will be behind us."

Clover's hands flapped at her sides like fish out of water. Mango pushed his head against her palm, and she exhaled the breath she'd been holding and drew in another.

"West is dead," Bridget said, taking her other hand. "Her brother is dead. You're hurting her."

"I'm sure I didn't mean to," Bennett said. "I'm just so grateful you both got away safe. Clover, can I have a word with you before we leave. Maybe in the guard station?"

Bridget tightened her grip on Clover's hand and said, "Daddy, really—"

"No," Clover said. "It's okay."

She let go of Bridget and walked with Bennett to the guard station. It extended from the city wall, forming one side of the gate opening, and had three glass walls. She'd be safe. Bennett opened the door and she went in.

"I know you missed your dose after your last mission, Clover," he said as soon as the door was closed.

"My brother took me outside the city." She hoped her shaking voice didn't give away her nerves too much. She should have stopped there, but the words kept tumbling out. "He was killed by a bear."

"You seem particularly well for someone who hasn't had her suppressant for so long."

Clover forced herself to inhale and willed her stomach to settle. "I guess I got lucky."

"A dispatch flyer went out on your brother two days after you left the city. We thought Miss Kingston was dead. That would have been the first murder in nearly fifteen years. Can you imagine if we'd made an announcement like that to the city?"

"Well, the system is working just fine now, isn't it? You would know if someone was still after her."

"Your brother was a virus survivor, wasn't he? That bear must have been a relief to him."

There was nothing Clover could say to that, so they were at an impasse. Bennett stared down at her; the scars on his own cheeks glowed white in the dim light of the guard station.

"You'll come back to the Company, now that you're home and safe, Clover. Where you're needed."

"Why am I needed there? What's so special about me?"

It was Bennett's turn to change the subject. "Most people in your position would be grateful."

Bennett turned his back to Clover and looked out the window that faced toward the forest where everyone was hiding, if they hadn't already left. And then she was positively certain they hadn't, because Marta came out of the trees about fifty feet away. She stood there a minute, fully exposed, and then lifted an arm and pointed at Bennett. Clover heard Bennett's breath catch when Marta turned her hand and flipped him the bird.

Marta was going to get herself killed. Where was West? Or Christopher?

Clover looked up at Bennett, expecting him to be on the verge of sounding some kind of alarm. Instead, he was as pale as—well, as a ghost. "Mr. Bennett?"

He looked over his shoulder at the others on the other side of the guard station. They couldn't see Marta from where they were. "Who is that? Who came here with you?"

Clover looked back to the trees, but Marta was gone. "Who is who?"

"You saw her."

West said Clover's face was transparent, but she did her best to be convincing anyway. "I didn't see—"

"A search was ordered for your brother," Bennett said. His voice sounded tight enough to play like a guitar string. "A search outside the city. The first ever. Dr. Stead vetoed it as a waste of time and resources."

Clover's head felt full of bees, buzzing and stinging and making it difficult for her to stay focused and in control of herself. She forced herself to stop rocking from foot to foot, but could not still her hands at her sides. "My brother is dead."

"We'll see about that."

"He was attacked by a bear."

"Then his body should be easy to find. Especially with you and Bridget Kingston to lead us to it. Dr. Stead will be pleased to learn that there will be no loose ends in this matter."

Bennett grabbed her arm and pulled her out of the guard station before she could react to his sudden, harsh touch. He didn't speak again until they were back to the others.

"It was awful. The bear—" Bridget was saying. Telling their rehearsed story. She stopped when she saw Clover and Bennett. "Clover saved me. We ran and she brought me here."

Kingston turned his attention to Clover. "Miss Donovan. I don't know how to thank you."

"I want to go to the Academy," Clover said.

Kingston shot a look to Bennett, whose mouth was drawn in a bloodless line over his big teeth. "We've already talked about this, Miss Donovan."

"If this girl passed the entrance exams, she deserves a place at the Academy," Bennett said.

"But she's already been assigned to the Mariner track," Kingston said.

"Not anymore."

"You're sure?" After a few seconds of silence and a look exchanged between the two men, Kingston nodded. "Very well. I'll look forward to seeing you at the Academy a week from Monday for the first day of classes."

"And Mango." At the last minute, she remembered something that seemed a lifetime away. "And I can't live with Heather Sweeney."

"Really, Miss Donovan—"

Bridget put a hand on Clover's arm. "She can room with me."

"Bridget," Kingston said. "You can't expect to return to the Academy. Not now."

"I have to." Bridget pulled away when he tried to put an arm around her. "I just need things to be normal again."

Clover watched Bridget turn into a spoiled rich girl. Her blue eyes brimmed with tears and her bottom lip pushed out.

"Bridget, please," her father said. "Control yourself. I can't let you live at the Academy until I'm sure you're safe."

"I'm safe. West is . . . he's—" Tears fell down Bridget's face.

"Please, I need to go back to school. I really need to. West is dead. Who do you think is going to come after me?"

Kingston didn't say anything. He didn't look at Bennett.

"What if she had a bodyguard?" All attention turned to Isaiah, and he cleared his throat before going on. "If she had a bodyguard, she'd be safe. Maybe safer than she'd be locked up at home. She was taken from your house, after all."

Bennett stepped in then. "Young man, you're out of bounds."

"I'm sorry, sir. West Donovan was my friend. We were neighbors. I feel responsible. I should have known he was unstable."

Clover didn't expect that, but as soon as he said it, she knew it was exactly the right thing. It would come out that Isaiah knew West, eventually.

"It's a good idea," Bridget said.

Kingston looked at Isaiah for a minute. "Bridget, you don't really want a guard with you all day. Think of the attention that would draw."

"He could pretend to be a student," Bridget said.

"How old are you?" Bennett asked Isaiah.

"Nineteen."

"He could pass for seventeen. Put him in my classes. Please Daddy, I've worked too hard to just *quit*."

"How do we know he isn't working with Donovan?" Bennett asked.

"My brother is dead," Clover said.

Bridget's tears were starting again.

"It's what you want?" Kingston asked Bridget. "You're sure, sweetheart?"

"It's what I want."

"All right." The headmaster turned to Isaiah. "Report to your supervisor at the end of your shift, son. Tell him to call my office tomorrow."

Kingston took a deep breath. "We'll drive you home," he said to Clover.

"I can walk. It'll be good for Mango."

"Don't be ridiculous. I'm sure your father is as upset as I have been," Kingston said. "Let's get you home to him."

Kingston wanted to talk to her father when he dropped Clover off at her house ten minutes later.

"I don't think he's here," she told him. "He's an executioner. I'm sure he's at the barracks."

"Not this late on a Saturday."

"Really, Mr. Kingston, it's okay. He's probably at the barracks. He'll be here soon."

"You'll be alone? Maybe you should come home with us."

"Don't be ridiculous, Adam. Take her to Foster City," Bennett said. "She'll spend the night in one of the emergency houses if her father doesn't come for her."

It took everything Clover had to keep her voice calm. "I'll go to my neighbor's house until he comes home. Thank you though. I'll see you tomorrow, Bridget."

She and Mango were out of the car before either man could argue with her. She bent to take the key from Mango's vest pocket, fumbling in her haste, and finally let herself into the house that she'd lived in her whole life. It felt foreign. A wave of loneliness washed over her as she peered out the window until the car drove away.

She went into her bedroom and opened the trunk at the foot of her bed. She packed a duffel with her mother's clothes. For some reason, she didn't care what Heather Sweeney and Wendy O'Malley and their friends thought about her wearing them.

She should go see Mrs. Finch. Let her know that she was okay and be the one to tell her that West was dead. Mrs. Finch had practically raised them. She loved West like she loved Isaiah. The idea of facing her grief tonight made Clover a little sick to her stomach.

She'd talk to Mrs. Finch later. Tomorrow. Right now, the only thing Clover wanted was to find Jude. She had two hours before curfew, plenty of time to get to the Dinosaur. She put the lead back on Mango and said, "Let's go home."

chapter 24

If we lose freedom here, there is no place to
escape to. This is the last stand on Earth.

—RONALD REAGAN,
"A TIME FOR CHOOSING" SPEECH, OCTOBER 27, 1964

Clover made it to within two miles of the Dinosaur. As soon as she saw Jude walking toward her, the stress of the last hour caught up to her and she had to gasp for air.

He closed the distance between them and wrapped his arms around her. He didn't pull away when she stiffened slightly, and then she melted into him, her duffel bag falling to the ground at her side.

"You made it," he said against her hair.

"So did you."

He kissed the top of her head, then pulled away and picked up her bag. "We should get to the Dinosaur before curfew."

"What was the train like?" Clover asked.

"It moves so fast. You'd love it."

"I can't believe you didn't get caught." Jude stopped walking, and she had to take a few steps back once she noticed. "What?"

"You really thought I'd get caught?"

"Didn't you?"

"Do you think I would have gotten on the train if I did?"

Clover wiped at her eyes with the back of her hand. "How did you do it?"

"I hid in the coal bin on the train, and then in the back of the truck."

An image, from an old movie she'd seen once, flooded Clover's memory. The inside of a train's engine car. A huge bin, full of chunks of heavy black coal, and a roaring fire that ate the coal like candy. "Under the coal?"

"Yes, under the coal, and then under some blankets in the back of the truck. Everything was fine, Clover. I promise."

"You could have died," she said, suddenly angry at the idea. "You could have been crushed. Or suffocated. Or caught. Or—"

Jude put up a hand to stop her. "I wasn't."

"You should have stayed on the ranch."

Jude put a hand on the side of her face and waited a few seconds for her to get used to the touch. "Do you really think that I would have let you come back into the city alone?"

"Bridget came, too."

"I promised West I'd take care of you."

"I don't need you to—"

Jude moved his hand from her cheek to her hair, smoothing it back. And then he kissed her. It lasted only a second before he dropped his hand and stepped back a little. "I was worried about you, too," he said.

"I'm never going to see my brother again," Clover said when they were almost to the Dinosaur.

"Of course you are."

"How? When?"

"We'll find a way."

Clover stopped walking. "Let's just go back now. Let's get Bridget and go back to the ranch."

"I have something for you." He opened his pack, pulled out one of Waverly's notebooks, and handed it to her.

"You shouldn't have taken this," she said, handing Jude her box so she could hold the notebook. "They need it at the ranch."

"Open it."

She did. Inside was Jude's neat printing. She thumbed through and saw that about two-thirds of the book was filled. "What is this?"

"I copied the letters for you. The first batch anyway."

Her emotions were too close to the surface, and for a second, she thought she might cry again. "You did?"

He shrugged. "Maybe for me, too. And Bridget. To remind us that we're still Freaks."

"We have to be careful with this."

"We will be."

They started to walk again, toward the Dinosaur. "This seems so huge. I don't even know where to start."

"Me, either. But we'll figure it out."

West sat in the rocking chair on the porch of the big house with Waverly's laptop computer balanced on his knees. The five of them still hadn't moved back to the smaller houses Waverly had gone to so much trouble to set up for them. None of them were ready to be so spread out yet.

The computer was opened and turned on. West stared at it and waited for his sister to open a communication between them.

Why had it taken so long to really hit him how dangerous it was for Clover, Bridget, and Jude to try to get back into the city?

Sure, he'd known that it was a risk. They all did. But until now, faced with their absence, it hadn't really sunk in.

If Bennett didn't believe that West was dead, who knew what he'd do? He'd already tried to kill Bridget once. All he'd have to do to Clover was force her through the portal and then not let her come back to her own time line. And Jude. Sneaking into the city in a train suddenly felt like the world's stupidest idea. Jumping-off-the-roof-of-the-Dinosaur-to-see-if-he-could-fly stupid.

It was his job to watch out for his sister, and he'd let her go back into the city. He'd sent her into a thousand possible dangers. He'd—

West?

epilogue

"Langston Bennett sent me to tell you that your daughter has been found."

James closed his eyes. The woman who'd knocked on the door to his barrack had straight dark hair, like Jane's only not as long, and he found he couldn't look at her. "And West?"

"Clover says that her brother didn't make it. Mr. Donovan, are you okay?"

James opened his eyes again. His heart felt twisted. Wrung, like a washcloth. "How?"

The woman looked up at him. She was much taller than Jane. And she looked close to Jane's age when she died. When he killed her.

"May I come in?" she asked.

He stepped back from the doorway, because suddenly he really didn't want to talk about this in the hall. "Tell me your name again."

"Leanne Wood. I'm—I was your daughter's trainer. She's going back to the Academy."

"Good," he said. "Good, she belongs there. She's so smart. Smarter than anyone else I know."

"She is very smart," Leanne said. "I'm so sorry for your loss."

If James had learned anything in the last sixteen years, it was that the only way to live with a wrung-out heart was to wrap it in steel. He said, "I lost my kids a long, long time ago."

"You still have Clover."

"Yeah," he said. "Yeah, I suppose I do. Where is she now?"

"Classes start next week."

"Have you seen her? Is she okay?"

Leanne shook her head. The ends of her hair glanced over her shoulders. "She's not a Messenger anymore. I'm not her trainer now."

"She's going to need a friend."

"Clover has friends. She needs her father. And my information is that she might have been less than truthful about her brother's fate."

Anger billowed around the steel in his chest, and he balled his fists against his thighs to keep from lashing out. "My daughter doesn't lie."

"I'm going to be dead in two years," Leanne said. The change of subject and the bluntness of her statement put James off-balance.

"What did you say?"

"In two years, I'll be dead. Of course, now that I know that, the future is back to what it should be, isn't it? A mystery."

"What makes you think you'll be dead in two years? That's— they don't keep track of that kind of thing."

"The real question is how I'll die."

James waited for her to tell him, but she just stared at him until he finally asked, "Fine, how do you die?"

"You kill me."

In another life, the idea of killing the young woman standing in front of him would have been so ridiculous, it would bounce off his brain in instant rejection. But this was *this* life. And in this life, he'd been on a firing squad for three years. "Then I stop you from killing someone else."

Leanne shook her head. "You stop me from helping the resistance. Maybe. No way of knowing now, is there?"

"Resistance to what?"

"You aren't very good at asking the right questions. The real question is, who is the resistance?"

James tilted his head and looked at her, putting off asking something he wasn't sure he wanted the answer to. She was patient. She waited until the question had wormed its way into him and he had to know. "Who is the resistance?"

"Right now, it's mostly your children."

In memory of Donna-lynn,
who taught me to read and made sure
I was always surrounded by books.

ACKNOWLEDGMENTS

I want to thank my agent, Kim Lionetti, and my editor, Michelle Vega, and everyone at BookEnds and Berkley who helped me make this story shine. I'm not sure how I got so lucky, but I did, and I'm so grateful.

I absolutely could not have written this book, or any readable book at all, if I hadn't been in the right place at the right time eight years ago to meet Melanie Harvey (and her children, who, as far as I'm concerned, are made of wonderful ideas). Mel held my hand while I learned to write, and then the universe took pity on me again and gave me Brian Rowe just when I needed him.

I have an incredible writing community and group of friends, who have given me invaluable support. Thanks, especially, Leanne, Tee, Kati, Josephine, Cheri, Nessie, Wes, and Shylah for being my first readers.

This book ended up being very much about siblings. That makes sense, since so much of who I am comes from being a sister to Jill, Russel, Alison, Kevin, Austin, Kyle, Patrick, and Ryan. If I ever start a revolution, you are the Freaks I want with me.

A special thanks to my brother Kyle and our dad, Keith Grimes, for putting so much time and effort into helping me make this book the best it could be. And to my sister Alison for making one of the scariest parts of this whole process fun.

My Adrienne and Nick inspired this story in so many ways. Thank you for growing up with me and making my life sweeter in every way than I ever thought it could be. And an extra big thank-you to Ruby, who was born bright as a jewel. It made all the difference, knowing the three of you believed, even before I did, that your momma was a real writer.

And to Kevin, for never once, in all these years, doubting that it was true.